A Death in a Snowstorm

by Joel Jurrens

For information, or to order additional copies, please contact:

Beacon Publishing Group
P.O. Box 41573 Charleston, S.C. 29423
800.817.8480| beaconpublishinggroup.com

Publisher's catalog available by request.

ISBN-13: 978-1-949472-07-3

ISBN-10: 1-949472-07-3

Published in 2020. New York, NY 10001.

First Edition. Printed in the USA.

Chapter One

Through the blowing snow and darkness, Deputy Jesse Gordon watched the pickup go around the section for the third time. Something had gone wrong. On the first trip, the truck had stopped on the shoulder of the state highway, the dome light had flashed for a moment and the pickup's taillights had disappeared down the highway going west. He had logged the time on his clipboard as 0012 hours. He had guessed the pickup had dropped someone off, and they were walking south across the plowed field into the farm service to steal anhydrous ammonia.

Twenty-eight minutes later, Jesse's heartrate went up a notch as the truck had come back and stopped at the same spot on the highway as before. He had waited for the dome light to come on again, but it never did. If it had, Jesse would have stopped the truck, because it would have meant the guy was back with the anhydrous. The anhydrous would have given Jesse enough evidence to make an arrest and get a search warrant. If they were ready for the anhydrous, the things they could buy for the meth lab—drain cleaner, starter fluid, pseudoephedrine, lithium batteries—would already be soaking in containers. But the dome light hadn't come on, and now the pickup kept circling the farm service. Something had definitely gone wrong.

Jesse had been with the Cossack County Sheriff's Department for a year and a half and running solo for the last six months. He had discovered the winter nights in rural Iowa consist of a lot of boring time when nothing happens. After ten o'clock, the traffic on the country roads disappears. There were long stretches when he didn't see headlights for hours, and the tires of his squad car were the only ones making marks on the frost-covered backroads. When he had ridden with his training officer, Sgt. Sanders, they had killed the dead time sitting at the law center swapping stories with the dispatcher and the Calvin Police Department officers. Jesse hadn't gotten a degree in criminal justice and become a deputy sheriff so he could listen to other people's war stories. Since being on his own, he had spent the slow times doing surveillance on the Raleigh Farm Service

Center. He would sit for two or three hours in his departmental Ford Explorer, watching from the dirt road that dead-ended just inside the Sandhill Slough Wildlife Refuge.

The farm service made an easy target for the local meth cooks. It sat smack dab in the middle of nowhere ten miles from the nearest town. Back when ephedrine was easy to get, the farm service had been hit on a regular basis, but not many people did small cooks anymore. These days most of the methamphetamine came across the southern border through Mexico, or from the big labs of the biker gangs. But recently the farm service had reported finding some valves on their tanks not shut tightly and leaking wisps of ammonia on some mornings. Someone was cooking meth and finding who was stealing the anhydrous had become Jesse's secret mission. Nothing had happened since he had been watching … until now.

The pickup went back out on the state highway, pulled off on the shoulder again and turned off its lights. The truck became a dark blob against a curtain of blowing snow.

Jesse decided he needed a closer look. Leaving his headlights off, he eased his Explorer forward, driving by feel, keeping his wheels in the two frozen ruts that made the one-lane road. When the wheels rose out of them, he would slow and drop them back in. He stopped the Explorer in a low spot with high elderberry bushes on both sides. They would hide the reflective sheriff's markings on the white SUV, he hoped.

He turned the defroster fan up a notch as the windshield clouded over. Snowflakes on the warm glass melted and turned into mini puddles that slithered down toward the Explorer's hood. Afraid the movement of the windshield wipers would give him away, he left them off and strained to see through the blurry windshield with his Bausch and Lomb binoculars.

A hundred yards in front of him, the steel buildings of the farm service squatted under an overhead light like giant alphabet blocks, like children would play with. The center office building looked back at him with square yellow eyes from its security-lighted windows, while the two windowless buildings flanking it were faceless cubes.

East of the buildings sat the big white tank holding the bulk anhydrous, and north of it, two lines of tank trailers were parked in neat rows. The spotlighted American and

Iowa flags on the flagpole thrashed furiously in the wind, but those and the blowing snow were the only movements Jesse saw.

Whoever was out there had to be a hardcore cook and a meth user. Northern Iowa was a bitch in the winter when it was this cold. He had started his shift at six and the temperature had been below zero. It felt as if it might have risen a few degrees since then, but the storm they'd been predicting had started. The snow was falling in big flakes and the wind had picked up until it was snowing sideways.

Sweat beaded up on his back, and Jesse turned the defroster fan down and looked out the windshield at the pickup again.

After a few minutes, a car went by on the highway, throwing snow and blotting out the pickup briefly in a swirling white cloud. The truck's headlights came on, and it pulled out onto the highway and fishtailed for a moment on the slick road as it turned south on the county blacktop.

Jesse watched it come towards him, He didn't have a clue what was going on, but it was time he found out. The truck went east passed the farm service again, and Jesse pulled the Explorer in behind it with his lights still off. As soon as they were swallowed by a dip in the road, he turned on his headlights and top lights.

The pickup slowly pulled off on the side of the road. When it was stopped, Jesse turned off his red rotating lights and turned on his forward amber flashers, hoping they would make him less noticeable if anyone was watching from the farm service.

Jesse grabbed his radio's microphone. "Cossack County from Car-seven."

No answer.

He waited a few seconds and repeated, "Cossack County from Car-seven."

"Traffic ... County?" It was Melonie's voice. She must have taken over the dispatching duties at ten. Jamie had been dispatching when Jesse came on at eight.

"Cossack County this is Car-seven. I'll be out with a brown Chevy pickup on the Refuge Road east of the Raleigh Farm Service Center." The license plate on the pickup was covered with snow. "No plate information at this time, Cossack County."

"Car-seven ... you are ... I have... you at ... Road."

Jesse blew out a frustrated sigh. The radio repeater was going out again.

Jesse repeated the information until he was sure Melonie at least knew where he was if he needed help. He slipped into his coat and put on his Russian-looking winter hat.

Outside the Explorer, the wind bit him, slicing through his coat as if he weren't wearing it. The snow stung his face like miniature pieces of shrapnel. Jesse cleaned the truck's license plate and checked the pickup's box. A few empty beer cans lay in it under a thin feathering of snow.

Jesse moved forward and checked the inside of the vehicle. On the rear fold-down seat sat a blue and white Igloo cooler. He shined his flashlight into the driver's face when he rolled the window down a couple inches.

"Roll the window all the way down, please," Jesse said.

"If I do, the cab will fill up with snow," the driver said in a highly nasal voice.

Jesse recognized him. They called him Pug because he had a severely flattened nose—Jesse didn't know his real name. He was in his early thirties and had a shaved head, now covered with a black stocking cap. Last year when Jesse had been riding with Sgt. Sanders, they had talked with Pug a couple times.

"What are you doing out here tonight?" Jesse asked.

"Just driving around checking the weather," Pug said and gave him a disingenuous smile packed with nervousness.

Jesse put his head by the open window trying to detect the odor of alcohol. He couldn't smell anything, but the wind was beating at his back. The guy could have been puke-faced drunk, and he wouldn't have smelled it. "May I see your driver's license, please?"

Pug already had it in his hand and handed it through the window. It identified him as Delbert Goebel.

Jesse motioned toward the backseat. "What's in the cooler?"

"Nothing," Pug said and turned around in the seat.

"Keep your hands where I can see them!" Jesse screamed. In one motion he had his Smith and Wesson .40 out of its holster and pointed at Pug. His heart pounded in his throat.

Pug eased back around and clutched the steering wheel with two shaking hands. "Hey man, I was just going to show you the cooler's empty." His nasal voice trembled.

Jesse shined his flashlight around inside the truck again, doing a detail check for weapons to give his heartrate time to drop back to normal. He couldn't see anything.

"I'll check the cooler myself, if it's okay with you?" Jesse asked.

The guy nodded with his hands still gripping the steering wheel.

Technically, Jesse needed Pug's permission before he could search the cooler, and technically he had gotten it.

Jesse holstered his weapon. He opened the front driver's door and the rear suicide door. The cooler was empty, but it would be a good way for transporting anhydrous.

"It's cold out here," Jesse said. He closed the rear door. "Shut off the truck and come back to my car."

"I ain't done nothing, man."

"Shut it off and get in my squad car."

"If I shut it off, the windshield will ice over," Pug said. "I got to get home. I got work tomorrow."

"You can leave it running," Jesse said. "But come back to my squad car."

Pug crawled out of the truck and the wind slammed the truck's door shut. He wore a red flannel shirt, jeans and black tennis shoes. His arms were wrapped tightly around his chest to keep warm

"Don't you have a coat?" Jesse asked.

"Didn't bring one," Pug said. "I didn't plan on getting out of the truck. It's freezing out here."

Any doubt Jesse had that Pug had dropped someone off vanished. He would not have lasted ten minutes out in this weather dressed the way he was. Someone else was out there.

When they reached the Explorer, Jesse patted Pug down for weapons and put him in the backseat. Jesse slid into the front seat, took a deep breath and still couldn't smell alcohol. He pulled his cell phone out of the holder on his belt—*screw the piece of crap radio*—and had Melonie run a wants and warrants check on Delbert Goebel: he was clean.

Pug had been in prison twice but had gotten married after the second time. Sgt. Sanders had said Pug's wife was keeping him on the straight and narrow. It had been awhile since he'd been in trouble.

"Can you turn the heat up, man? I'm freezing back here," Pug said.

Jesse cranked the heater fan to full speed.

"So tell me again what you're doing out here?" Jesse asked, talking louder to be heard above the roaring fan.

"I told you. I'm just driving around looking at the weather."

"You dropped someone off," Jesse said, watching him in the rearview mirror.

"No, I didn't."

"Don't call me a liar," Jesse said. "I saw you do it."

A surprised look jumped on Pug's face, but he didn't say anything.

Jesse turned in his seat and looked at Pug. "So who was it?"

More silence.

"Who was it?"

"It was just some guy I picked up who wanted a ride," Pug said. "He got to be a pain in the ass so I kicked him out."

Jesse didn't believe it. It was absurd. You didn't give someone a ride and drop them off in a snowstorm. He motioned toward the pickup. "Whose truck is that?"

Another pause.

"Is it yours?"

"Yeah, it's mine."

The times when they had talked with Pug before, he had been driving a rusted-out piece-of-crap Grand Prix. Jesse called the law center on his phone again and had Melonie run the tags on the pickup.

"The truck belongs to Walter Hemper," Jesse said, looking at him in the mirror. "Is he the one you dropped off?"

More silence and Jesse knew the answer.

"You know I'll find out," Jesse said.

"Okay man, listen, I'm going to level with you," Pug said. The surprise had abandoned his face. He looked worried now. "Wally showed up at my place and said he needed a driver. I thought we were going to pick up another car. He drove out here, stopped on the highway and got out. I don't have a clue what he's doing."

"He got out in the middle of nowhere in a snowstorm?"

"I thought maybe he had to piss or something."

"Do I look that stupid?"

"Hey, I don't know what he's doing," Pug said, "and that's all I know."

Jesse wouldn't get anything out of him. Once they had done time, they didn't give someone up easily. He didn't have anything on Pug right now. Until he caught Hemper with the anhydrous, he couldn't file charges on anyone. He had hoped there would be anhydrous in the pickup when he made the stop. Now if Hemper saw him, he would toss the anhydrous, and with this snow, it could be spring before they found it. Sgt. Sanders had some kind of connection with Pug. Jesse guessed he might have used him as an informant at one time. If Jesse did Pug a favor, it was possible Sanders could get him to rollover on Hemper.

"I tell you what I'll do," Jesse said. "I'll give you a break tonight. You get in the pickup and go straight home. I'll have the Calvin PD go by your house in 15 minutes. If this pickup isn't there, I'll get an arrest warrant for you. Understand?" It was a bluff. He had nothing on Pug—parking on the highway wasn't illegal—but he didn't want Pug hanging around and picking up Hemper.

"What about Wally?" Pug asked.

"You let me worry about him," Jesse said and turned around and looked at Pug again. "And don't try calling him either."

"It wouldn't do no good," Pug said. "He ain't answering."

"Why?"

"Don't know. I haven't been able to get ahold of him. He ain't answering his phone or texts." Pug leaned forward until his flattened nose touched the security cage between the front and back seat. "Tell me the truth. Your boy Sanders has him already, right?"

"What do you mean?"

"Wally called earlier and said he thought someone was out there with him. That's Sanders, right?" He flopped back in the seat. "Man, I'm screwed. My old lady is going to divorce my ass."

Jesse was the only deputy working. If someone had a tail on Hemper, it was not someone from the sheriff's department, and the state police were focused on heroin and fentanyl. He doubted they would waste manpower on a rinky-dink local cook like Hemper.

Jesse put his shoulder against the driver's door and forced it open with the wind doing its best to keep it closed. The citation books and log sheets in the console ruffled and snapped as the wind dove inside the vehicle. He stepped out into the raw weather and braced a hand against the door frame to keep from being blown back inside the Explorer.

Jesse opened the rear door and handed Pug his driver's license. "Remember, go straight home." He almost laughed because he sounded like a mother talking to a little boy. "I'll have the police department check on you in 15 minutes."

"Man, it's going be at least a half hour before I can get home in this crap," Pug said. "It's really coming down."

The storm had picked up. The wind shook the Explorer as if trying to tip it over. The windward doors had snow plastered on them like stucco.

"Okay, 30 minutes, but no more," Jesse said.

Pug ran to the truck hunched over with his arms wrapped around him. He got in and Jesse followed him out onto the state highway.

It was tough driving with the visibility less than 50 yards. Jesse followed the pickup's taillights until he was sure it was headed for Calvin. At the first intersection, he turned around and went back to the farm service. He parked the Explorer in the sheltered area east of the buildings by the bulk anhydrous tank.

Jesse pulled his cell phone out of its holder and called the dispatcher.

"Melonie, this is Jesse again. Could you have the city officers run by Pug's place in about a half hour and check if the pickup I just stopped is sitting there?"

"Will do."

"I'll be out at the Raleigh Farm Service Center," Jesse said. "I think Walter Hemper is here stealing anhydrous. I'm going to try and find him."

"Be careful," Melonie said. "The storm is getting worse. I can't even see across the street here in town."

"It's that bad?"

"We have a full-scale blizzard, and it's headed your way," she said. "The state pulled the plows off the roads."

"It shouldn't take long," Jesse said. "I'll follow his tracks and get him out of here."

"Okay," she said. "But keep in mind Jesse, if you need help, it will take a while to get someone to you."

"Thanks for the warning."

He hung up the phone and put it back in his belt holder. Melonie had sounded worried. Jesse wondered if he shouldn't be, too. At the law enforcement academy, they had said that cops got in trouble when they let courage trump common sense. He hoped he wasn't doing that now.

Jesse dug his snowmobile suit and black bunny boots out of the duffle bag in the back of the Explorer and put them on. He locked the SUV's doors, pulled the flaps on his winter hat around his ears and buckled the chin strap.

The anhydrous tanks stood in the shelter of the farm service buildings. The snow came more or less straight down back there without being drifted into piles by the wind. Hemper's tracks hadn't filled in yet; finding them was easy under the overhead light. A single set of tracks came from the direction of the highway and went between the two rows of tank trailers. A mass of footprints covered the ground between the trailers where Hemper had gotten the anhydrous—it was why he hadn't seen Hemper from his hide—and another set of tracks went back toward the highway.

Jesse checked the time: 01:40 hrs.

Walking across the plowed field from the highway would take ten minutes. Getting the anhydrous would take another ten minutes, and it would take ten minutes to get back to the highway. It had been almost an hour and a half since Pug dropped Hemper off. Something had definitely happened to him.

Chapter Two

Jesse peeked out from the behind the shelter of the buildings into the open field that stood between him and the highway. Melonie was right; it had become a blizzard. He did not relish going out into the full force of the storm, but Hemper could be lost out there in the field. He might be wandering around looking for the highway, or, depending on how he was dressed, he could have been overcome by the cold and be lying on the ground somewhere covered with snow and freezing, maybe near death. Catching him stealing anhydrous had suddenly become the secondary objective.

Jesse turned on his flashlight. The beam of light was alive with blowing snow. Each snowflake reflected the light back at him in glowing white specks. Beyond five feet, everything swirled in a wall of whirling dots that brought him a moment of vertigo.

Jesse braced himself and stepped out from the protection of the buildings into the full force of the storm.

The tracks that had been sharp and clear in the shelter of the buildings were indistinct out in the open field. A foot and a half of snow had been on the ground before the storm started, but Hemper's tracks were filled in until only indentations were left, two side-by-side shallow drag lines in the snow where he had shuffled his feet.

After the first fifty yards, the tracks changed. They were four drag marks: two small ones in the middle as before and bigger marks on the outside. It looked as if Hemper had fallen and was crawling on his hands and knees. Everything was too drifted in. Jesse couldn't make sense of any of it, but he quickened his pace. If Hemper was crawling on the ground, he was in big trouble.

Suddenly the tracks cut sharply left. After ten yards they went back right before cutting left again. All the zigzagging back and forth made following his trail even harder. In places the snow had washed the tracks out. A couple times Jesse couldn't find them and searched blindly until he found the trail again. He finally lost it for good.

Jesse stopped and shined his flashlight in all directions, finding nothing but the whirling white kaleidoscope of blowing snow.

Jesse stood in the open field with no tracks to follow. It had been a huge mistake coming out there. His own footprints were already filled with snow, and he had jogged back and forth so much following Hemper, he wasn't sure what direction he was facing or where the farm service sat. He strained to catch the glow of the lights by the buildings. There was nothing but the white wall of blowing snow in all directions.

The cold crept inside his snowmobile suit and sent a shiver through him.

From his emergency medical training, Jesse knew shivering was the first sign of hypothermia. It was the body generating heat by creating motion. Next would come uncontrollable shaking, then mental confusion. If he stood in the wind much longer, the cold would paralyze him, and he wouldn't be able to move or figure out how to get back to the Explorer. He didn't want to be found frozen to death less than a quarter-mile from safety. Finding Hemper would have to wait until he could get more people to help.

Jesse jerked the zipper on his snowmobile suit to his chin and pulled his cap farther over his ears and neck. The farm service was south of him. The wind was out of the northwest. If he walked crosswind with the wind blowing into the back of his right shoulder, he would be going in a southerly direction.

Keep the snow blowing at a 45-degree angle away from me and to my left.

If he missed the farm service, he would at least run into the blacktop running on the south side of it. From there he could find the farm service and his Explorer.

He had walked a few steps in that direction when a whiff of anhydrous hit him.

The smell couldn't be from the farm service—the wind was coming from the wrong direction—and the only anhydrous out in the field would be the stuff Hemper had stolen. It was coming from directly upwind or Jesse never would have smelled it with the wind blowing that hard. He thought about getting back to safety and getting help. Instead he turned into the wind and followed the smell.

With each step the odor grew stronger. At times when the wind hit him right, his eyes watered and burned. Ahead of him, the beam of the flashlight picked up something thin and dark sticking out of the snow. It looked like a bicycle inner tube. The scent of anhydrous was overpowering.

Jesse took a step and his foot hit something soft. He jumped back. Before he looked, he knew it was Hemper.

He lay face down in the snow wearing all white, white coveralls, a white stocking cap and white tennis shoes.

Hemper's feet must be frozen with nothing but tennis shoes covering them. Jesse dropped on one knee beside him.

"Are you okay?" Jesse yelled against the wind as he shook him by the shoulder.

No response. He took off his right glove and reached around the side of Hemper's neck, checking for a carotid pulse. His hand plunged into something warm and sticky. Jesse jerked away and stared in horror at the blood on his hand glistening in the beam of the flashlight. He grabbed Hemper by his coveralls and rolled him over.

Jesse jumped back, his heart pounding against his sternum.

Hemper's head lay flopped back at a weird angle with his throat spread open like a gaping mouth. Dull, sightless eyes looked at Jesse. Shredded skin and red meat sparkled wet and grotesque from where Hemper's Adam's apple should have been. Dark blood was everywhere on his face, coveralls and the snow under him. Jesse could see the bone of his spine and look down the horribly white, severed windpipe sticking out of his chest like a ribbed vacuum cleaner hose. Pale arteries, like the cut ends of rubber tubing, still oozed drops of blood. Hemper's spine and the nape of his neck were all that held his head and body together.

What happened? What the hell happened?

He grabbed his epaulet mic and screamed into it. "Cossack County from Car-seven. Emergency!"

Nothing.

Of course nothing, you idiot. The repeater isn't working.

The fingers on his uncovered right hand were wet with blood and already numb from the cold and wind. He wiped them on his snowmobile suit, but they had already lost feeling. His glove had fallen on the ground when he jumped away from the body. Now it was buried somewhere under the snow. He looked for it frantically for a few seconds and couldn't find it. Screw the glove, he decided. Getting help moving his way was the important thing right now.

He moved the flashlight into his numb right hand so he could work the zipper with the hand that still had feeling in it. Awkwardly he dug inside the snowmobile suit and found the cell phone holder on his belt. It was empty. He checked again … definitely empty. The snowmobile suit rubbing against the phone must have worked it out of its holder.

Jesse leaped to his feet and frantically patted his pants' legs from his waist to his ankles, hoping it was trapped in one of them. Nothing. He searched the area around him, kicking the snow. Nothing.

Something above Hemper's bloody head caught his attention. He let the flashlight's beam rest there for a moment.

Footprints. Huge footprints. Footprints way too big to have been made by a person and so fresh the snow hadn't filled them in yet. Footprints made only minutes ago, maybe seconds ago. Footprints something had been standing in when Jesse walked up to the body.

Suddenly Jesse knew why there had been two sets of tracks. What had Pug said?

"When Wally called, he said he thought someone was out there with him."

That's why his tracks had zigzagged. Something had been chasing him.

Jesse shined his flashlight out in the direction the tracks went. Nothing but blowing snow. Another shiver went through him that wasn't from the cold. He fumbled inside his suit and dug out his Smith and Wesson and pointed it at the storm. His right hand was so numb he could barely hold the pistol. It could never have pulled the trigger. He stuffed his hand in the side pocket of his snowmobile suit for protection against the weather, hoping it would warm enough to regain feeling. With his gloved hand he zipped his snowmobile suit closed. He had to get help.

Melonie's words came back at him: *"Keep in mind, Jesse, if you need help, it will take a while to get someone to you in this weather."*

Jesse headed toward where he thought the farm service was, keeping the wind against his back right shoulder and glancing over that shoulder frequently. His progress was frustratingly slow, even with the wind pushing him. The shivering came in waves as the cold blew through his suit. He walked hunched over with his numb right hand in his pocket with the pistol, and the hand with the flashlight wrapped across his chest holding in body heat.

After a few minutes, he tripped on something under the snow that made a sharp sound like glass shattering when he went through it. He sprawled face first on the ground. Snow covered his head and slipped down his neck. The shivering became shaking. His frozen right hand screamed with pain when he tried to catch himself. He dropped his flashlight.

For a moment he lay on his belly stunned and shaking, unable and not wanting to move. The urge to curl into a tight ball and lay there until the shaking stopped overwhelmed him. But something from deep inside a still warm part of his mind told him if he did, he would freeze. He forced himself to a sitting position.

The flashlight was on his left, glowing white under a veil of snow. With his gloved hand he dug it out. Snow melted on the hot lens forming a tiny puddle on the glass. He put his uncovered right hand above it and drew the warmth from the flashlight into it. His hand tingled as it warmed, finally stinging with a thousand needles, but at least he had some feeling in it. His little finger stuck sideways at a funny angle. Something had happened to it during the fall. Now that he had feeling in the hand, he could pull the trigger on the .40 … unless he had dropped it.

The hard steel of the pistol greeted him when he patted his pocket. Jesse struggled to his feet and put his frozen hand back into the pocket with the pistol. He shined the flashlight on the ground and saw he had stumbled into a frozen grass waterway—a strip of grass the farmer had left in the field to prevent soil erosion. The dried blades of grass were covered with ice. When he moved his feet, it sounded like wind chimes tinkling.

Jesse needed to get moving. The shaking had become constant after the header into the snow. His thoughts were jumbled. Lying in the snow and curling into a fetal position was still an overwhelming urge. He forced himself to put one foot in front of the other and moved in the direction of the farm service.

Put the wind on my right back and get going.

He quickened his pace, hoping the extra movement would generate body heat.

After a minute, he heard something behind him. He stopped and listened through the howling wind. The sound came again, louder this time. A crashing sound like glass breaking. It took a moment for his slowed brain to figure it out, and when it did, a chill went through him that was far worse than anything the cold could bring. Something had gone through the grass waterway behind him. Something was following him … coming after him!

He pulled the pistol out of his pocket. It didn't matter if his hand froze. A frostbitten hand was gravy compared to what had happened to Hemper.

Jesse walked backward, his heart racing and the gun and flashlight pointing at where the sound had come from. The wind blew in his face. Tears froze on his cheeks. His hands shook and his joints ached from the cold. He couldn't feel his face from looking into the gusting wind. His nose and cheeks were numb, maybe frozen, and he didn't care. No matter what, he wouldn't turn his back on whatever was out there.

When it touched his back, he fell to the ground screaming.

Three more times he screamed, high-pitched like a little girl, before he turned and pointed the pistol at the side of a farm service building. He put a hand on the metal wall and sobbed with relief. He'd made it.

You're not there yet.

It came through the fog in his brain and hit him like a hammer. He was a long ways from being safe. Until he was in the Explorer—out of the wind, getting warm and behind locked doors—he wasn't safe.

He looked back into the blowing snow. There wasn't any way of getting in touch with the sheriff's office. His cell phone was gone and the radio was down. He'd have to drive back to Calvin, if he could even get there it in this weather. He was a long ways from having made it.

Using the side of the building for support, he regained his feet. He hurried around the building the best he could because his legs didn't work right. His knees and hips were freezing and wouldn't bend. He moved like the Tinman from *The Wizard of Oz* before the oil can.

When he came around the corner of the building and saw the Explorer sitting under the light, his heart leapt. He attempted a sprint, but the most he could manage was a stiff-legged waddle.

All the Explorer's windows were frosted over. A quarter inch of ice covered the windshield where snow had melted and froze. In the shelter of the buildings and with the security light, Jesse could see fifty feet. He felt better, safer. Nothing could sneak up on him. He fumbled under his snowmobile suit, found his keys and worked them awkwardly out of his pocket with his left hand.

He fought with the frozen door, opened it and struggled into the vehicle, his stiff muscles making him an invalid. Before he put the key in the ignition, he locked the doors. When he turned the key, the engine gave out a sick groan. Jesse's heart stood still for an instant until the motor roared to life.

Jesse grabbed the radio microphone. "Cossack County from Car-seven."

Still nothing.

All of the windows were too frosted over to see through. He cranked the defroster fan to full speed. The cold air bounced off the windshield's glass and back into his face. He slouched against the door, getting below the draft of cold air, and watched the windshield, willing it to clear so he could get out of there.

After a couple minutes, a thin line of unfrosted glass with water drips of melted ice slowly running toward the bottom of the windshield appeared. The temperature gauge on the dash display had moved off the C.

The vehicle warmed and so did Jesse. His face hurt. His frozen hand felt as if it was on fire, and his little finger still stuck out at an unnatural angle.

A four-inch window had cleared above the dashboard when something bumped into the back of the Explorer.

Jesse came upright in his seat and froze when he looked out the back window. The Explorer's frosted rear window was filled with a dark shapeless form silhouetted in the farm service's overhead light. Jesse tried swallowing and couldn't. His hands shook. The injured right one bumped hard against the console. He barely felt it. Frantically he dug the pistol out of his pocket. When he looked back, it was gone.

His head moved continuously as he checked all the windows trying to find it again. Nothing.

The cleared area on the bottom of the windshield had grown to six inches. It was enough. Jesse threw the pistol on the passenger's seat and slammed the Explorer into drive. He floored the accelerator. The rear wheels spun uselessly on the slick snow, and the Explorer's rear end slid sideways. Jesse dropped the Explorer into four-wheel drive and did a wide U-turn. He headed the Explorer toward the blacktop. As he passed the office building, he caught a glimpse of something as it disappeared between two of the buildings. Jesse gasped and stomped the accelerator to the floor.

Chapter Three

Aaron Barnum ended the call with his attorney and sat in his car for a moment. They needed one more meeting with his soon-to-be-ex-wife, Natalie, and her attorney before the judge signed the dissolution of marriage decree. At their last meeting she had brought her new boyfriend, "Bryan with a Y." He was a tall skinny college kid, ten years younger than her. She had brought him to get under Aaron's skin. They had agreed to have an amicable divorce, but he didn't think that creature existed.

Aaron wouldn't be 33 for another four months and already he'd tanked a marriage. He took full responsibility for it. When he'd quit the Davenport PD and became an investigator for the Department of Criminal Investigation, the marriage was finished. It just took a few years for both of them to realize it. Nat was high maintenance and needy. It had been fine when he was a patrol officer, and even three years later when he made detective, because he could be home every night listening to her problems and telling her how beautiful she was. But when you're living in motels most of the time, you can't do that. And it became harder and harder finding outrage because some beautician had cut off a half inch too much of Natalie's red hair, when he had come from interrogating a guy who had beaten his girlfriend's face off with a baseball bat, and the only remorse he had was that he'd spend the rest of his life in prison.

Aaron would get through the divorce. He was six-feet tall with blue eyes and brown hair he kept cut short for efficiency. People said he was good-looking, and he believed them—he had to be or Natalie would have never gone out with him. Eventually he'd find someone else who wasn't so needy and could take him being gone so much.

Aaron stepped out of his car and went into the Cossack County Law Center. A wall of bullet-proof glass stood immediately in front of him, separating the control center from the rest of the world. On the left was a door with a sign that read: Calvin Police

Department, and a door on the right that read: Cossack County Sheriff's Office.

Aaron chose the one on the right. It opened into a narrow hallway with another closed door at the far end. Halfway down on the right was a customer service window. Over the top of the window a sign with a gold sheriff's star announced Cossack County Sheriff's Office.

A bone-thin woman with black hair pulled back harshly in a bun sat at an oak desk in the center of the room. She had a sickly pale face with bronze lipstick and coal-like dark eyes peering out from behind round tortoiseshell glasses. The glasses magnified her eyes and made her look like an emaciated owl, an image heightened by the black and white houndstooth shirt she wore under her gray pantsuit.

"May I help you?" She had a crackly voice and not a hint of a smile creased her face.

"I'm looking for Sheriff Thompson," Aaron said.

"Do you have an appointment?"

"He's expecting me."

Aaron pulled out his flat badge in the leather case with his ID. The woman came over and took the badge from Aaron. She was short, no more than five-three even with her exaggerated black heels. She took the badge from him and scrutinized it as if hunting for a terrorist using fake credentials.

"I will let him know you are here," she said, keeping the badge when she went back and sat at her desk again.

The entire reception area was impressively neat and had a thick smell of air freshener, something floral. Nothing was out of place. The desk had a stapler, stacked gray plastic IN and OUT boxes and a desk pad calendar with no writing on it. Not even a stray pen lay on the desk. Nothing cluttered the counter or the tops of the file cabinets standing in perfect alignment throughout the room.

The woman picked up the phone and hit a few buttons. "Cal, there is a Special Agent Aaron Barnum from the Iowa Department of Criminal Investigation here to see you," she said, reading from the badge. She nodded at the phone. "I will let him know."

She came back and handed Aaron his badge. "He will be right out."

In a moment a door on the right opened and Sheriff Thompson rushed into the reception area. He was tall and lanky, Aaron guessed about six-three, in his late 40s with curly brown hair that had crept back over the top of his head, giving him a major league forehead. A BB-sized mole stood out on his right cheek like a beauty mark on an actress from the 60s. He smiled and his cheeks squeezed his green eyes closed until they were nothing but slits. It was the smile of a used car salesman, someone they'd call Tex or Buck—Aaron guessed *Cal* would fit that category, too. Aaron had looked into Sheriff Thompson's background, and he *had* been a car salesman before he became a loan officer at the local bank. Three years ago, without prior law enforcement experience, he was elected Cossack County Sheriff.

The sheriff extended his hand. "I'm Cal Thompson." He wore a tailored brown uniform with sharp, professional creases, but his green clip-on tie had a dime-sized ketchup stain. "Dina said your name's Aaron? I don't think I've met you before."

Aaron shook his hand. "It's my first time here."

"Normally we deal with Cassie Baker from your department."

"Cassie works narcotics," Aaron said. "I'm a homicide investigator."

"So you think it's a murder?" Panic flashed across the sheriff's face for an instant.

Aaron gave him a smile to put him at ease. That, and "be diplomatic with the locals," were the only things he had learned from his former partner, Frank Turner. Frank had been two years away from retirement and a functional alcoholic when Aaron joined the DCI. Frank never touched a drop when he was working, but within an hour after they'd gotten to the motel at night, he was hammered. Usually he was hungover until noon, and the last six months before he retired, he had the shakes by late afternoon.

After he retired, Frank had become a non-functional alcoholic. Aaron had seen him twice since then. Both times he was ploughed with a water tumbler of Hiram Walker's Ten High in his hand. He had an ex-wife, two kids and a grandkid. He hadn't seen any of them in years. Aaron hoped he wouldn't be him in 25 years, but soon Aaron would have the ex-wife.

"I can't even guess if it's a murder or not yet," Aaron said. "But if there's a possibility, they send me."

"Personally, I think it was all a freak accident," the sheriff said. "Too much doesn't make sense for it to be a murder."

"Is there someplace we can talk?" Aaron said, glancing at the skinny owl. He didn't want to discuss the case standing in the hallway where anyone passing by could hear.

"Of course. We can use my office." He opened the door wider. "Dina, we'll be in my office for a little bit."

"Remember, you have a meeting with the safety board at three," Dina said.

Aaron glanced at his watch: 1:30.

"We should be done by then," the sheriff said and went into his office.

Sheriff Thompson's office smelled musty, as if there was a colony of mold hiding somewhere. It was the polar opposite of the outer office. A gray metal desk sat in front of a shaded window. Several layers of papers and Manila folders covered the top of the desk except for a small area in front of the high-backed office chair. Against the wall opposite the desk, black hard rifle cases, ammunition boxes, pepper spray canisters and empty cardboard boxes lay in piles with no semblance of order. A thin walkway led to the desk, but the rest of the floor was littered with stacks of books, piles of old uniforms and more boxes. It seemed as much a storage closet as an office.

Aaron sat in a swivel chair wedged between boxes of outdated code books.

"I was expecting two of you," the sheriff said. "I thought you guys worked in pairs."

"Budget cuts," Aaron said. "They decided we could work as well by ourselves." They had reduced the size of the department by attrition. When an agent retired, they didn't replace them. Most of the other agents had hollered like hell, but Aaron had been glad to see it happen. He was tired of babysitting Frank. It was nice not making excuses and having to cover for a partner.

"So what do you need from me?" Sheriff Thompson asked after he'd closed the door and took a seat at the desk.

"I'd like to see the original file on the case."

"I emailed everything to you." The sheriff's beauty mark raised in a smile, but it seemed forced.

"I know," Aaron said. "But I always check the originals."

He had found from past experiences that often things like handwritten notes didn't get passed on. Sometimes original reports were put into the file along with the final report and only the final report was sent. And sometimes officers made handwritten notes, put them in the file and forgot about them or left out little details because they might be embarrassing to the officer or the department.

"I should have it here somewhere." The sheriff dug through the papers on top of his desk.

It didn't surprise Aaron the report would be buried somewhere in the mountain of papers instead of in an alphabetized file cabinet. Given the condition of the office, it seemed perfectly natural.

"Here it is." The sheriff held up a thick manila folder. "It's big. Everyone involved did a report."

Aaron had read the reports he had been sent. Most of them read as if they were written by an eighth grader who had flunked English.

Sheriff Thompson thumbed through the file briefly and laid it atop the papers piled on the desk in front of Aaron.

Aaron moved it closer, but never looked at it. "Thank you. I'll go through it later and get it back to you when I'm finished."

"Leave it with Dina when you're done," the sheriff said. "Anything else?"

"I'll need a place where I can work," Aaron said. "Someplace private if possible." Small departments had stuck him in basements and even hallways the general public walked through. He needed a place where suspects and witnesses could be interviewed without worrying someone might overhear.

"You can use the room across the hall," Sheriff Thompson said. "It even has a lock on the door, so you can leave all your stuff there at night."

Aaron wouldn't be leaving his *stuff* there. Spare rooms always had extra keys, and the janitor usually had a master key. He wasn't leaving his things laying out where a deputy, or even the sheriff, might be tempted to check out how the case was progressing.

Aaron followed a strict need-to-know policy when he worked.

The sheriff paused for a moment and studied Aaron. It seemed he had a question he was debating whether or not to ask.

"Would you mind if I assisted you?" he asked. "I'd like to observe your investigation." The mole raised in a salesman's smile. "I don't have much experience at it. I went through the academy after I was elected, but they don't teach you much about investigating." He smiled even more broadly, squeezing his eyes shut. "I thought maybe I could learn something from you."

"I'd be glad to have the help," Aaron said. It was unusual for a sheriff to assist. Usually the department's detective or some officer assisted. They knew the locals and could help with background information on any possible suspects or friends of suspects. The sheriff or chief of police also wanted someone from their department in on the investigation as an early warning system if the department had screwed something up. This time it was different because the sheriff had already decided it was an accidental death. Coming to any other conclusion would be proving him wrong.

"Since you're going to assist me, maybe you can explain a few things," Aaron said.

"Such as?"

"As I understand it, your deputy found Hemper's body early on a Thursday morning?"

"Sometime between two and two-thirty," Sheriff Thompson said. "He never logged it anywhere so I'm guessing."

"But the body wasn't recovered until Saturday afternoon?"

"Right," the sheriff said, nodding.

"And why was that?" Aaron asked.

"Our radio repeater was down, and Jesse … Deputy Gordon … lost his cell phone, so the dispatcher couldn't get a hold of him," the sheriff said. "When Melonie Briggs, the dispatcher, didn't hear anything from him, she got worried and called me.

"I live two miles outside of town, and the storm was so bad I couldn't make it out of my driveway, let alone into town or out in the county where Jesse was. I had Melonie get some off-duty Calvin Police Officers with snowmobiles to go out and find him. They found Jesse about four miles east of Calvin in the ditch. He had driven off the road because of the zero visibility and got stuck."

"Is he okay?"

"He frostbit his face and right hand," the sheriff said. "The face will heal, but they're still not sure about the hand."

"I hope it works out for him," Aaron said.

"I hope so, too," the sheriff said. He looked worried. "I talked with Jesse on the phone that night, and he said there was no doubt Hemper was dead. The storm was supposed to end about noon on Thursday. It was already five in the morning. I couldn't see sending people out into the storm and having them get lost or worse trying to recover the body." The sheriff paused and tapped his fingers nervously on the top of his desk. "I'm still not sure I made the right decision, but it's the one I went with."

Aaron smiled to put him at ease. "It was your call." He didn't second-guess decisions made on the ground unless they were grossly incompetent, and this didn't fit that category. The safety of live people always took precedence over dead people. "So that brings us to Thursday noon."

"We spent all Thursday afternoon and some of the night doing a detailed search of the field where Jesse said he found Hemper."

"And you didn't find him?"

The sheriff shook his head. "The storm had dropped two feet of snow with high winds. There was a snow drift over ten feet high running from one side of the field to the other. We brought out a couple front-end loaders from the county road crew and moved the snow off the whole field."

"That must have been a job."

The sheriff smiled. "Tell me about it, but we had to do it to make sure Hemper wasn't under the snow drift."

"But you didn't find him on Thursday?" Aaron asked.

"After we'd cleared about two-thirds of the field, it was after ten at night and another storm blew in. It got bad, so I suspended the search," the sheriff said. "We marked the area of the field we hadn't searched, and I had a deputy guard the scene until we could come back and finish. On Friday we went back and cleared the rest of the field, and we still didn't find the body."

"What happened?"

"At first I thought someone had gotten sloppy and didn't check the loader buckets well enough," the sheriff said. "I figured we'd moved Hemper from one place to another. Which meant we'd have to redo the whole field."

"That had to suck?"

"I wasn't looking forward to it. I'll tell you that much," Sheriff Thompson said. "Melonie sent a teletype around the area and found a cadaver dog in Minneapolis. They came on Saturday and found Hemper's body around sunset. It was in the field east of where Jesse had said it was. So we cleared the wrong field."

It didn't make sense. "How did that happen?"

The sheriff smiled. "Jesse said Hemper's tracks zigzagged back and forth, and he couldn't see more than ten feet in front of him. I figure he got turned around and didn't know he was in the other field."

Maybe it made sense and maybe it didn't. "I saw the body at the state coroner's in Des Moines," Aaron said. "It was in pretty rough shape." Not much was left but the bones. Most of the muscle had been chewed off.

"The coyotes got at it," the sheriff said. "There's a ton of them around, especially in that area right by the wildlife refuge."

"Do you think coyotes could have done that much damage so quickly?" Aaron wasn't a wildlife expert. He knew little about coyotes.

"One of my deputies shot a buck last deer season," the sheriff said. "It was right at sunset, and he lost the blood trail in the dark. He came back the next morning at first light to look for it. When he finally found it, there was nothing left but some of the hide and the antlers. The coyotes had cleaned it up overnight." The sheriff paused for a moment. "They worked on Hemper for over two days, and it was in the middle of winter when food is hard to come by. So yeah, I have no doubt they did it."

"I hope the coroner can give us something to go on," Aaron said. "There's not much physical evidence if he was murdered."

"You think he was murdered?" The sheriff asked again, and his nervousness came out in how quickly he asked the question. "I'm pretty sure it was an accident.

He fell on something and that's how he cut his throat."

"You might be right," Aaron said and smiled to put him at ease again. "Did you find a tool or weapon under the body?"

"No. But he might have fallen on it and staggered around in the snowstorm bleeding," the sheriff said. "Maybe it's why he was zigzagging back and forth … because he couldn't see."

Doubt covered Sheriff Thompson's face. Aaron wasn't sure if even the sheriff believed his own theory.

The sheriff smiled with his forehead still wrinkled with concern. "Since Jesse wasn't right about what field it happened in, we can't know for sure where the weapon, or whatever, might be," he said. "Of course, I'll have people scour the entire area looking for it when the snow melts this spring."

Way too late. If they found the weapon, or whatever, three months from now, it would prove it was an accident. But if they didn't find it, the murderer could be on the other side of the world by then.

The sheriff stopped and studied Aaron for a moment before he spoke again. "I'll level with you," he said. "I wasn't sure whether to call you guys in on this case or not."

Aaron wasn't surprised. He'd read the sheriff's report.

"Like I said, I'm convinced it was an accidental death," the sheriff said. "But I guess you can't be too cautious."

"It's always good to be cautious with deaths like this," Aaron said. Anytime there was an unattended death you had to be certain what caused it. You couldn't guess at it.

"The county attorney is the one who had me call your department," the sheriff said. "She got nervous about some of the things Jesse was saying."

"Such as?"

The sheriff's beauty mark raised in a grin. "I'm sure you'll talk to him. I'll let him tell you himself," the sheriff said. "Personally, I think it's cut and dry. Hemper was overcome by the anhydrous and fell on something."

Aaron had found nothing was ever cut and dry until you had the evidence to support it. Assuming anything when it involved a death was stupid, but he didn't say anything, because he was trying to be diplomatic.

"Hemper stumbled into the refuge, fell on something and cut his throat," Sheriff Thompson said. "There's all kinds of junk in the refuge he could've cut it on."

The sheriff kept adding things to fit his story. It was all rationalization.

"Aren't there fences around the refuge?" Aaron asked. "I don't remember the deputy reporting going over a fence?"

"Jesse said he lost Hemper's tracks a few times," the sheriff said, defending his theory. "Maybe Jesse didn't go into the refuge and Hemper did. Jesse might have found him when he staggered out of it again."

"You might be right," Aaron said. *But again, it's all speculation without one shred of evidence to back it up.*

"I'm sure once you look into this, you'll see this being a murder doesn't make sense," the sheriff said.

Aaron smiled. "One person killing another seldom makes sense."

Sheriff Thompson smiled back, but it was a nervous smile. "I know," he said, "but there's no motive, and who would go out and murder someone in the middle of a snowstorm?"

It was the first thing about the case the sheriff had said that made sense.

Aaron stood. "Can you show me the room where I'll be working? I'd like to get started."

The sheriff looked at his watch. "I have a meeting at three."

"I'm going to be reviewing the files, that's all." Aaron couldn't believe he expected him to put off the investigation until he could be there. "I won't be interviewing people until tomorrow."

"Are you sure it's necessary? Either my deputies or I have talked to everyone."

"I know," Aaron said. "But I want to do it again and make sure everything was covered."

"Okay," the sheriff said as if he were giving Aaron permission. "But we were pretty thorough."

Aaron left the sheriff's office and went out into the lobby. He needed a Coke. He didn't drink much coffee, but he went through way too many bottles of Coke a day.

He pushed the black call button under the bullet-proof glass and got the attention of the blond dispatcher on the other side of the glass. She was turned away from him watching a TV on the wall.

"May I help you?" she asked when she'd rotated her chair so she could see him. Her voice sounded tinny through the speaker as if he'd ordered a Big Mac.

Aaron guessed she was in her mid-twenties. She reminded him a little of Natalie. Not the way she looked, Nat was a redhead and bustier, but they were both like human mannequins whose main job was looking good. The blonde behind the glass had a thin face surrounded by long, bleached hair. Blue eyes looked out from a face covered with thick, hooker makeup that hid any flaws. Her demeanor was serious, all business. He guessed she called it *professional* while others called her a bitch.

"Is there a pop machine around?" Aaron asked.

"You can get pop down the street at the convenience store," she said wearing a smile with no feeling in it.

He gestured at the area beyond her. "There isn't one back there somewhere?" These small departments always had some kind of a squad room, and there was always a pop machine.

Again the emotionless smile. "I'm sorry, it's for law enforcement personnel only."

He took his badge out of the inside pocket of his sports coat. "I'm sort of a member of the club," he said, holding the badge against the glass.

This time her smile was genuine. "Sorry, I didn't know who you were. Come on in."

She pushed a button in front of her. The security door on the left clicked, and Aaron went through it into the control room. The blonde stood from the bank of radios, phones and monitors and extended her hand. Her brown sheriff's department uniform hid the details, but he guessed she was thin. "I'm Jana."

"I'm Aaron Barnum."

They shook hands, and she held onto his longer than he considered normal.

"I imagine you're here about the Hemper case?" she asked, still holding his hand.

"Right," Aaron said. It was starting to get awkward.

"We've been expecting you," she said, the smile at full spread showing ultra-white, straight teeth.

"So where's the pop machine?"

"Back in the squad room," Jana said and finally released his hand when she pointed at an open doorway at the rear of the control room.

The squad room was little more than a wide hallway with a door on one end and a window at the other. A metal table with six worn red chairs sat under the window. Along the left side were an ancient avocado refrigerator, a sink and a pop machine. A white microwave and Bunn coffeemaker took most of the counter beside the sink. The opposite wall held a line of beige lockers. One of the lockers was covered with newspaper clippings. Most of them were from supermarket tabloids with frantic headlines screaming in all capital letters: I'M HAVING BIG FOOT'S LOVE CHILD! And, CIA CLAIMS ABOMIINABLE SNOWMAN KILLED TALIBAN LEADER!

Aaron got a Coke out of the machine and went back into the control room.

Jana was touching up her lipstick.

"Did you see his body?" Jana asked as soon as he walked through the door.

"What body?"

"Hemper's of course."

"Yes, I've seen it," Aaron said. "Have you?"

"I saw the pictures," she answered with a child-like fascination showing in her blue eyes. "The coyotes really got to it."

Aaron couldn't believe they had shown a dispatcher pictures from a crime scene. Sometimes the smaller departments considered everyone working in the building as law enforcement. They shared information with people who had no business knowing anything about the case. Aaron had run into jailers who had criminal records. Some of these civilians had good friends and relatives who had done time. Aaron shared information on a need-to-know basis, and he didn't see how this dispatcher needed to know anything. If the details of the case got out, how could he determine if any leads were legitimate? Rumors flowed like beer at a college kegger in these cases. You had to be able to separate fact from something someone had heard on the street.

Jana studied him for a moment as she put the lipstick back in her purse. "You know you might be wasting your time coming here."

"Why?"

"Cal says this was all a freak accident," she said.

"I hope he's right," Aaron said and smiled. "It'll make my job easier." He abruptly changed the subject. "What's a good motel in this town?"

"There are only two," she said. "The Sleepy Inn and the Starlight."

"Which would you recommend?"

"The Sleepy Inn," she said without thinking about it. "The Starlight is filled with the low-class dirt bags and construction workers. We get calls four or five nights a week out there."

"I could do without that."

She smiled. "Where are you from?"

"Des Moines." He actually lived in Urbandale, but most people outside the metro area considered the whole area to be Des Moines.

"How many nights are you staying here?"

"It depends on how things go," Aaron said. He hoped it wasn't long.

59

Chapter Four

The room they let Aaron use was some sort of meeting room. It smelled faintly of spoiled food. Aaron guessed they celebrated people's birthdays and had potlucks there. Two long metal tables with simulated wood-grain tops and six green plastic chairs at each table sat in the middle of the room. Simple gray paint covered three of the walls with a whiteboard on the other and a black telephone mounted beside it. A hand-drawn diagram of a building with several outbuildings in black, red and blue erasable ink filled the board. It looked like the plans for a training exercise or the execution of a search warrant.

Aaron set up his laptop and spent the afternoon going through the file. It was massive. A report had been done by everyone even remotely involved in the investigation, including each of the fire department and county road crew people who had participated in moving the snow when they searched the field for Hemper's body. Most of those reports read: *Moved snow looking for the body for two days and didn't find nothing.* They were useless, because if anything had been found, it would have been noted by whoever was in charge and whoever found it. Having every bit of information you could get your hands on was always a good thing, but some departments thought a thick file made a good investigation. A thick file full of relevant information made a good investigation.

Aaron made a list of the people he wanted to interview: Deputy Jesse Gordon for sure; Delbert (Pug) Goebel; Melonie Riggs, the dispatcher the night Hemper was killed; and the county road crew foreman, Roland Poland—Aaron needed a different perspective on the search than the sheriff's. There would be more as the investigation went along, there always was, but those people would be a good starting point.

His cell phone rang and Aaron pulled it out of his jacket pocket and looked at the ID. It was the state medical examiner's office.

"Hello, this is Aaron Barnum. How may I help you?"

"Hi, Aaron. This is Chantel. How's everything going there?"

"Hi, Chantel." Chantel was Dr. Chantel Moore, deputy coroner for the state medical examiner's office. "Everything's going as well as can be expected." She was a tall, ultra-thin brunette with fascinating violet eyes. Her premed and medical school had been paid for with modeling jobs she had done while in high school and college. They had even considered her for the *Sports Illustrated Swimsuit Issue* at one time, but they went with a better-known model with bigger breasts.

"Is it cold there?" the doctor asked.

"Cold enough," Aaron said. "It gets below zero at night."

"Brrr," she said. "Better you than me."

He laughed. "Thanks."

"It's funny how being a half a state away can make so much difference," she said. "It's still above zero here."

"Once you cross Highway 20 you're in the Arctic Circle," Aaron said.

She laughed. "Watch out for Polar bears."

"Not a problem," Aaron said. "I'd have to go outside to see them. I'm staying indoors."

She laughed again. "Good idea," she said and paused for a second. "Aaron, thanks again for going with me to the theater the other night. I had a good time."

"Me too."

They had developed a friendly relationship from working on various cases together. Three nights ago, she'd had two tickets to the musical *Wicked* in Des Moines. The guy who had gotten the tickets had been called out of the country on business, and she'd asked Aaron to go with her. He didn't know what relationship she had with the guy who had gotten the tickets, but Aaron was sure if he asked her out again, she'd accept. He didn't plan on asking. She made more money than him, was way smarter than him, and she dated guys important enough to get called out of the country on business. He hated admitting it, but she intimidated him.

"So why am I honored with your phone call?" Aaron asked.

"It's not much of an honor," she said. "It's about your case. I have a note saying you wanted the results of my examination of the victim as soon as I had them."

"I thought Dr. Timmons was doing the autopsy?"

"He was, but they found a body in the Missouri River," she said. "The hands were tied behind its back. It's an obvious murder victim and high profile—some state senator's son. The water stuff is Ben's specialty, so they sent him and gave me your case."

"Welcome aboard," Aaron said. She didn't have Dr. Timmons' experience, but she knew her stuff. "What do you have for me?"

"What do you want?"

"Let's start with cause of death," Aaron said.

"Exsanguination."

"He bled to death?"

"Right," she answered. "And from the lab results, fairly quickly. There were few signs of hypovolemic shock." Aaron scribbled a note to look up *hypovolemic*. "The report said when the deputy found the victim he had extensive throat injures?" Chantel asked.

"Right," Aaron said. "The deputy said his throat had been cut all the way to the spine."

"My guess is both of the carotid arteries were severed," Chantel said. "The subject would have bled out quickly. Much of that is speculation. The cadaver was in a bad condition. Most of the neck area was gone."

Subject. Cadaver. It was pathologist speak. They didn't work with people. They worked with specimens. "He laid out in a field for a couple days," Aaron said. "The coyotes got to him."

"It was more than coyotes," the doctor said. "I found bite marks from skunks, opossums and raptors."

"Dinosaurs?"

She laughed. "I love your sense of humor, Aaron."

He blushed. She was talking about birds of prey: hawks, eagles and vultures, not some *Jurassic Park* creature.

"I found some teeth marks I can't identify, too," she said.

"What do you mean?"

"They are some of the earlier marks, and most of them are covered with bites from other animals," she said. "It's like the bites are in layers and these are in the first layer. None of the bite marks are clear enough to identify the species, but they are the biggest of the teeth marks."

"Any ideas?" Aaron asked.

"I don't know. Maybe a wolf?"

"Are there wolves in Iowa?"

She chuckled. "You're asking the wrong person. I'm the least outdoorsy person you will ever meet."

"I'm right there with you," Aaron said. He hadn't even been a boy scout. "Maybe it was a wild dog?"

"Does it make a difference?"

"I guess not," Aaron said. "I'm a stickler for details. Is the toxicology done?"

"I have it right here," she said.

He heard a couple clicks of a mouse. He figured she was bringing the results up on her computer screen.

"You can look at them on the lab's site," Chantel said. "They've been posted."

"I'll look at them later and print them off," Aaron said. "Give me an overview for now."

"There were traces of methamphetamine."

"A lot?"

"No," she said. "If this guy was a hardcore user, he was going through withdrawals. There was also alcohol in his system."

"Was he over the limit?"

"Not even close," she said. "I'd say he had maybe a beer or two a couple hours before he died."

"Anything else?"

She paused for a moment. "Not that I can see."

Damn. It would have been nice if he had something he could turn into a lead. "How about your examination? I'll read your report later, but did you find anything interesting I should know about?"

"Nothing that sticks out," she said. "What are you looking for?"

"Is there any way of knowing if it was an accidental death or an intentional act?" Aaron asked. "The local sheriff thinks it was an accident. I'm skeptical because of what the deputy at the scene saw with the neck."

"The body had been damaged extensively post-mortem," she said. "The location where the initial injuries were reported had been destroyed by wildlife feeding on the carcass."

Now she was calling it a carcass. "Thanks anyway," Aaron said.

"Sorry I can't help?"

"It's okay," Aaron said. "I get paid to figure this stuff out. But it would have been nice if you could have said, 'This guy died accidentally,' or even 'This guy was murdered.'"

"If it helps, I have seen accidents where the throat of the victim was ripped open and the carotids were cut."

"Really?"

"I worked a case where a teenager was standing in the back of a pickup when the driver went under an extended eave of a corrugated metal roof," she said. "The metal caught him in the neck and shaved off his neck and face. The other was a farmer on a four-wheeler who hit an uncovered utility pole guy-wire."

"So it is possible?"

"It's possible," she said. "But keep in mind, both victims in those cases were traveling in excess of 20 miles per hour when it happened."

"So I'm back to square one," Aaron said.

"Sorry," she said again. "I've sent you my report. Read it when you get the chance. Maybe you'll see something I didn't."

"I'll take a look at it the first chance I get," Aaron said.

"If you need something else, the body is still here," Chantel said. "Nobody has claimed it."

"I'll let you know after I go through your report," Aaron said.

"Okay. And thanks again for the other night," she said. "We should do it again sometime."

"It sounds like a good idea." He still didn't see it happening.

They hung up.

Aaron was disappointed. The only thing he'd learned from the autopsy was the victim wasn't drunk or stoned, and he had bled out, which Aaron had already suspected. So he was back where he started. He opened the file again.

~*~

Around five, Aaron went out to the control room for another Coke. A different dispatcher sat behind the glass. Aaron pulled his badge out, but she opened the security door before he showed it to her.

"Hi. I'm Agent Aaron Barnum," he said walking into the control room. It had a definite vanilla smell from a glass jar with a burning candle in it sitting on the countertop in front of the radios.

"I know who you are," the dispatcher said. She was an older woman, mid-forties at least, with dirty blond hair and streaks of gray showing through. "Jana was working when you came. Everyone knows about the 'dreamy detective'." She put her fingers up in air quotes and smiled.

"I haven't been called dreamy in a while." He stretched his hand toward her. "And you are?"

"I'm Melonie Riggs." She rose and they shook hands.

She had been the dispatcher the night Hemper died.

"You're on my list," he said.

"List?" She gave him a puzzled look. You're not Santa, so it can't be a naughty list."

Aaron smiled. "You're one of the people I need to talk with about the Hemper case."

She studied him for a long moment.

"I already did a report," she said finally.

"I know. I read it," Aaron said. "I want to go over it with you and make sure I understand everything."

"Okay," she said. "As long as I don't end up testifying in court."

"Right now, I'm not sure there will be a court," Aaron said.

Everyone hated testifying in court. He didn't know yet if there was even a crime, but it relaxed people if they weren't worrying about one day sitting in front of a judge and jury telling the story again.

"Can we talk now?" he asked.

"We can, but it'll cost you." She picked some money off the counter in front of her. "I have a pork tenderloin basket waiting for me at Smitty's. The Calvin PD officers were supposed to get it for me, but I sent them on a domestic call." She held the money out to him. "You want to talk, you have to go get my food."

Aaron smiled. "I've never had to bribe a witness before."

"You've never had me as a witness."

~*~

Aaron got her food at Smitty's Bar and Grill. It was a small lounge with a Western theme a few blocks from the law center. He got himself a burger, too, because he hadn't eaten, and it would be awkward interviewing her if she was eating and he wasn't.

He handed Melonie the white Styrofoam container along with her change.

"Thanks," she said and opened the container. It was brimming with fries and a tenderloin sandwich eight inches across. She motioned at his container. "What did you get?"

Aaron opened the container. "I got the Smitty Burger."

She grinned. "Good luck with that."

"Have you had one of these?"

"Everyone has had one of those … but just one."

He laughed. "Okay, I get it. Give the out of town guy a bad time."

"If only that was true," she said and took a bite of the tenderloin.

Aaron sat beside her at the control console in front of the vanilla-scented candle.

"Can I put this somewhere?" he asked, nodding toward the candle.

"Sure, blow it out and put it anywhere," she said. "I keep it here for self-defense. Some of these guys get gas and aren't shy about sharing."

Aaron laughed, blew out the candle and put it in a corner out of the way. He took a bite of the burger. It was by far the worst burger he had ever eaten, something like meatloaf without seasonings. "What kind of meat is this?"

"You were expecting meat?"

He laughed. The French fries were good. He nibbled on them.

"Are you ready for some questions?" he asked.

She shrugged. "Go ahead."

Aaron took his digital recorder out of his jacket pocket and laid it on the counter between them.

"What's that?" Melonie asked.

"I'm going to record everything," Aaron said. He had learned that even handwritten notes weren't always accurate. They didn't relay the pauses and voice inflections he would forget if he reviewed it six months from now. "Does it bother you?"

"I guess not," she said and took another bite.

"So how long have you worked here?"

She held up her hand while she chewed and swallowed. "Since I was 23. It was 22 years last month." She looked at him over the top of her sandwich. "To save you the math, I'm 45."

Aaron smiled. He liked her attitude. "The night Deputy …" He forgot the name for a moment.

"Jesse Gordon," she answered and took another bite.

"Right," Aaron said. "The night Deputy Gordon found Hemper's body, did you know he was doing surveillance on the farm service?"

"No. I knew he was doing something, but I didn't know he was sitting on the farm service."

"How did you know?"

"Most new guys think the job is about writing tickets," Melonie said. "On the weeknights, they go out and stop everything with wheels until ten when the traffic dies down. After ten, they'll sit in the law center and wait for calls. They can't see any reason for being out there if they're not making traffic stops." She set the tenderloin back in the box and adjusted the top of the bun which had slipped to the side. "Jesse wasn't like that. He never came in here unless he had something to do." She picked up the sandwich again.

"So he was proactive?"

"I think he was trying to make a name for himself." She took another bite.

Aaron had found there were two types of rookie cops. The arrogant ones who wanted the glory, and the righteous ones who wanted to get the bad guys off the streets. Aaron wasn't sure which cubbyhole Deputy Gordon fit into. "When was the first time you heard from him that night?"

Melonie swallowed and took a drink from a bottle of Pepsi on the counter before she answered. "When he stopped Pug. It surprised me."

"Why?"

"I knew we had a blizzard coming, and I and didn't think anyone would be out."

"When he called in, did he seem nervous or scared?" Aaron asked.

"No," she said, shaking her head. "He seemed frustrated because the repeater wouldn't work, and so was I." She gave an angry growl. "That damn thing needs replaced before someone gets hurt. The road crew has the best repeater money can buy because they get federal and state money as well as county funds. The infinite wisdom of the board of supervisors decided the SO could get by with a repeater from the lowest bidder."

"The repeater breaks down often?"

"About any time we have a storm with wind," she said. "There's a bad seal on the casing somewhere. Snow blows in and the heat from the repeater melts it. It shorts out a circuit or something—I'm not an electronics wizard. The company the county bought it from keeps looking at it. When they leave, they always say it's fixed, but it never is."

"So Deputy Gordon used his cell phone when he made the traffic stop?"

"Right. That's what we've been doing when the repeater is down."

"According to the reports he called you again later?"

"Before he went looking for Hemper," she said. "He let me know he'd be out of the vehicle at the farm service."

"Did he sound scared?"

"I think I was more worried than he was."

"Why?"

"I never had babies, and I hate cats," she said, smiling. "These young officers are my kids. If it had been me, I'd have let that crackhead Hemper freeze to death."

"And the phone call was the last contact you had with Deputy Gordon?"

"Right." she said. "I always check on an officer every fifteen minutes when they're out on a call. You never know what could happen, even on a simple traffic stop. I worry until I know everything is okay."

"You're a good mom," Aaron said.

The comment brought a smile. "I couldn't reach him by radio or phone. The sheriff has GPS tracking units for the squad cars—he got them with a grant—but he's never had them installed. I imagine they're still in boxes back in his office, along with the in-car computers the guys should have in their cars so they can run their own license checks."

Having seen the sheriff's office, it didn't surprise Aaron. "So what did you do?" Aaron asked to get her back to the story.

"I waited another fifteen minutes hoping he'd call," Melonie said, "and still nothing. That's when I called a couple off-duty Calvin Police Officers with snowmobiles and asked them if they'd go look for him."

"I thought it was the sheriff's idea?"

"He thinks so, too." She laughed. "I called Cal after the guys were on their way and suggested we have someone look for Jesse. It works better if you can make him think it's *his* idea."

Aaron liked her more and more all the time. "And they were already looking for him?"

"Right," she said. "Cal said he'd look for Jesse himself. A half hour later he called back and said he couldn't get out of his driveway."

"And that's when he had you send the guys on snowmobiles."

She snorted. "At first he wanted someone from the road crew to get him with a snowplow. He planned on looking for Jesse with the plow."

"You didn't do it?"

"There was a semi across the highway on the east end of town," she said. "They couldn't have gotten the plow around it, and the wreckers weren't going out until the storm stopped. Cal finally decided I should get someone with a snowmobile to look for Jesse."

Aaron laughed.

"As soon as I hung up with the sheriff, I got a call they'd found Jesse," Melonie said. "I waited until they had him at the hospital before I let the sheriff know."

"The sheriff said you're the one who got the cadaver dog they found the body with, too."

"I'd met a dispatcher from Cherokee County at an update school last spring," Melonie said. "They had gotten a dog out of the Twin Cities to find a body once. I suggested it to Cal before they started searching the first field, but he said they needed the area cleared to find whatever Hemper had fallen on that cut his throat."

The sheriff had developed his accident theory early, before all the evidence was in, even before the body had been recovered. It was not what Aaron considered good police work. It wasn't even mediocre police work. Everything the sheriff had done had been geared toward proving his theory.

"After they cleared the field and didn't find the body, the sheriff had me get the dog," Melonie said.

"Getting people moving the deputy's way was quick thinking on your part, as was coming up with the idea of getting the cadaver dog," Aaron said. "You should have been a cop."

She smiled. "I wanted to be at one time. I have a degree in criminal justice."

"So why are you dispatching?"

"My first husband got an accounting job here in Calvin," she said. "I took this job thinking it'd give me a better chance when a deputy's job opened up."

"Again, why are you sitting behind bulletproof glass instead of in a squad car?"

"Long story," she said. "Two years after I got this job, they had an opening for a deputy. I scored the highest on the written part of the civil service test, but they never even gave me an interview."

"Why?"

"Turns out the sheriff at the time wouldn't even consider hiring a woman as a deputy.

The only thing he cared about women was how nice of an ass they had." She looked at Aaron for a moment with the hint of a smile. "By the way, at the time I had one sweet little ass."

Aaron laughed before he got serious. "You should have done something about it. That's discrimination."

"I know," she said. "Hubby number one was outraged. He got a lawyer and wanted to sue."

"But I take it you didn't?" Aaron asked.

"I squashed it," she said. "The lawyer said I could have won, but what good would it have done? The court could have ordered them to hire me—wouldn't that have been fun working conditions—or I could have gotten a few bucks from them. But if I wanted to be rich, I wouldn't have gone to college to be a cop."

Aaron laughed.

"And if I filed a discrimination lawsuit, my chances of getting hired somewhere else would have gone down considerably," Melonie said. "I still wanted to be a cop, and who would hire someone who sued their department?"

"And that was that?"

"No," she said. "Fast forward eight years. We have a new sheriff and another opening. The new sheriff was the sergeant when I tested the first time. Before the test, he pulled me aside and told me I should've had that last job. He guaranteed me if I passed the test, the job was mine."

She paused and Aaron studied her for a moment. "And you didn't pass?" he asked.

She snorted again. "Oh ye of little faith." She blew on her fingernails, shined them on her shirt and looked at them. "Number one again."

"But you're not a deputy. What happened?"

"I rushed home in a daze and told hubby number two I'd gotten the job," she said. "And guess what? He didn't want a cop for a wife."

"*You* married a sexist?"

"The problem wasn't that I was a woman," she said. "He was older than me and had been in law enforcement for a long time. Sitting at the supper table with a rookie cop bubbling over with enthusiasm for something he was sick of wasn't his idea of a good time."

"So you turned it down?"

"We'd been married less than a year at the time, and I was in that stupid first-year-of-marriage love," she said. Her voice went to a sickly-sweet little girl's voice. "I will do anyting my widdle Hunny Bunny wants."

Aaron smiled. He could still remember that kind of love.

"The funny thing is, less than five years later, we were divorced, and I'd moved on to hubby number three," Melonie said.

"And you never tried again?"

"I was getting a little old to be a rookie," she said. "And husband number three had some health problems."

"Are you still with husband number three?"

"I buried husband number three six years ago."

"Sorry," Aaron said. "Is there a husband number four?"

"There's a Jim," she said, smiling. "He's a good guy, smart, treats me well, and every week or so he tickles my fancy—if you know what I mean. I can't ask for much more."

Chapter Five

"So what did you get done yesterday?" Sheriff Thompson asked.

Aaron sat across his desk from him in the sheriff's office. Other than removing the case file from its top when he gave it to Aaron, the desk hadn't been straightened.

"I went through the file and made sure I had everything," Aaron said. He couldn't see a problem with keeping the sheriff updated.

"And did you have everything?"

"There were a few odds and ends missing," Aaron said.

The sheriff looked perturbed. "Didn't I send you everything?"

Aaron smiled to put him at ease. He was touchy about even the little things. "There were some early reports and handwritten things."

"I didn't send those because they were duplicates of stuff already in the report." His voice was filled with defensiveness.

"Most of it was," Aaron said, still smiling. When you did investigations, details were everything. Nothing was unimportant until it wasn't. "I like having copies of everything."

The sheriff seemed satisfied. "So where do we go from here?"

"I'm going to re-interview people," Aaron said. "I already talked with Melonie Riggs yesterday."

Again the sheriff looked perturbed. "I would have liked to have been there."

"It was an unscheduled talk," Aaron said. He could see working with Sheriff Thompson would be difficult. "We talked over sandwiches last night in the control room. I didn't find anything new." *Nothing that changed the case, or that she would have told me if you'd been there.*

"So, who else do you need to interview?" the sheriff asked.

"Deputy Gordon, Delbert Goebel—"

"Pug won't talk," the sheriff said. "My deputies tried. He lawyered up."

That's because you threw him in jail.
"I'm still going to try," Aaron said.

"He's in his cell", the sheriff said, grabbing the phone. "I'll have the jailer bring him into your office across the hall."

"Not yet," Aaron said. "I have a few things I need to do before I interview him. I'd like to start with Deputy Gordon."

"He's off-duty for a while because of his hand," the sheriff said. "I'll give him a call and have him come in." He looked at his watch. "How long will this take? I have a meeting with the board of supervisors in a half hour. Can you wait until tomorrow?"

"It shouldn't take long." Aaron wasn't delaying anything for the convenience of the sheriff.

"Okay," Sheriff Thompson said. "I guess I've already heard everything Jesse has to say. I'll call him and have him come over to your office across the hall. The sheriff reached for the phone. "Although it would be fun hearing him tell about Bigfoot again."

"I'm not sure what you mean?"

The sheriff smiled. "You'll find out."

~*~

Deputy Gordon's frostbite had been severe. His cheeks and forehead swelled with pus-filled blisters, some of them bloody, making them dark, almost black. His right hand was wrapped loosely in a white gauze bandage, and he held it gingerly against his chest to keep from bumping it on anything.

"Hi Jesse," Aaron said as soon as he walked through the door into his makeshift office. "I'm Agent Barnum." Without thinking he offered his hand.

Jesse displayed his gauze covered right hand and forced a smile.

"Sorry," Aaron said. "How bad is it?"

"They don't know yet. They figure my face will be scarred, but it'll heal. My hand's the problem." His face suddenly wore a worried expression. "I broke my little finger that night when I tripped and fell. My hand was so numb I didn't know it was broken until I was at the hospital. They might have to amputate the little finger … and maybe the one next to it, because it was pretty badly frostbitten, too." He said the last part in a shaky whisper and stopped suddenly. He looked scared.

Aaron felt sorry for the young deputy. He could qualify with a pistol without a little finger, but it would be hard, if not impossible, with two fingers missing. He was still young and his career in law enforcement could already be over.

Aaron quickly moved passed it. "Have a seat, Jesse."

Jesse sat at the table, and Aaron took the seat directly across.

Aaron took his recorder out of his briefcase, turned it on and set it on the table. "I hope you don't mind Jesse, but I'm going to record our talk." He always called it a *talk* with a witness. It relaxed them more than if he called it an *interview* or *questioning*.

"Sure," Jesse said.

Aaron dug Jesse's report out of the file and paged through it briefly. It was a good report. The kid knew his stuff. He had all the details and didn't use big words to impress people.

"I've read your report several times," Aaron said. "How often did you do surveillance on the farm service?"

"I don't know. It wasn't anything regular," Jesse said. "I did it after 2200 hours during the week when there wasn't much traffic on the highways."

"That was good thinking," Aaron said. "It shows incentive."

"I'd heard people had stolen anhydrous from there a few times over the years," Jesse said.

"Did you have any information anyone would be there that night?"

"No. I figured with the storm coming in, it would be a good time for someone to hit the place. The snow would cover their tracks."

They went through the incidents of the night with Jesse retelling it. Aaron didn't find out anything he hadn't read in the report. Jesse had seen the pickup, made a traffic stop on Goebel, went looking for Hemper in the snowstorm, found his body and went back to get help. The exact thing he had put in his report. Almost word for word what he had put in his report. It was as if he had memorized it.

"Is there anything else you might have thought of since you did the report?" Aaron asked.

Jesse's looked at his lap for a moment before looking back at Aaron. "No. That's it. I put it all in my report."

He seemed suddenly nervous.

"Jesse, are you sure there isn't something else?"

"No. That's everything," Jesse said looking at him. His face was blank but his eyes were worried.

"Are you sure?"

Jesse suddenly glared at him, his eyes boring holes through Aaron. "The sheriff told you, didn't he?"

"Told me what?"

"About the tracks," Jesse said. He looked away. "Go ahead laugh. I was cold and disoriented. I wasn't thinking clearly." He paused and looked at Aaron again. "I panicked. I was scared, okay? There I said it. Are you happy?"

Aaron suddenly remembered something the sheriff had said. "Sheriff Thompson said you saw Bigfoot?"

Jesse shot him a death scowl.

Bingo. He'd hit a nerve.

"I didn't see *Bigfoot*," Jesse said with anger seeping into his voice. "The guys came up with that, not me."

The anger surprised Aaron. He figured Jesse might be embarrassed about going in the ditch and getting stuck, but the anger caught him off guard. "What did you see, Jesse?"

"It was nothing," Jesse said, speaking in a monotone voice, making an effort to keep the emotion out. "It was cold. The wind was blowing. It was nothing. Just some tracks."

"Where were they?"

"They were by Hemper's head," Jesse said.

Aaron leafed through Jesse's report. "You say in the report they were Hemper's footprints?"

"Maybe they were," Jesse said. "Some of the guys said the wind can do funny things with snow. It can fill in footprints, or it can grab the edges and make them bigger."

Aaron knew the wind could enlarge footprints, but it didn't happen often. The conditions had to be perfect. "You should have put it in your report."

"I did," Jesse said. "When I was working on the report, John Sanders read it over my shoulder and started calling me the Bigfoot hunter. He spread it around the rest of the department."

"Do *you* think they were Hemper's footprints?" Aaron asked.

"I guess." Jesse shrugged. "I don't know. It seemed funny that there would be snow in the bottom of the tracks while the wind made the edges bigger. Wouldn't it have blown the snow out of the bottom of the footprints too?"

"I don't know," Aaron said. "I don't have much experience with that kind of thing." If Jesse had taken pictures of the tracks, some lab tech could have figured out if they were Hemper's footprints or not, but he hadn't. "So what did these footprints look like?"

"Not like Bigfoot's, I can say that much," Jesse said. "They were bigger and rounder."

"Like an elephant's or a mammoth's?"

"I'm not saying I saw mammoth tracks," Jesse growled. "Don't go spreading that around."

"I'm not saying you did," Aaron said. "I'm trying to find something to compare it with."

"It was more oblong than round," Jesse said. "Just round on the edges."

"Like a bear's track?"

"Maybe. I've never seen a bear's track," Jesse said. "But it would be the biggest bear ever."

"How big are we talking?"

Jesse held his hands out in front of him. "Maybe two feet long and a foot or foot and a half wide with rounded edges on the top and bottom."

Off the top of his head, Aaron couldn't think of anything that would make footprints that size, or anything even close. "Any idea what made them?"

Jesse paused for a moment and looked as if he was going to say something, but he didn't.

"I don't know," he said finally. He looked across the room at the white board. "I guess they were Hemper's, like the guys said."

The pause bothered Aaron. Days had gone by since it had happened. Jesse would have gone over everything from that night numerous times, especially what had made those tracks. He wouldn't stop and think about it now. He was hiding something. Aaron had done enough interviews and interrogations to know that much.

"Jesse, did you see something else?"

"I didn't see Bigfoot," Jesse said.

It wasn't the question he had been asked. Which meant it was the question he expected. He sat with his hands in his lap looking at the whiteboard on the wall and occasionally glancing at Aaron. Aaron remembered the newspaper clippings about Bigfoot and Yeti stuck on the locker in the squad room. He'd bet Jesse had been teased mercilessly about the tracks. Aaron tried a different approach.

"Have you ever seen a ghost?" Aaron asked.

Jesse's head snapped around, and he gave Aaron another death glare. "No. I've never seen a ghost. Don't get that started."

"Well, I've seen one," Aaron said.

The deputy's face broke for a second. It was filled with skepticism, but also curiosity. "You're giving me crap, aren't you?"

"I swear it's the truth," Aaron said. "Do you remember the Harley Cooper case?"

Jesse nodded but Aaron couldn't see any real recognition on his face.

"It was a couple years ago over in eastern Iowa," Aaron said. "They found Cooper's body burned and stuffed in the back of a cave. He'd been dead a week in the middle of the summer. The body was very decomposed by the time it was found."

"I remember it, now" Jesse said. "His son killed him, right?"

"His stepson," Aaron said. "It was his first wife's son from a previous marriage."

His face lit up with recall. "Okay, I do remember," Jesse said.

"They called me in the day the body was found. The lab boys were done and the body had been removed," Aaron said. "We had crime scene tape blocking off everything and two uniforms by the road making sure nobody wandered into the scene.

"I'm on one knee examining where the body had been. When I looked up, there was a fat old guy in bib overalls standing at the cave's mouth.

"You can't be here, I told him. This is a crime scene. I was ready to chew some uniform's ass for letting him through."

Aaron couldn't read anything from Jesse's face, but he was paying attention so he went on. "'I heard that,' the guy said. 'I bet it's Harley Cooper. Nobody's seen him for a while now.'

"At the time, we didn't know who the victim was. There wasn't any identification on the body.

"You might be right, I told him, but you can't be here.

"'Harley's young wife and his stepson have been playing slap and tickle, if you know what I mean,' the guy said and winked at me. 'If I was looking for someone who wanted to get rid of Harley, I'd start with those two.'"

Aaron blew out a snort. "After I ran him out of the cave, I went and ripped on the uniforms for a few minutes for letting him through. They said they never saw him.

"A couple days later the coroner identified the body, and it was Cooper. I got his driver's license picture from DOT." Aaron paused a moment for effect. "It was the same guy who came in the cave."

Jesse looked at him with wide eyes, but a hint of skepticism peeked out around the edges. "I thought the stepson confessed?"

"Sure, after I told him I knew about the affair, he confessed," Aaron said.

Jesse looked at him suspiciously, still not believing it. "So how come I never read anything about this in the papers?"

"Do you think I would tell people a ghost helped me solve a case?" Aaron asked smiling. "Do you know how much ridicule I would have faced?"

Jesse looked at the tabletop and nodded. "I think I do."

Aaron didn't believe in ghosts. He'd never seen one, and one had never helped him solve a murder case. (Cooper's wife had come forward and told Aaron about the affair. She was afraid the stepson had done something stupid when she'd ended it. When Aaron told the stepson the love of his life had ratted him out, he broke down and confessed.) But if Chantel found something suggesting anything but an accidental death, he would need every lead he could get. If it meant telling a young deputy a ghost story, then so be it.

Jesse motioned towards the recorder on the table. "Can you turn that thing off?"

Now they were getting somewhere. Aaron switched off the recorder. As soon as Jesse left, he would make detailed notes. "What did you see, Jesse?"

"I'm not sure," Jesse said. "It was windy, and I was cold and a little shook up after finding the body … like I said, I was scared, okay?" He looked back across the room at the wall as if he was focusing on the diagram on the whiteboard. His good hand rested on the table and his wrapped hand lay in his lap. After a moment he looked back at Aaron. "I could hear something behind me when I was on my way back to the farm service, but it might have been the wind."

"What do you mean you heard something?"

"I don't know," Jesse said. "It sounded like something went through the grass waterway behind me. But I can't be sure, because it was windy, and I was a little freaked out with all that had happened."

He was trying to find an explanation for it. Aaron had seen it before in victims who had gone through traumatic events. They rationalized things to make sense of the situation. "So you thought you heard something?"

Jesse nodded and put his good hand in his lap with the injured one. "Whatever it was—if there was something—might have been following me." His voice had a tremble in it.

Aaron watched him for a moment. Jesse wouldn't look at him at all, and he looked scared. "Why do you think that?"

He glanced at Aaron and back at the whiteboard. His lower lip was between his teeth and he bit it hard once before he answered. "Don't tell anybody this, because I haven't said anything about it to the other guys," Jesse whispered, looking back at Aaron before looking at the recorder and making sure it was still off. "Something bumped into my Explorer when I was sitting at the farm service." His tone changed suddenly and he forced a weak smile. "But thinking about it now, maybe it was the wind rocking the vehicle. Or maybe the wind blew something into it."

He was still rationalizing, trying to explain what he couldn't explain.

"So you didn't see anything?" Aaron asked.

Jesse fidgeted in his chair, shifting his position. "Maybe there was something in the back window for a moment, but it could have been a newspaper or something blown there by the wind. It was only there for a second or so."

"And you didn't see it again?"

He shook his head. "That's it."

Aaron didn't believe him. Fear covered the young deputy's face. His left hand held his injured right hand to keep both from shaking.

"Jesse, if you saw something else, I need to know," Aaron said. "It won't go past this room." If it was important, it would go into his report, but first Aaron needed to know if it was important.

Jesse chewed on the inside of his lip for a moment. "You can't tell any of the guys about this. Okay?" he said finally. "And not the sheriff either."

"I work on a need to know basis," Aaron said. "I don't see how they need to know any of this."

Jesse seemed satisfied and finally looked Aaron in the eye. "When I was pulling out of the farm service, maybe I saw something go between the buildings." His voice broke a little.

"Something? Like what?"

"I don't know, maybe it was nothing," he said. "It was blowing snow, and I was a little scared, and I was looking through an iced-over windshield, okay?"

His hands shook no matter how tightly he gripped them. Tears glistened in his eyes.

"What did you see Jesse? I need to know."

"All I saw was some fur," Jesse said. "I didn't get a good look at it so it might not have been anything."

He was trying as hard as he could *not* to tell the story, but nobody was scared from not seeing *anything*. "What did it look like?"

"I only saw part of it as it went between the buildings," he said, talking softly now, but his eyes were wide. "It was white and covered with long hair."

"Could it have been a person?"

"No," Jesse said immediately. "It wasn't someone's coat. It was fur, long shaggy fur. And too big to be a person. Way too big."

"What do you mean?"

"The part I saw was eight or nine feet tall … maybe ten," Jesse said.

Aaron let it sink in for a moment. It couldn't be. "How well did you see it?"

"I just saw it for a second," Jesse said. "It was a flash of fur."

Aaron studied Jesse as he looked across the room at the wall. He was definitely upset and at least *he* believed he had seen something. "You should have put all of this in your report."

"I was going to," Jesse said. "As I said, I wrote about the tracks in the first report," Jesse said. "I was advised to take it out."

"Why?"

"Sgt. Sanders, my old training officer, said if a defense attorney ever got wind of it, he'd use it against me, and I'd never have credibility with a jury again," he said. "Sanders said every jury would know I was the deputy who saw Bigfoot's tracks."

"You still should have mentioned it in the report," Aaron said. "It should have been documented."

Jesse looked at him. "The way you put being helped by a ghost in your report?"

There was the problem with making stuff up. "How sure are you about seeing this thing?" Aaron asked.

"I don't know," Jesse said. "Sitting here now, safe, warm, and after getting all the crap from the guys, I don't know."

"How about that night? How sure were you about seeing it then?"

Jesse looked across the room for a few moments before looking at Aaron.

"You can't tell anybody," Jesse said and looked at the tabletop. He looked like a little boy who was ashamed of what he'd done, more than a young deputy sheriff. "But when I saw it … I pissed myself." He raised his head and looked at Aaron. A glistening tear slithered on his damaged right cheek. "Is that sure enough for you?"

Chapter Six

After Jesse left, it was almost two. Aaron thought about calling the sheriff and letting him know what he had found from Jesse, but he doubted the sheriff would keep it confidential. He would definitely tell the skinny owl, and who knew who else. Aaron didn't want Jesse getting any more ribbing from the rest of his department. He decided to keep Jesse's sightings on a need to know basis, and he didn't see any reason the sheriff needed to know. Aaron had decided the sheriff's main objective was making sure his department didn't look foolish. The sheriff had staked so much on it being an accidental death, anything else would make him seem incompetent. Although Aaron could see why the sheriff was convinced it wasn't a murder. Someone would have had to have been waiting for Hemper at the farm service in a snowstorm. Where would they have parked their car? Deputy Gordon had been watching the farm service and hadn't reported any other vehicles stopping that night. The only other options would be, there were two other people in the pickup with Goebel—two had gotten out to get the anhydrous and one had killed the other; or Bigfoot had killed Hemper. Aaron didn't believe in ghosts or Bigfoot. He needed to talk with Goebel.

Aaron left his office and went down the hall to the county attorney's office. Debra Bachman was a thin overworked woman with straight gray hair hanging to the middle of her back. It looked odd on a woman in her mid-sixties. She'd heard about the footprints Jesse had seen and had demanded the sheriff contact the DCI. Aaron had the impression she did not think highly of Sheriff Thompson.

Aaron brought her up to speed on what else Jesse had seen. She had a need to know, because if the case ever went to court, she would be part of it. He liked bringing prosecutors in on everything early so they could prepare. She went ballistic that Jesse hadn't put what he'd seen in his report. Aaron settled her down by telling her he didn't think Jesse had seen Bigfoot or any other monster. Stress and terror wreaked havoc on the imagination. Things were magnified. It turned house cats crossing the road into mountain lions and a glimpse of fur from a dog or a deer into Bigfoot. It was why witnesses at homicides and violent accidents sometimes told different stories.

After leaving the county attorney, Aaron went to the control center for another Coke. The dispatchers were going through shift change. Jana stood with her faux fox fur coat on and her red purse over her shoulder while Melonie sat in the chair in front of the radios.

"Well hi, Aaron," Jana said as soon as he entered the control room. "How's the investigation going?"

"The way they all go, a little at a time." He wasn't sharing anything with her.

"You know, Sgt. Sanders has let me sit in on a couple interrogations," Jana said.

"That was nice of him." Aaron knew what she was hinting at. It wasn't going to happen.
"By the way, if you get tired of restaurant food and are looking for some home cooking, I make a mean lasagna," she said.

Aaron smiled. "I appreciate the offer. I'll let you know." He didn't intend to take her up on it. He figured she was nosey and wanted information about the case.

The blonde beamed. "Let me know when, so I can have it ready."

"I'll do that."

Her smile widened. "I have to get home and let my dog out," Jana said. "I'll see you tomorrow. Let me know when you're coming over."

"Goodbye," Aaron said and watched her disappear out the back door.

When he turned back, Melonie was trying her best to stifle a laugh.

"What's so funny?"

"I should have warned you," she said. "Our little Jana is a bit of a badge bunny. You go over to her house, and there will be more than lasagna on the menu."

Aaron's face blushed, but he recovered quickly. "I've always liked a good lasagna."

Melonie laughed. "Well, the way I hear it, it could be the best lasagna you've ever had. Any flavor you want and as much as you can eat."

"That good?"

"The only problem is you have to talk with her before and afterwards," Melonie said. "Or at least that's what my boys tell me."

Aaron feigned shock. "What kind of boys are you raising who would tell their mother those kind of stories?"

"What are you talking about?" Melonie asked her face blank with feigned ignorance. "I'm just talking about food."

Aaron laughed.

The back door opened and a young girl who couldn't have been more than five feet tall came into the law center. She wore the brown uniform of the Iowa DNR with a baseball cap and a pecan-colored braid hanging out the back. Bangs covered a forehead sitting on top of a well-tanned face. Aaron guessed she was a junior high school kid who had a part-time job with the DNR. She took off her brown winter coat revealing a thin body. When she turned sideways and closed the door, he saw a pistol on her hip. This was no teenager.

"Hi, Summer," Melonie said when she saw her.

"Hi," the girl said. She had a voice containing a slight rasp and way too deep for such a tiny girl.

"This is Aaron Barnum," Melonie said. "He's with the DCI. Aaron, this is Summer Conrad."

"Nice to meet you," Aaron said.

She shook hands crisply, a quick squeeze and release.

"You're the game warden?" Aaron asked.

"We haven't been called that in decades," she said without the hint of a smile. "We prefer conservation officers."

"Of course." Aaron knew that. He didn't know why he'd used the other term.

"Aaron is investigating the Hemper case," Melonie said.

"Of course," Conservation Officer Conrad said, but still no smile. She could have had a competition with the skinny owl in the sheriff's office as to who smiled the least. "How's it going?"

Aaron couldn't detect any real interest. It seemed the required question. "I'm doing the background stuff right now."

"Maybe Summer can help you find Bigfoot," Melonie said and laughed. "I'm sorry, but I know you talked with Jesse."

Aaron assumed everyone in the department knew about the tracks Jesse had seen.

"I'm not looking for Bigfoot," Aaron said.

Summer gave a bored nod. "Well, you'll have to excuse me. I have court."

She left abruptly.

"She's a tiny thing," Aaron said after she had left. "How does she do her job?"

"Don't let her size fool you," Melonie said. "She's assisted on some calls, and the boys say she's tough as nails."

"She doesn't seem very friendly," Aaron said. "Maybe it's me,"

"It's not you," Melonie said. "She doesn't do much with anyone around here. Keeps to herself most of the time. Never comes to any department parties or associates with anyone off-duty."

"I suppose it's what you get from working by yourself so much," Aaron said.

"Personally, I think she's a stuck-up ice princess," Melonie said.

Aaron laughed. "Whoa. Sounds like there's a little bitterness there."

"You bet," Melonie said. "Any woman who looks younger at 30 than I did at 17, I'm bitter about."

"She's 30?" It was ten years over Aaron's highest guess.

"She might be 31 by now. I'm not sure when her birthday is."

Sheriff Thompson walked through the law center's front door.

"Are you finished with Jesse?" he asked coming into the control room.

"Just finished," Aaron said. "I was getting ready to call you."

"So who are we going to talk to now?"

"The head of the county road crew that cleared the field looking for Hemper."

"Why?" Sheriff Thompson asked. "They didn't find anything. Hemper was in the next field over."

Aaron smiled, but it irked him that this guy was trying to tell him how to do his job. "I know. I like to cover all my bases."

Sheriff Thompson dug his cell phone out of the holder on his belt. "I'll give Bud a call and have him meet us here."

"Find out where he is," Aaron said. "We need to go out to the scene so he can show me what happened when they cleared the field."

"We don't need him," the sheriff said. "I can show you everything. I was there the whole time."

"I know, but I already have your story in the report," Aaron said. "I'd like to get another perspective." He knew the sheriff would tell him what fit the department's storyline. The foreman shouldn't have anything invested in how this case came out, so he should tell what had happened without slanting it one way or the other.

The sheriff shrugged and made the call.

~*~

Roland "Bud" Poland was the county road crew's shop foreman. When Aaron and Sheriff Thompson walked through the door of the gas and oil scented county shed, two men stood looking under the hood of an orange gravel truck with a snowplow blade mounted on its front.

Aaron knew which one was the foreman immediately. He was pointing at the truck and giving instructions to a thin younger man beside him. When he saw them come through the door, he picked a rag off the fender of the truck and came over wiping his hands.

"Hi, Calvin," he said, still wiping his hands on the rag. He was a short sturdy man who reeked of grease and cigarettes. Uncontrolled salt and pepper hair stuck out from under a filthy black baseball cap. His bushy eyebrows flared above dark framed glasses and a trimmed gray beard hung from his chin like a squared off throat protector on a catcher's mask. "What do I owe the *privilege* of you coming out here personally?"

His angry dark eyes and the sarcastic ring in his voice made Aaron guess that Bud and the sheriff did not get along.

"This is Investigator Barnum with the DCI," Sheriff Thompson said, motioning toward Aaron.

Aaron stepped forward and shook his hand. It was greasy. "Call me Aaron." He wanted to keep things informal and put the witness at ease.

"So what can I do for you, Aaron?" Bud asked.

"There are a few questions we need to ask you about when we cleared the field looking for Hemper's body," Sheriff Thompson said.

"Ain't much to tell," Bud said. "We wasted two days clearing the wrong field and didn't find nothing. You made me write a report saying I didn't find nothing, remember Calvin?"

"I'd like to go over everything with you," Aaron said.

"And we need you to go out to the scene with us," the sheriff added.

"I ain't got time for this crap right now," Bud said. "We're in the middle of winter. I've got plows busted, and I got to get to Luther this afternoon yet. I can't put everything on hold."

"It would be a big help," Aaron said. He could see this witness would not be cooperative. "And it shouldn't take long."

"Right. I know how that works," Bud said. He glared at the sheriff. "You already burned up my overtime budget by wasting two days clearing the wrong field. I was told *that* would only take a couple hours."

"Look," Sheriff Thompson said bluntly. "We're just being polite. We can haul you to the law center and do the interview there."

"Go ahead," Bud said his voice rising. He stuck his wrists out in front of him. "Cuff me up."

"Let's all take a deep breath and settle down here," Aaron said. He didn't know what the sheriff was doing. You didn't rile up witnesses. "We know you're busy, and we're sorry about the interruption. I know winter must be a busy time for you."

Bud snorted with disgust. "You don't know the half of it," he said. "I only have so much money in my overtime budget, and the storms always come on the weekends."

"It must take some planning to make it work out," Aaron said.

Bud let out a loud huff. "Sometimes it don't work out. I've got the union yelling at me because they worry about seniority and not what needs done, and the supervisors screaming because they think you should always be under budget. Not to mention every farmer in the county thinks their road should be cleared first. We have a system for clearing roads: The blacktops first then …"

Aaron let him vent for a few minutes.

"So why do you have to go to Luther?" Aaron asked when Bud paused for a moment.

"I got to climb up on the elevator and see about building a shed around the sheriff's piece of crap repeater." He shot a glance at the sheriff that would have speared him through if it had been solid. "They paid a company good money for the repeater, and now *I* have to fix it."

"Isn't Luther east of here?" Aaron asked.

"It's about twenty miles east on the state highway," Sheriff Thompson said. Aaron wished he'd shut up.

"And isn't the farm service where Hemper was killed east of here?" Aaron asked, looking at Bud and ignoring Sheriff Thompson.

Bud nodded. "It's about ten miles."

"I tell you what," Aaron said. "When you're ready to go to Luther, why don't I jump in with you, and we can stop at the farm service on the way. Any questions I have, I can ask on the way there. That way we kill two birds with one stone."

"It'll be five or after before I get back here," Bud said. "You sure you got that kind of time to waste waiting for me at Luther?"

"Sheriff Thompson can follow us in his car," Aaron said. "When we're done at the farm service, I can ride back with him."

"I may have some more questions for Bud," the sheriff said.

"I've talked with you all I need to about this," Bud said.

"You can always talk with Bud some other time," Aaron said. "If I find out anything new, I'll let you know."

Aaron turned back to Bud. "So when are you planning on leaving?"

Chapter Seven

They headed east out of Calvin with Aaron squinting against the sun's rays bouncing off the bright white snow. Even with the sun behind him, the glare made him wish he had brought his sunglasses.

"What time did you start moving snow at the scene?" Aaron asked.

"A little after noon," Bud said. He drove the orange Cossack County pickup with the heel of his left hand laying nonchalantly over the top of the steering wheel. It made Aaron nervous. Patches of glare ice dotted the road. He would have been more comfortable if Bud had a firm grip on the wheel. "The storm was over, and I was getting guys out clearing the roads when I got the call from Murphy."

"Murphy?"

"John Murphy. He's the county engineer," Bud said, looking at Aaron when he talked and ignoring the road. "He said the sheriff needed our help finding a body. I told him to get the fire department. We had roads blown shut, and I couldn't spare the manpower." He looked back out the windshield.

"But you went?"

Bud looked at Aaron again. "Murphy said they already had the fire department, but they needed a frontend loader to move snow. I finally jumped in a plow and had Tim Schwartz follow me in a Payloader."

Aaron clutched his armrest until Bud looked at the road again. "Tim is one of your men?"

"He works in the shop doing repairs," Bud said. "They told me it wouldn't take more than a couple hours. I was hoping nothing would break before we got done."

"How many people were at the scene when you got there?'

"A ton," Bud said, not looking at the road again. "The Calvin and Luther fire departments, Cyril Powers—the emergency management director—the sheriff and every deputy." He glanced out the windshield.

"At least they had plenty of help."

Bud gave out a sharp snort. "As soon as I get there, Cal's pissed," Bud said. "He thought I'd bring my whole crew. The minute I got out of the plow he *ordered me* to get everyone there and all the equipment, right now." He huffed out an angry laugh. "I told him they were busy working on getting roads open. Cal says, if I didn't get everyone there right away, he'd throw me in jail for failing to obey a peace officer. I said, go ahead. I could use the vacation."

"What happened?"

"Cal called Murphy, and Murphy said to leave two plows for the blacktops, and we'd get the gravels after they found the guy." Bud stopped talking as he gave a quick glance at the road and looked back at Aaron. "I had every farmer who lives on gravel bitching at me for three days."

He looked back through the windshield. "There's the farm service," Bud said. He motioned toward some red metal buildings south of the state highway. "Beyond it where you see the trees and hills is the refuge."

The refuge was a mile or so south of the highway. It started abruptly the way the shore rises from the ocean. In front of it lay acres of flat treeless farmland blanketed with snow like a white sea. All of it divided neatly into the parallelograms of civilization by fences and roads with straight edges and sharp right-angle corners. Beyond the farmland, the refuge towered like a diseased growth working its way across the land. Snow-covered hills with rounded tops like the worn teeth of a giant rose into the blue sky. Thick, disorganized growths of stunted dark trees, scraggly brush and bulrushes stood out against the white snow, blotting out everything between the hills and making its own wall that separated it from civilization. Nothing was straight or uniform. Even now, with all the leaves gone and looking like a forest of dead trees, it appeared impregnable.

Aaron figured the hills were some sort of glacial phenomenon, like the Loess Hills in western Iowa. Except these glaciers had dumped the hills in swampland. Thick areas of cattail-infested sloughs ran between the hills. It was useless land. The pioneers would have ignored it. The hills were too steep to farm and there was too much muddy wetland between the hills to even use them for grazing cattle.

"I've always thought in the winter it looked like something from the ice age," Bud said when he saw Aaron studying the refuge.

Aaron agreed. It had a prehistoric beauty. Something he'd just as soon look at from afar.

They turned south at the next county blacktop and pulled into the farm service with Sheriff Thompson following in his departmental Crown Victoria.

Bud stopped the pickup behind the buildings and left it running when they got out.

Aaron zipped his insulated coat. It was cold, close to zero. Sheriff Thompson came over stomping his feet as he joined them at the front of the pickup.

"Okay, explain to me what happened," Aaron asked.

"Right over there is where Jesse found Hemper's first tracks," the sheriff said and pointed at some portable anhydrous tanks on wheels. He put his hands back in his coat pockets.

A door at the office building opened, and a bald guy came out, slipping into a grey flannel parka.

"What you guys doing?" the bald guy asked, fumbling with the parka's zipper.

"This is Agent Barnum from the DCI, Will," Sheriff Thompson said. "He wants to look at the scene."

Aaron pulled off a glove and extended his hand. "It's Will?"

Will finished zipping the parka and shook Aaron's hand. The guy's hands were freezing, and as soon as they finished shaking hands, he stuffed them into the parka's pockets.

"I'm the manager here," Will said, flipping the parka's hood over his head. "You're with the DCI?"

"Right," Aaron said smiling.

"Maybe you can answer a question," Will said. "Are we going to get sued over this?"

"That's civil law," Aaron said. "I work the criminal side."

"We didn't do anything wrong so we shouldn't, right?" Will asked. "But people now days are always looking for a quick buck."

Chantel had said nobody had claimed Hemper's body. It was unlikely anyone would bring a lawsuit. But Will was right. You never knew when it came to money.

"You might ask your attorney," Aaron said.

"I already have," Will said. "He says we shouldn't have any liability, but we'll have to wait and see what happens."

A short fat man came through the office door wearing a moss-colored jacket over black Carhartt bibs. Curly red hair stuck out from under a Minnesota Vikings stocking cap and two days' growth of beard stubble covered his cheeks. Aaron didn't want a bunch of civilians hanging around, but he guessed they already knew more about the location than he did.

"What you guys doing?" the guy in the Carhartts asked. His lower lip bulged with a wad of snus, making his words garbled.

"They're looking at the scene again, Andy," Will said. "This guy's an agent from the DCI."

"Aaron Barnum." Aaron slipped off his glove again and offered his hand to Andy.

Andy shook it without removing his leather glove.

"Did you two help in the search?" Aaron asked.

Will grinned. "We helped by drinking coffee and watching through the office window."

Andy spit a stream of tobacco juice on the ground leaving a brown strip in the snow. "It was quite a show," he said smiling, displaying brown teeth covered with flecks of tobacco.

"Andy found the cell phone," Will said.

"What cell phone?" Aaron asked.

"The young deputy's," Andy said. "I was plowing snow and saw it laying on top of the snow. I must have rolled it out on one of the passes with the plow."

Aaron couldn't remember it being in any of the reports. "Where did you find it?"

Andy pointed over a few yards by one of the buildings. "Right about there."

Aaron pulled a digital camera out of his coat pocket and snapped a couple pictures.

The cell phone had fallen out of Jesse's holder early. Aaron guessed it had been knocked loose when he put on his snowmobile suit. In a dozen steps it had worked its way out of his pant leg and onto the ground.

"We tried finding it through its GPS," Sheriff Thompson said. "But laying out in the cold so long had drained the battery."

"So run me through this," Aaron said. "Tell me how you figure this happened."

"I'm going back inside where it's warm," Will said. He walked away hunched over with his hands still in his pockets and disappeared into the office.

Aaron wished the other guy would leave, too, but it appeared he would stick around for a while.

"Okay," Sheriff Thompson said. "The way I have it figured, Jesse and Hemper both went this way out into the field." He pointed north along the east side of the last building. "The wind was out of the northwest that night and they couldn't see anything, so it would have pushed them to the east. It's the first field east of here where we found Hemper's body."

"And you cleared this field out here?" Aaron asked, motioning out at the field between them and the state highway.

"We took off every flake," Bud said. He pointed out at where a mini Himalayan mountain range of snow was piled on the far side of the field. "You can still see on the west side where we put it all after we checked the loader buckets."

Aaron snapped a few pictures of the field and the line of snow at the far end. "That's a huge pile of snow."

"Tell me about it," Bud said.

"There was a ten-foot drift running from north to south across the field," the sheriff said. "It took forever getting through it."

"There's a strip of grass running through the field," Bud said. "It acted like a snow fence and piled the snow there."

"Is that the waterway Jesse said he tripped on?" Aaron asked.

The sheriff shook his head. "No. He tripped in the ditch by the road and thought it was the waterway."

"I don't understand," Aaron said.

Sheriff Thompson gave him one of his car salesman's smiles, raising the mole on his cheek. "I can explain it to you," he said. "Let's jump in our vehicles, and I'll show you."

Aaron got in the pickup with Bud again, and they followed the sheriff's Crown Vic out of the farm service and east on the county road. Andy was behind them in a white Ford truck with *Raleigh Farm Service Center* written on the doors in red letters.

"Did you find anything in the field when you were clearing it?" Aaron asked Bud when they were in the truck.

Bud's glasses had frosted over when he had gotten back in the warm pickup. He looked at Aaron over the top of them. "Like what?"

"I don't know. Something sharp. A weapon or tool or some debris."

"We found a bunch of stuff. Beer cans and everything else. The closer we got to the state highway, the more stuff we found—from people throwing it out car windows, I imagine. We even found a disc harrow blade. It must have fallen off something when the farmer was turning soil last fall. Maybe he had a spare one sitting on his tractor, because those things don't come off on their own."

"That's one of those heavy round things, right?" Aaron asked. "I'm not much of a farmer."

Bud smiled. "Right."

It was possible Hemper could have fallen on it and cut his neck open. "Was it ever checked for blood?"

"I don't know. Ask Cal," Bud said. "He made us put everything in the back of a pickup when we picked it up."

"Where is it now?"

"When they found the body in the other field, Cal told us to throw it away."

"Where?"

"We put it in the dumpster at the county shed in Calvin," Bud said.

"Is it still there?"

"It should be. The city doesn't do garbage until tomorrow."

Aaron made a mental note to check on it when he got back to Calvin.

The road on the south side of the farm service went a quarter mile east and made a sharp left turn to the north where the blacktop changed to gravel. The sheriff went halfway to the state highway on the gravel, pulled to the side of the road and stopped. In a moment, Andy joined them.

"See this," Sheriff Thompson said pointing at the west ditch. "It's a field access."

It was a simple driveway for the farmer to get his equipment in and out of the field.

The sheriff walked across the road. "There's another one on this side. It doesn't happen often that you find field accesses directly across from each other, but in this case they are."

"And your theory is?" Aaron asked.

"The wind was pushing him east," Sheriff Thompson said making a wide motion east. "Jesse walked through the west field access, across the road, through the east field access and out into the other field." He pointed out toward the east field. "The road is gravel here. It was covered with snow and it has some pretty good ruts in it. Jesse says he couldn't see more than a few feet. He would have gone from one field and into the other without ever knowing he'd done it."

"Okay, but what about the grass waterway he tripped on?"

"The ditch," the sheriff said. "There aren't any fences here. Jesse went into the ditch, tripped on the grass and thought it was the waterway in the other field."

"But wouldn't he have gone through the grass, crossed the road and tripped on the grass in the other ditch, too?"

"The ditch on the west side ain't got no grass," Andy said. "They burned it off last fall."

Sheriff Thompson smiled. "You can't see it because it's filled with snow, but the east ditch has knee-high grass and the west one is bare."

Aaron snapped a few pictures of everything, including the first field and farm service from the different angle. He didn't know about any of it right now. The sheriff was making the evidence fit his theory of what had happened instead of looking at the evidence and letting it form the theory. "So where was the body found?"

"It was out there where the orange flag is, right?" Andy asked, pointing into the east field.

"Right," Sheriff Thompson said.

"I figured that's why you guys put it there," Andy said.

The flag was 100yards east of the road and 50 yards north of the refuge border. It waved from the top of a metal pole a couple feet above the snow.

Aaron snapped a picture. "Let's go take a look."

"I got to get to Luther," Bud said looking at his watch. "If you don't need anything more from me, I'll be taking off."

"Sure. Go ahead," Aaron said. He took off his glove and they shook hands. "Thanks for your help, Bud."

"Not a problem," he said.

Bud got in the pickup and left. Aaron hoped Andy would leave, too, but when they went into the field, he followed.

"There's a blade on the front of my truck, and it's four-wheel drive," Andy said motioning back towards his pickup. "Why don't we jump in it and drive out there?"

"We'll walk," Aaron said. He didn't want to take the chance of ruining even more evidence with a snowplow.

It was slow going across the field. The snow was knee-deep in most places and in some places it was waist-deep. It made 100 yards seem more like a quarter mile. Aaron was glad he had switched to his boots before getting in the pickup with Bud. By the time they reached the flag, sweat soaked his t-shirt from the exertion.

"We put this flag right where Hemper's body was," the sheriff said, panting from struggling through the snow. "It's in a stand held down with sandbags."

"And you didn't find anything under him he might have fallen on and caused his injuries?" Aaron asked.

The sheriff shook his head. "We shoveled this whole area by hand 40 yards in all directions down to bare dirt, and we didn't find anything.

"Right across the fence in the refuge is a bunch of junk: machinery and corrugated metal from old buildings," the sheriff said, pointing toward the tangle of trees in the refuge.

Andy nodded in agreement. "There used to be an old access road running southeast off where the road turns sharp to the north," he said. "People dumped stuff in the refuge all the time before the DNR blocked it off."

"I think Hemper wandered into it, tripped and hit his neck on something sharp," Sheriff Thompson said. "It's how he got the injuries Jesse saw."

Aaron snapped some pictures. "Did you have anybody check the refuge and see if there was blood anywhere?"

"I had two deputies back there for a full day," the sheriff said. "They didn't find anything, but there's been two snowstorms since it happened, so everything was covered."

It didn't matter. Standing at the scene, Aaron saw the absurdity of the sheriff's theory. Chantel had said Hemper had severed both carotid arteries and bled out quickly. He might have made it a few feet before collapsing, but he wouldn't stumble around for fifty yards. If he had sliced his throat in the refuge, they would have found him in the refuge.

"Okay, we're done here," Aaron said. He shivered from the wet t-shirt touching his skin. "Andy, where does the grass waterway through the other field run?"

"There's a culvert running under the state highway to the west," Andy said. "It runs from there to an intake by the farm service buildings. There's a tile that runs underground from there and dumps into the refuge. Why?"

Aaron smiled. "I like details. Let's go take a look at it."

He would have to sit and rethink all of this when they got back to his makeshift office. If Hemper had run into something and cut his throat, it would have been something within feet of where they found him, and they had shoveled everything for 50 yards in all directions.

~*~

Sheriff Thompson dropped Aaron off at the law center and went back to his office. Aaron got in his car and slipped back out to the county garage.

The sun had touched the tops of the trees in the late afternoon when Aaron pulled into the county garage's parking lot. Shadows covered the dumpster on the east side of the building where they had first met Bud.

Aaron slipped on a pair of latex gloves and opened the lid of the dumpster. He shined his flashlight into the dark inside. He couldn't see the disc harrow blade, but being heavy, it would have worked its way to the bottom.

He dug stuff out of the dumpster and laid it on the ground. There were cans, bottles, sheets of plastic and grocery bags, but he couldn't find the disc blade.

"Hey! What are you doing over there?" a tall young man with longer blond hair yelled as he came out of the walk-in door of the building.

"I'm Agent Barnum with the DCI," Aaron said. He dug his badge out of his jacket.

"Okay. I recognize you from earlier," the guy said in a more relaxed voice.

Aaron remembered seeing him bent over the truck with Bud when they were at the county garage earlier. "And you are?"

"Tim Schwartz. I work here in the shop."

He was the guy Bud had taken out to the scene with him.

"Maybe you can help me," Aaron said. "I'm looking for the things your guys cleared off the field by the farm service when you were looking for the body."

"It should be right there in the dumpster," Tim said. "I put it in there myself."

Aaron dug some more out as Tim walked over.

"That's it," Tim said looking at the pile on the ground. "All those cans and stuff."

"Do you rember a disc blade?" Aaron asked, still rummaging around in the dumpster.

Tim didn't answer for a second.

"It might be evidence," Aaron said. "Do you remember seeing it?"

"Yeah," Tim said and paused again.

"Do you know where it is?"

"*I've* got it." He looked nervous. "They said they were going to throw all the stuff away," he said, his nervousness showing in how fast he talked. "I do a little junking on the side, so I took it. It's good heavy scrap metal. I didn't think taking it would hurt anything." He stopped and licked his lips. "Am I in trouble?"

Aaron smiled to put him at ease. "You're not in trouble, but I need to see it."

"Sure." Tim said. "It's right over there in the back of my truck,"

Aaron followed him to a gold Dodge Ram pickup with a rusted silver bumper. Tim opened the tailgate, hopped into the box and quickly dragged a heavy piece of metal onto the tailgate.

It looked like a giant brown Frisbee with a square hole in the middle. If it had been sticking out of the ground on its edge and Hemper had fallen on it, it might have sliced his neck open.

Aaron bent over until his face was inches from the metal and looked it over carefully with his flashlight. He couldn't see any blood. He flipped the disc over. No blood on that side either.

"I need my investigation kit," Aaron said. "It's over in my car. I'll be right back."

Aaron grabbed the blaze orange plastic box out of the trunk and went back to the pickup. He took a bottle of luminol out of the box and sprayed the disc. If there were any traces of blood, it should have glowed blue. It didn't. Aaron flipped it over and sprayed the other side. Nothing. He was disappointed, but things rarely came that easy.

"Well if you still want it, it's all yours," Aaron said, nodding at the disc as he put the bottle of luminol back in the box.

"It's okay," Tim said. "It makes me nervous just to touch it now. I'll put it back in the dumpster."

"I'll get it," Aaron said, hefting it off the pickup's tailgate. "I have to put all the stuff I took out back anyway."

"Okay," Tim said. "Do you need anything else? Otherwise I'm headed home."

"Go ahead," Aaron said. "Thanks for your help."

Tim closed the tailgate, got in the truck and drove away.

Aaron lugged the heavy blade back to the dumpster and dropped it in. He picked up the cans and plastic on the ground around it and stopped.

A black bicycle inner tube lay on the ground at his feet.

He picked it up in his latex-covered hands. It had been cut in two and one end was tied with a yellow nylon rope while the other end was open. But the open end had creases and lighter striations in the black rubber where it had once been tied with the rope. Meth cooks transported anhydrous in inner tubes all the time. They didn't leak. They were cheap, and they could be thrown away when they were done with. Deputy Gordon's report had said he had seen a bicycle inner tube laying by Hemper's body and smelled an overpowering smell of anhydrous ammonia.

Aaron studied the inner tube for a moment, looking at it from different angles in the fading daylight.

A cardinal safety rule in investigations was you never smelled or tasted anything. There was too big of a chance of poisoning or contaminating yourself. You sent all suspicious materials to the lab or tested them with a field testing kit. Aaron's investigation box contained kits for testing most drugs, blood and gunshot residue, but nothing for testing anhydrous.

He gingerly lifted the inner tube toward his nose. When it was still a foot away, he could clearly detect the smell of anhydrous ammonia.

Aaron dug a big plastic evidence bag out of his investigation kit, put the inner tube in it and labeled and sealed it. He still wasn't sure whether it was an accident or a murder, but the sheriff's theory of what had happened the night Hemper died had been blown to pieces.

Chapter Eight

The jailer who brought Pug into the room was a short, chubby Hispanic with fine curly hair, like black peach fuzz, covering his head. His cologne overrode the room's usual smell of stale food.

Pug wore a blaze orange jumpsuit with the words *Prisoner Cossack County Jail* stenciled across the back in black letters. His nose was as flat as any bad boxer's. Three days' growth of dark stubble rimmed a glistening U-shaped bald spot on the top of his head. He was well-restrained in handcuffs with a belly chain and leg irons that jingled when he sat at the table.

"Take those off him," Aaron said, motioning at the chains.

"We should leave them on," Sheriff Thompson said as he leaned against the wall behind Pug.

In basic interrogation school that the sheriff would have gone through at the law enforcement academy, they recommended you make the suspect feel as helpless and pressured as possible, but Pug had become a witness. Aaron wanted him as comfortable as possible.

"Take them off," Aaron said again.

The sheriff did not look happy as the jailer removed the hardware. Aaron was past caring whether the sheriff was happy.

"Do you need me anymore?" the jailer asked.

"You can go, Al," the sheriff said. "We'll let you know when Pug's ready to go back in his cell."

The jailer left the room, taking the restraints and his cologne with him.

Aaron smiled. "Okay, Pug. You don't mind if I call you Pug?"

He shrugged. "Everybody else does."

Aaron pulled out his badge. "I'm Agent Aaron Barnum with the DCI," Aaron said, showing Pug the badge. "I'd like to ask you a few questions about the night Hemper died."

"You need to read him his rights," Sheriff Thompson said.

"It doesn't matter," Pug said. "I ain't saying nothing without an attorney."

Aaron put the badge back in his pocket and opened a manila folder on the table in front of him. "Maybe this will change your mind." He took out a piece of paper and slid it across the table.

"What's this?" Pug asked, turning the paper around so he could read it.

"It's an order dropping all charges and ordering your release," Aaron said. "As soon as a judge signs it, you're out of here."

"What?" The sheriff looked confused and upset. "Those were my department's charges. Why wasn't I consulted?"

"The county attorney didn't think there was enough evidence to support a conviction," Aaron said without looking at him.

"I still should have been consulted," the sheriff said.

Aaron didn't respond. The charges had been ridiculous: burglary, theft, criminal trespass and first-degree murder, because Hemper had died in the commission of a felony. They couldn't prove any of them. Maybe some lesser charges would have stuck, but Aaron was working on a possible murder. He needed Pug's side of the story, and he didn't have a problem with trading away minor charges for it. The county attorney was more than willing to get rid of the charges and let Aaron take the heat from Sheriff Thompson.

"Is this for real?" Pug asked looking at Aaron again. "You're not setting me up?"

"If it isn't real, anything you tell me wouldn't be admissible in court," Aaron said. "You know that. It's why I didn't read you your rights." Most prisoners became jailhouse lawyers quickly. Aaron couldn't see how Pug would be any different.

Pug thought about it for a moment. "What do you want to know?"

Aaron turned his digital recorder on. "I'll be recording this, if it's okay?"

Pug shrugged.

"First of all, how did you meet Hemper?" Aaron asked.

"In prison."

"How did you end up in prison?"

"Pug did a strong-armed robbery of a convenience store," Sheriff Thompson said.

Pug glared at him. "I didn't do the robbery."

"What happened?" Aaron asked.

"I don't remember most of it," Pug said. "I was with Pat Pattison. We were both drunk and out of beer and money. We stopped at the Grab and Go, and I was supposed to get the beer while Pat distracted the clerk. When I tried leaving, the clerk saw me, so I took the beer and ran."

"That's misdemeanor shoplifting," Aaron said. "They don't send you to prison for that."

"They do when you try to kill the clerk," the sheriff said.

This time Aaron glared at the sheriff. "Why don't we let Pug tell the story?" Aaron said.

Pug seemed pleased with the rebuke of the sheriff. He was grinning.

"So what happened?" Aaron asked.

"I guess after I ran out of the store, Pat pulled a knife on the clerk and took the money out of the cash register."

"You guess? You've seen the surveillance video," the sheriff said. "Pattison tried to stab the clerk. If he hadn't been so drunk, he would have killed her."

"I was outside before any of that happened, and you know it," Pug snapped.

"So threatening her with a weapon made it armed robbery?" Aaron asked, ignoring the sheriff.

"I didn't know anything about the knife until the next afternoon when the cops showed up at my place with a warrant and dogpiled me," Pug said.

"They nailed him for being an accessory," the sheriff said.

"Pat got a 25 with an enhancement for being a habitual felon," Pug said. "It wasn't his first time. He'd went down a couple times before."

"And you got off easy and still couldn't keep your nose clean," Sheriff Thompson said.

"I had a drinking problem at the time, okay?" Pug shouted at the sheriff.

"You were the biggest drunk in the county," the sheriff said.

"That's enough," Aaron said, looking at the sheriff. Sheriff Thompson looked shocked, but Aaron wasn't going to referee a match between them. "Let's let Pug talk." He looked back at Pug. "What did you get?"

"They gave me ten years."

"And you met Hemper there?"

"No," Pug said. "I did two years at Anamosa, and they paroled me."

"Until you got sent back." the sheriff said.

"I already said I was a drunk," Pug growled.

"Don't get mad at me," Sheriff Thompson said, grinning. "I didn't pour the beer down your throat."

"This thing is over." Pug folded his arms in front of him. "If I'm a free man, take me back to my cell 'til the release order gets here."

This needed to stop. Aaron stood and smiled at the sheriff. "Can I talk with you out in the hall for a minute, sheriff?"

Before he could answer, Aaron left the room. In a moment Sheriff Thompson joined him.

"You and Pug don't seem to get along," Aaron said.

"We've had some run-ins in the past," the sheriff said. "Things that happened before I was sheriff."

Aaron nodded, trying to be diplomatic the way his training officer had told him. "He has information I need," Aaron said. "And he won't tell me anything with you in there." *And constantly antagonizing him.*

"The guy's a scumbag," the sheriff said. "He always has been."

"Most of the people we deal with are scumbags," Aaron said, keeping a smile on his face. "And riling them up is not how you get information from them. You have to relate to them."

"I was taught you intimidate them."

Where did you learn that? Some TV cop show?

"Well, this is my investigation, and we'll use my methods," Aaron said. The smile left his face, and he didn't put it back. Sometimes diplomacy didn't work.

The sheriff looked frustrated. "I guess it's hard for me to get with the program when I know it was an accident."

"It wasn't an accident," Aaron said. "Of that much I'm sure."

The sheriff's face went pale. He looked as if he'd been punched in the gut.

Aaron suddenly knew why the sheriff had so quickly rationalized Hemper's death as an accident. Next year was an election year. Having an unsolved murder and maybe a murderer still on the loose would not look good. Right now they didn't even have a suspect. Aaron didn't believe the sheriff was doing anything devious; it just worked out better for him if he called the death accidental, so he had found a way to do it.

"How do you know it's not an accident?" Sheriff Thompson asked softly.

"I don't have time to explain right now," Aaron said. "Why don't you go to your office, and I'll finish talking with Goebel. When I'm done, we can sit and discuss it."

The sheriff walked down the hallway without saying anything.

Aaron watched him go until he disappeared through a door. He went back into the room with Pug.

"Where's the sheriff?" Pug asked.

"He had something come up."

"He ain't coming back?"

"No."

"Good. He's an asshole."

Prisoners always tried playing officers against each other. Aaron wasn't going there. "I've only known him since a few days ago."

"Well, I've known him for fifteen years, before he was even the sheriff, and he's an asshole," Pug said. "I bought my first car from him. It was a piece of junk, and he knew it when he sold it to me." Pug's jaw was set. He looked mad. "My folks beat his ass in court and got my money back. He's been pissed ever since."

The sheriff should have told him all this before he ever stepped in the room with Pug. Aaron would have never let him sit in on the interview. Now he'd have to let Pug settle down before they'd get anywhere.

"The only reason he's sheriff is because he married the banker's retarded daughter," Pug said. "Daddy-in-law got tired of him screwing up at the bank, so he talked him into running for sheriff and bankrolled his campaign. Rumor is, he had a couple people follow the guy he was running against. They saw him come out of a bar and called the state patrol. He got arrested for OWI, and the guy's chances of winning were pretty much over. The sheriff's an asshole."

Aaron smiled, still not taking sides. He wasn't getting into local gossip.

"Anyway, the sheriff is gone and won't be coming back before we're done here," Aaron said. "We were talking about how you met Hemper."

"I got released from Annie and sent to Ft. Dodge for breaking parole when I got arrested for drunk driving. Wally was my cellmate for the last six months in Fort Dodge."

"What was he in for?"

"Cooking meth. He'd been paroled, too, and got thrown back in for a dirty piss test," Pug said. "He had 18 months left when I got out."

"Where did he come from?"

"Not sure," Pug said. "He moved around a lot. Originally he was from somewhere south along the Missouri border."

"Did you plan on him coming here when he got out?"

"We talked about meeting up, but there was nothing definite," Pug said. "By the time he got here, I was on the wagon, married and had our little girl. I was a working guy. I was trying to start over clean." He paused and a serious look crossed his face. "My old lady told me before we got married, if I didn't straighten up, she'd take our baby and leave my ass. She probably will now that I got thrown in jail. She ain't answering her phone."

"Maybe she'll change her mind," Aaron said.

"I hope you're right," Pug said. He looked worried.

If Pug had been a suspect, Aaron would have used his wife against him. But Pug was a witness. All he needed from him were the details of what had happened. "What happened when Hemper got here?"

"He lived with us for a little while," Pug said. "My old lady thought she could reform him like she did me. Her dad was a drunk. She had sympathy for addicts."

"Did it work?"

Pug coughed out a laugh. "The day after he moved in, I caught him smoking a rock in the garage. I chewed his ass. The old lady would have thrown us both out if she'd caught him."

"How long did he stay with you?"

"Two weeks. He was wasted all the time and didn't even try finding a job. The old lady finally kicked him out."

"How often did you see him after he left?"

"Once or twice a week he'd stop by. Nothing regular." Pug said. "When my wife's car was gone, he'd stop. He didn't want to run into her."

"Did you guys do anything together?"

"No," Pug said shaking his head adamantly. "I didn't really want to see him.

He was hanging out with local dopers, cooking and selling again."

"How do you know?"

"Sometimes he'd have ten thousand dollars cash on him, and a week later he'd borrow money for smokes," Pug said. "It ain't like that unless you're cooking and using. It ain't good cooking meth when you're an addict. You use more than you sell. You're lucky if you break even."

"The night he died, what happened?" Aaron asked.

Pug paused for a moment before he spoke. "Wally stopped by after dark," he said. "My old lady was out of town for the night at a baby shower for her sister. He said he needed someone to go to Luther with him and get another car. He wanted me to drive it back to his place," Pug said. "I don't think he could find anybody else, and I think he was afraid if he told me we were going to get something for a cook, I wouldn't have gone."

"Would have you?"

"No," he said immediately. "And Wally knew it, too. I was never much into dope, and I wouldn't have screwed up everything I had by helping Wally with a cook."

"Why couldn't he have gotten the anhydrous by himself?"

"I don't know for sure, because he never said," Pug said. "My guess is he didn't want the truck sitting there while he was getting the anhydrous. Wally was a doper, but he wasn't stupid."

"And it was you and him in the truck?"

"If there had been someone else, I wouldn't have gone with him. He said he was getting another car. The other guy could have driven it."

"Okay," Aaron said. He believed him. It wouldn't take two people to get the anhydrous. "When did you figure out what he was doing?"

"When he turned off the highway and went by the farm service," Pug said. "I knew right away he was getting anhydrous for a cook. I told him I didn't want any part of that crap."

"What did he say?"

"He didn't say anything," Pug said. "He stopped the pickup on the highway and jumped out."

"Did he have anything with him when he got out of the truck?" Aaron asked.

"I don't know what you mean. Like what?"

"A weapon or tool? Something big and sharp?" *Something he could have fallen on and cut his throat with?*

"He grabbed a bicycle inner tube off the floor in the back," Pug said.

"Nothing else?"

Pug thought a moment. "He might have had a wrench or something in his pockets."

"But nothing big?" Aaron asked.

"No."

"What did you do after he got out?"

"What could I do?" Pug said. "I figured I better move before a cop came by and stopped to see what I was doing. Wally must have seen me leave, because he called me on my cell phone."

"What did he say?"

"He said he'd call me when he needed to be picked up."

It must have been when Jesse saw the pickup move the first time and disappear west. So far what Pug was saying fit Jesse's story. "Where did you go when you left?" Aaron asked.

"I was pissed, and I was going to go home and leave him there," Pug said, "but it was snowing hard. Wally wasn't dressed very warm, and I knew he'd freeze if I left him. I went a couple miles west and sat on a gravel road until he called."

"What did he say?"

"He said to meet him at the same spot on the highway where he got out."

That would be when Jesse saw him come back. "Anything else?"

Pug thought for a moment. "He said someone was out there with him."

"Who?"

"I don't know," Pug said. "I figured nobody. Wally got paranoid sometimes from the meth. He always thought the cops were after him."

"And the phone call is the last you heard from him?"

Pug nodded, then stopped in mid-nod. "Wait. He called me again a couple minutes later."

"What did he say?"

"He didn't say nothing. I think he butt dialed me," Pug said. "I could hear him panting."

"Panting?"

"You know, like he was running. Out of breath. It kind of sounded like he was crying, too."

"What do you mean, crying?"

"You know, like whimpering, sobbing, that kind of thing," Pug said. "It was hard to tell. Maybe it was the wind. I could barely hear him. The phone must have been in his pocket."

"But he never said anything?"

"No. I tried yelling in my phone to get his attention, but he never answered," Pug said.

Aaron studied him for a moment. "What do you think happened to him?"

Pug looked puzzled. "What do you mean?"

"What do you think killed him?"

"Killed him?" A confused look covered Pug's face. "I thought he froze to death?"

"He had severe injuries."

Pug digested the information for a moment. "Like what?"

"The deputy who found him said his throat was cut."

"What?"

"You haven't heard this?" Aaron couldn't believe they wouldn't have let him know.

"Hey, nobody's told me squat," Pug said. "They brought me in and started asking questions. I knew Wally was dead, but they didn't say nothing about how he died."

Pug had been sitting in jail without knowing what had happened. Aaron couldn't believe it, but it gave his story more credibility. At least he wasn't making things up to fit the evidence the way Sheriff Thompson had done. "Did anyone have something against Wally?"

Pug's eyes got wide. "Are you saying he was murdered?"

"I don't know," Aaron said. "It's what I'm trying to find out. Did he have any enemies?"

"I don't know," Pug said. "When Wally was cranked he could be a dick, and I guess it's possible he could have owed people money." He stopped again, thinking. "But why would they kill him out in the middle of nowhere? How would they even know he'd be there?"

It was the part Aaron couldn't figure out either. Whoever killed Hemper would have had to know he would be getting anhydrous at the farm service, and according to Pug, nobody did.

"Well I don't have any more questions for you," Aaron said, turning off the recorder. "You've been a big help. Do you have any questions for me?"

"Who killed Wally?"

"I'd like to know that, too," Aaron said. "If you think of anything else, let me know." Aaron dug his business card of his jacket pocket and handed it to Pug.

"I'll let you know," Pug said and looked at the card briefly before tucking it in the breast pocket of his jumpsuit.

Aaron went over to the phone on the wall and buzzed the dispatcher. Jana answered.

"Could you send the jailer back here?" Aaron said. "I'm done with Pug."

"Right away," she said. "Have you decided when you're coming over for lasagna?"

"Not yet," Aaron said. It was tempting. "I'm pretty busy right now with the investigation."

"Okay. Let me know when."

"Will do."

"How's the investigation going?" she asked.

"A little bit at a time." Aaron hung up before she could ask any more questions.

"You weren't putting me on about me getting out of here?" Pug asked.

"As soon as the judge signs the papers, you're a free man," Aaron said and smiled.

Pug smiled back, but the smile fell from his face quickly. "Now I got to try and mend fences with my old lady."

"Good luck," Aaron said.

"I'm hoping since the charges were dropped, she'll see I didn't do anything wrong," Pug said.

"If you want, I can explain it to her," Aaron said. He figured it was the least he could do.

"Thanks," Pug said smiling. "I appreciate it. We'll see how it goes."

"I do have one more question," Aaron said.

"Yeah? Go ahead."

"Did you see anything unusual the night you dropped Hemper off?"

Pug's high forehead wrinkled with puzzlement. "What do you mean?"

"The deputy reported seeing something the night you were out there with Hemper."

"Like what?"

"I don't know," Aaron said, smiling. If he suggested anything, it would put ideas in Pug's head. Aaron wanted him to find his own answer. "He saw a flash of something. It was a bulk. Nothing he could identify. Did you see anything?"

Pug thought for a moment. "We did see something cross the road when we went by the farm service the first time."

"What was it?"

"I don't know. It was a ways ahead of us and hard to see because of the snow," Pug said. "Wally said it was a deer, but the eyes didn't shine in the headlights the way a deer's do, and it looked taller than a deer."

"What do you think it was?"

Pug snorted a laugh. "It was coming out of the refuge, so I told Wally it was a mountain lion."

"A mountain lion?"

"There's been rumors about mountain lions in the refuge forever," Pug said. He smiled. "I think it was a deer like Wally said."

Chapter Nine

After Al took Pug back to his cell, Aaron wrote some quick notes on his laptop about the interview. He hadn't learned anything earth-shattering, mainly background information. Pug had confirmed Hemper had not been carrying a weapon or tool that could have caused his injuries and getting the anhydrous seemed like a spur of the moment thing. Hemper hadn't made plans with Pug to get the anhydrous, so nobody should have known he would be there. Those were the main things Aaron had gotten from Pug.

Aaron closed the laptop and went across the hall to the sheriff's office.

Dina sat at her desk looking at her cell phone. Not a single paper lay on the desktop.

"Is the sheriff in?" Aaron asked from the hallway.

She laid the phone on her desk. "He's expecting you." She picked up the phone on the desk, with not even the hint of an emotion crossing her bone-white face. "Cal, Agent Barnum is here to see you," she said. After a slight pause she hung up. "He says go right in."

The sheriff's office now had a stop and a yield sign leaning against the wall behind the sheriff's chair. Nothing else had been straightened or moved. Aaron took a seat.

"What did you find out from, Pug?" Sheriff Thompson asked. The worry covering his face hinted it wasn't the question he wanted answered.

"It was just Pug and Hemper in the truck," Aaron said. "I thought maybe someone had gone with them, went out in the field with Hemper and killed him."

"I never thought of that," Sheriff Thompson said. "Or maybe Pug is the one who killed Hemper? Maybe he went out in the field with him, killed him and went back to the truck? Maybe we've had the murderer in jail all along?"

More wild theories. The sheriff was grasping at straws. "It couldn't have happened that way," Aaron said, crushing the sheriff's new theory. "Jesse did a good job of noting the times the pickup stopped on the highway. Pug couldn't have walked into the farm service with Hemper, killed him and gotten back to the truck. There wasn't enough time. And why would he have come back once he drove off? If he killed Hemper, why wouldn't he have gone home? It doesn't make sense."

The sheriff paused for a moment, thinking about it.

"But he didn't have to walk into the farm service," the sheriff said. "Hemper died a hundred yards east of the gravel road. Let's say Pug was supposed to pick him up on the gravel road. He could have chased him in the field and killed him. That's why his tracks zigzagged. He was being chased by Pug."

The sheriff wouldn't let his theory go no matter how ludicrous. "First of all," Aaron said. "Pug didn't even have a coat with him when Jesse stopped him. If he had gone out in the storm dressed the way he was, he would never have made it back to the truck. Second, Hemper wasn't killed in the field where he was found. He was killed in the field by the farm service and moved to the other field."

The information visibly shocked the sheriff. His face went limp for a moment. "How do you know?"

"Do you remember the things you had them gather when they were clearing the field by the farm service?"

"Yes?"

"I went through it all last night," Aaron said. "I found a bicycle inner tube like the one Jesse said he saw by Hemper's body. It smelled of anhydrous. Pug also said Hemper had one with him when he got out of the car."

The sheriff thought for a moment and a small light of hope came into his eyes. "It doesn't mean anything," he said. "They've been stealing anhydrous from the farm service for years, and an inner tube is a common way for cooks to transport it. It could be an inner tube from someone who stole some months ago."

"I have a state trooper running it to the lab so they can check it for Hemper's fingerprints," Aaron said.

"There won't be any fingerprints," Sheriff Thompson said. "Hemper was wearing gloves."

"Have you ever tried tying a knot in rope wearing thick gloves?" Aaron asked. "I guarantee you he took his gloves off before he tied the knot, and I'm guessing he tied the knot in the one end before he ever went out in the field."

Aaron paused for a moment as he dug into his jacket pocket. He took out a clear plastic evidence bag and laid it on top of the clutter on the desk. "I also found this in the stuff from the field."

The sheriff examined the bag. "It looks like a leather glove."

"A black, right-handed, leather glove," Aaron said. "It's the one Jesse lost when he found Hemper's body. Jesse has already confirmed it's his. So it was the field by the farm service where Jesse found Hemper."

A stunned look froze on the sheriff's face as he stared at the glove in his hands. He fingered it for a moment through the plastic bag but didn't say anything. He slumped in his chair and laid the glove back on the desk.

Sheriff Thompson had made a huge mistake not having someone check the pickup load of stuff they gathered from the field before having it thrown away. Aaron figured Jesse hadn't done the written report when they were clearing the field. The sheriff only knew the basics Jesse had told him over the phone. He wouldn't have known about the inner tube or Jesse's glove at the time. They were looking for a weapon or a tool Hemper might have fallen on, not an inner tube and a glove.

"When we found Hemper's body in the other field, I figured the stuff from the farm service field wasn't important," the sheriff said softly. "I had them throw it away." He looked off across the room at the wall behind Aaron for a moment. "I've already sent out a press release saying Hemper's death was accidental." He looked back at Aaron. "I'm going to look stupid."

Sheriffs had guaranteed four-year jobs, and the public looked at the failures more than the accomplishments. If they lost an election, it meant they'd have to start from scratch somewhere else doing something different.

"It happens with cases like this," Aaron said. "Sometimes people make mistakes." But it shouldn't have happened. Sheriff Thompson should have let one of his experienced deputies handle the case. He had what Aaron called Politicians' Disease. He believed when he won the election, he suddenly became smarter and knew more than everyone else in his department.

"So Hemper was murdered?" Sheriff Thompson asked.

There was the question everyone would ask, and Aaron couldn't answer. "I don't know yet," Aaron said. It was the only answer he had right now. "There are still people I need to interview. I'll let you know when I have the next interview scheduled."

"It's okay," the sheriff said. He looked defeated. "I have other things to do. Let me know if you find out anything new. Okay?"

The sheriff wouldn't be participating in the investigation anymore. His main objective had been finding out if he had screwed up, and that had already been determined. Sheriff Thompson was so shaken he never asked how the body got in the other field, which was a good thing, because Aaron didn't have any idea.

Chapter Ten

After Aaron left Sheriff Thompson, and was back in his temporary office, he opened his laptop and went online to the lab's website. He found the Hemper case file and went through the lab and autopsy reports again. The body had been moved from one field to the other, but why, and by who or what? He was missing something.

He looked at the toxicology report again. It was pretty straightforward. Nothing there. He looked at the pictures of the clothes Hemper had been wearing white overalls, white stocking cap, blue insulated nylon gloves, socks, tennis shoes, white hooded sweatshirt, t-shirt and jockey shorts.

The picture had an overall view of them laying on a table along with the cellphone that had been in Hemper's pocket. Most of the stuff had been chewed to shreds by animals. Aaron studied the phone trying to find something. After five minutes, he realized he was grasping at straws. There was nothing.

He clicked over to the autopsy report. Nothing different from what Chantel had told him over the phone. The pictures in the file showed Hemper's naked body lying on a stainless-steel table. Not much muscle left on the bones. Most of it had been eaten by animals. The feet and the hands were about the only things left untouched. Aaron figured the wildlife went for the meaty stuff first. He paused for a minute on a picture of Hemper's right hand, enlarged the photograph and re-centered it in the middle of the screen.

He studied it for a long time. Finally he pulled out his cell phone, opened its address book and punched a number.

"Medical examiner's office. This is Dr. Moore," Chantel said.

"Hi Chantel, this is Aaron."

"Hi Aaron." Her voice softened and lost the professional crispness. He imagined her beautiful violet eyes narrowing with a smile. "Are you still in the Arctic?"

"Yeah."

"Is it still cold?"

"Yeah, but it's supposed to warm up tomorrow afternoon."

"That's good."

"Then we're having a snowstorm."

She laughed. "It figures," she said. "What can I do for you?"

"Maybe nothing," Aaron said. "I was going through your report, and I noticed from your photos Hemper had some scratches on his right wrist."

"Wait a second. Let me bring up the report." He could hear the faint clicks of a mouse. "Okay, I see what you're talking about. Some minor abrasions on the top of his hand and wrist area. It looks like the cuff of his glove was pulled back exposing his skin. What do you need to know?"

"Do you know what made them?"

She blew out a thoughtful exhale he could hear through the phone. "They were made post-mortem, if it helps," she said. "My guess would be they were made when they took the body out of the field. Some of these departments get sloppy when handling bodies. I once had a volunteer fire department accidently drop a body off the roof of a three-story building. When I called them on it, they didn't think it was a big deal. 'Hey, what's the problem? The guy was dead already'," she said in what Aaron took as an attempt at a hillbilly accent.

"It didn't happen when they moved the body," Aaron said. "There was two feet of snow on the ground. Dragging a hand through snow wouldn't have made those marks."

"Ben did the examination before the body was cleaned," Chantel said. "Let me check his notes and see if he found anything." Some more mouse clicking. "Okay. I have Ben's report. It's in the file labeled, *Dr. Timmons-Hemper initial exam.*"

Aaron found it and opened it.

"It says there were bits of dirt and small rock particles in the abrasions," Chantel said. "My guess would be gravel."

The only gravel in the area was the gravel road between the two fields. It would have been cleared of snow after every storm, so there couldn't have been much snow on it the night Jesse found Hemper's body.

"What's this all about, Aaron?" Chantel asked. "Do you have something?"

"The body was moved," Aaron said. "It was about a quarter to a half mile from where the deputy originally found it. I can't be sure of the exact distance because nobody marked anything in the one field."

"How would it get moved and why?"

"There's the million-dollar question," Aaron said. "I think it was dragged across the gravel road, and that's how the hand got the abrasions. The white overalls the guy was wearing have dirt streaks on the right sleeve, too. Originally I thought they might have been made before that night, but now I don't know."

"Do you think an animal feeding on the carcass could have dragged it?" Chantel asked. "Maybe the coyotes?"

"I don't know," Aaron said. "Could a coyote drag a person that far? How big is a coyote?"

"As big as a dog, I guess," she said.

"Are we talking a cocker spaniel or a St. Bernard?"

"You're asking the wrong person," Chantel said. "You need a wildlife expert."

"I know," Aaron said. "I'll have to find one." He needed someone who knew about the large predators in the area.

"Are you classifying this as a murder?" Chantel asked.

"Not yet," Aaron said. He didn't know how Hemper ended up in the other field, but if it was an animal that could have dragged him that far, it was an animal that could have killed him. If Hemper was killed by an animal, it wasn't a murder. "Chantel, is Hemper's body still there?"

"Let me check." He could hear more mouse clicking. "It's scheduled for cremation tomorrow—no one ever claimed it—but it's here now."

"Could you do me a favor?"

"Sure. What?"

"Remember you said there were some teeth marks on the body you couldn't identify?" Aaron asked. "You said they were larger than the others."

"Right. I remember," Chantel said. "They were covered by other bite marks so there were only partials. I thought they might be a large dog or a wolf … Have you found out if there are wolves in Iowa?"

"Not yet," Aaron said. He needed the wildlife expert. "Could you identify what made those teeth marks through DNA?"

"If there's enough material, I can do a test," she said.

"I'd appreciate it if you'd do it for me."

"Sure. I'll go get a sample right now," Chantel said. There were a few more mouse clicks. "I put the body's cremation on hold in case you need something else."

"Thanks."

"Not a problem," she said. "Let me know if you need anything more."

"Will do," Aaron said. "Thanks again."

He hung up, picked up the intercom phone and punched in the code for the dispatcher.

"Dispatch," Jana answered.

"Hi, Jana. This is Aaron. Could you get in touch with the DNR officer?" Aaron asked. "I think it is Summer something."

"Summer Conrad," Jana said. "What do you need from her?"

"I have a few questions," Aaron said. "See if she can meet me here sometime this afternoon." He hung up before she could ask any more questions.

Aaron went to the county attorney's office. He figured he better keep her up to speed on what he'd found. If this was a murder, she would be the one who would prosecute it. She needed to know the sheriff had screwed up by throwing evidence away. It wasn't a surprise she needed right before she went to trial. The sooner she got the information, the sooner she could deal with it.

Nothing he told her surprised her. Aaron guessed she had never bought the sheriff's theory about Hemper dying in a freak accident. Her main question was the obvious one: Is it a murder? A question he still couldn't answer. She suggested he send Jesse's glove to the lab and see if they could confirm it as Jesse's through DNA, in case the lab couldn't lift Hemper's prints off the inner tube. He agreed, although he didn't have any doubt Hemper had died in the field behind the farm service and was dragged to the other field.

Aaron went back to his office and arranged to have a trooper run it to the lab. By the time he was finished, it was after two. He hadn't eaten since breakfast and decided this would be a good time to take a break. When he went out to the control room, Melonie was sitting in the chair behind the bullet-proof glass.

"Do you know if Jana got in touch with the DNR officer?" Aaron asked.

Melonie picked a yellow sticky note off the counter. "It says here, 'Summer will be here to meet with Aaron at 1630 hrs.'" She handed the note to Aaron.

Aaron checked his watch. 2:15. "I'm going to grab something to eat. Do you need anything?"

"I'm good," she said, smiling. "But thanks for asking. You were easier to train than most of the guys."

Aaron laughed. "Where's a quick place to eat besides Smitty's? I couldn't handle another one of those burgers."

Melonie grinned. "If you're hungry for lasagna, Jana's home. She keeps wondering when you're coming over."

"I only have two hours," Aaron said.

"Now you're bragging," Melonie said and laughed.

~*~

Aaron grabbed a meal from a fast food joint, and before three, he was back in his makeshift office going through the lab reports again.

At exactly 4:30 a hard double-rap came on the door. When he opened it,

Conservation Officer Conrad stood in the hallway looking more like a teenage girl than ever without her coat or cap. Her hair still hung in a long single braid.

"I was told you wanted to talk to me?" she said walking into the room. Aaron heard a hint of annoyance in her raspy voice.

"I need a little information," Aaron said. "Have a seat."

"Is it going to take long?" she asked. "Because if not, I'll stand."

She definitely sounded annoyed.

"Suit yourself," Aaron said. "I thought there was something you could help me with."

"What do you need?" she asked, direct and to the point.

"You know that Sandhill thing?"

"You mean The Sandhill Slough State Wildlife Refuge?" she asked, sounding more annoyed than ever.

"Yeah, that thing," Aaron said. "I'm sorry. I'm not from around here."

"What about it?"

"Can you tell me what large wildlife would be in there?"

"Are you looking for Bigfoot?" The hint of a smile raised the corners of her mouth.

"I'm not looking for Bigfoot." Aaron figured she must have heard about the tracks Jesse saw.

"Well, I'll tell you this much, if Bigfoot lives in Iowa, he would live there," Summer said. "It's 150 miles long and 30 miles wide in spots. It's the most isolated, uninhabited place in Iowa."

"Okay, but I'm not interested in Bigfoot," Aaron said. "What other big wildlife lives in there?"

"All the normal Iowa wildlife," she said. "I don't know what you're looking for."

"What kind could drag a person a quarter-mile or so?" Aaron asked. "Could a coyote?"

"No," she said. "A *huge* coyote around here weighs maybe fifty pounds, and most of them are closer to thirty. Plus, unless it's small like a rabbit, a coyote will eat its prey where it lays."

"How about wolves?" Aaron asked. "Are there any in Iowa?"

She nodded. "The department recently confirmed a wolf in Iowa by DNA," she said. "But wolves are like coyotes. They eat their prey where it goes down. They don't drag it."

"So what does drag its prey?"

She thought for a moment. "A mountain lion will drag a kill off to hide it so it can feed later. So will a bear."

"Are there mountain lions in Iowa?"

She nodded again. "Every now and then a hunter will shoot one, and we get tons of reports of sightings."

"How about bears?"

"There have been some bears reported in Iowa. Most of them were farther east along the Mississippi River. They follow the river from northern Minnesota or Wisconsin."

"Would there be any grizzly bears?"

She flashed a quick smile, revealing a gap between her front teeth. "The nearest grizzly bears are a long ways away," she said. "I doubt they'd make it this far without someone noticing."

"So what would be in the refuge that is big with long white hair?" Aaron asked.

She showed her gapped teeth again. "Now you're talking polar bears. They're in the Arctic."

"I didn't mean a bear," Aaron said. "Deputy Gordon said he saw something the night he found Hemper."

"I heard about it," she said. "He says he saw Bigfoot's tracks."

"He said it wasn't Bigfoot," Aaron said. "It was something big white and hairy. Any ideas?"

She thought for a moment. "The Abominable Snowman?" she deadpanned.

"Can we be serious? This is important." But he was glad she had cracked a joke. He had thought of her as a humorless bitch.

"I don't know what to tell you."

"Pug said they saw a deer cross the road on the night Hemper was killed," Aaron said. "Could it have been what Deputy Gordon saw? Or maybe something chasing the deer?"

"I doubt he saw a deer," she said, sounding confident.

"Why?"

"In the winter when the snow gets deep, the deer yard up," Summer said. "They have trails running between their bedding areas and their feeding areas. They don't do much wandering around. I seriously doubt if a deer would have left the shelter of the refuge in a storm. They would lose more calories trying to stay warm out in the wind and cold than they would gain."

"So if it wasn't a deer Pug saw, what did he see coming out of the refuge?"

"You need to ask Wildman Bob," Summer said.

"Who?"

"He lives in a cabin in Sandhill Slough," she said, "If anyone knows what's in there, he does."

"How do I get in touch with him?"

"You don't," she said. "He has a cell phone, but he only turns it on once a day to check messages or if something comes up and he needs to call out. He keeps an eye on the refuge for the department."

"Can you give me directions to his cabin?" Aaron asked. "I'd like to talk to him."

"You go 20 miles east of Calvin on the blacktop, turn south until you run into the refuge and walk from there," she said. "The cabin's about ten miles as the crow flies."

"There's no road?"

"There are only three roads going across the refuge, and none running its length."

"Is there a map or something so I can find my way?"

She looked at him for a moment with an amused expression on her face. "You're serious about going out there?"

"I want to talk to this … Wild Bob. I like being thorough."

"Wildman Bob," she corrected. She studied him some more. "You have anything besides a suit jacket to wear?"

"I have a snowmobile suit in the trunk of my car," Aaron said.

"How about boots and mittens?"

"I have those, too," Aaron said. "I don't spend all my time sitting at a desk."

"You look like you've never been in a winter woods in your life, city boy," she said without a smile.

"I went ice fishing once."

"Once? I'm impressed," she said without sounding impressed. She thought for a moment before she spoke. "I'm running some supplies out to Bob tomorrow afternoon. I guess you could tag along if you can operate a snowmobile."

"That's not a problem." Aaron had never been on a snowmobile, but they had rented Jet Skis on their honeymoon. There couldn't be much difference.

"I'll pick you up here, tomorrow afternoon at one," she said and opened the door. "I have a meeting with the county attorney." She went out the door but poked her head back in before the door shut. "You might want to get a pair of long underwear and maybe some heavy socks." She pulled her head out of the room and shut the door.

He looked at the closed door for a moment. Wildman Bob? If he lived in the refuge he'd know what was in there. Specifically, what was in there that could potentially kill somebody?

~*~

At six Aaron called it a day. On the way out of the law center he stopped by the control room.

"Did Summer tell you where Bigfoot is?" Melonie asked, grinning.

"I'm not looking for Bigfoot," Aaron said. "But I did get a date with her."

"Really?" She seemed genuinely surprised.

"Tomorrow afternoon she's taking me out to the refuge."

Melonie grinned at him. "If you're expecting lasagna, the rumor is she's a lesbian."

"Rumor?"

"I can't say for sure. I don't go that way," she said. "I have Jim. Remember?"

"So why do you think she's a lesbian?"

"When she first came here, every single guy in the PD and SO asked her out. She turned them all down flat."

"And that makes her a lesbian?"

Melonie shrugged. "I don't start the rumors. I just spread them."

Aaron laughed.

"Nobody has ever seen her with a guy … or a woman either," Melonie said.

It didn't matter who Officer Conrad spent her nights with. Aaron wasn't looking for romance. He was trying to solve a murder case.

Chapter Eleven

At noon Aaron grabbed a quick bite at Smitty's—the pork tenderloin instead of the Smitty Burger this time—and was dressed in warm clothes, his new long underwear, snowmobile suit, stocking cap, and mittens by 12:45.

Ten minutes later he wished he hadn't put the snowmobile suit on as sweat beaded on his forehead. He stepped outside to wait for Summer Conrad.

The day was bright, clear and cold. Aaron squinted against the glaring sun's rays bouncing off the snow. He decided he'd need his sunglasses, and he went toward his car when a tan DNR pickup pulled into the parking lot. When it stopped, Summer Conrad hopped out. She had on sunglasses and a green stocking cap but wasn't wearing a coat.

"Get your snowmobile suit off, city boy" she said as a greeting. "You sweat and you'll freeze."

"I thought—"

"No, you didn't think," she said. "If you had thought, you wouldn't be all bundled up like that. We still have to load the sleds and drive 20 miles before we get on the snowmobiles. You'll get overheated riding in the pickup and moving around when we hook up the trailer."

Aaron didn't argue. He pulled off the snowmobile suit and stuffed it in the rear seat of the club cab pickup. They got in and Summer pulled the pickup out of the parking lot and headed east.

"So tell me about this Wildman Bob," Aaron said.

"What do you want to know?" she asked, concentrating on looking out the windshield.

"For starters, what's his real name?" Aaron asked. "I doubt Mr. and Mrs. Bob named their son Wildman."

"His name is Robert Milton," she said. His joke didn't even buy him a smile.

"So why is he the only one living in the wildlife refuge?"

"The department made a deal with him," she said, still looking straight out the windshield. "They let him stay at the refuge, and he keeps an eye on it for them."

"Do they pay him?"

"No. He has his pension from the state and social security."

She still hadn't looked at him, and it bothered him.

"So why does he stay out there?"

For the first time she glanced at him. "Because, he'd be out there even if he didn't have the deal."

"What do you mean?"

"He was the officer for this area before me," she said, looking out the windshield again. "They say a few years before he retired, he was spending all his time in the refuge. He'd sleep out there in a tent most nights and even in the middle of winter sometimes."

He was one tough SOB if he slept outside in the middle of winter, Aaron decided. "Why did he do that?"

"Who knows?" she said. "It's just Bob. But there's no cellphone service in the refuge. To make or receive a call, you have to climb to the top of one of the hills. The department couldn't contact him most of the time. He was pushing 55, retirement age. The department figured they'd let it go until he retired. But it didn't work out that way."

"He didn't retire?" Aaron guessed.

"He just kept working," Summer said. "Pretty soon a couple years have passed and he's still going strong. Mandatory retirement isn't until 70."

"So what happened?"

"One winter he caught a guy trapping muskrats in the refuge," Summer said. "There's no hunting or trapping allowed in there. You can fish, but hardly anyone does because the mosquitoes are so thick in the summer, and it's so choked with weeds you'd have a hard time getting a line through them. Anyway, the guy said Bob handcuffed him to a tree and shot at him. Bob denied it of course."

"Do you think he did it?" Aaron asked. "Was he trying to kill him?"

She shook her head. "He did it, but Bob wasn't trying to kill him," she said. "He shot combat pistol competitions when he was younger. He's an excellent shot. If Bob wanted him dead, the guy would be dead, and his body buried somewhere in the refuge where nobody would ever find it."

It amazed him how casually she said it. "So why'd he do it?"

"I don't know for sure," she said. "But this was the third time Bob had caught the guy trapping in the refuge over the years. The punishment is a fine, liquidation of damages and loss of trapping privileges for a couple years. My guess is, Bob wanted him scared enough that he'd never come back."

"What happened?"

"The guy threatened a lawsuit, so the department gave him a settlement and fired Bob," Summer said. "But the union went in and fought for him. They were afraid of establishing a precedent. Anytime the department got a complaint from a citizen, they could get rid of the officer. Because when you got down to it, it was the perp's word against Bob's."

"And they got him back on?" Aaron asked

"They settled on a 30-day suspension without pay, because Bob hadn't done a wildlife survey the previous fall," Summer said. "They also demanded a psychological examination." She looked at Aaron again. "I think the department was scared to put him back out there. Most people already thought he was a little crazy."

"How'd the psych test come out?"

"I don't know," she said. "But there couldn't have been anything major in it, because they sweetened his retirement package. They offered to pay his insurance premiums until Medicare kicked in."

"I take it, it didn't work?"

She smiled, again showing her gapped teeth. "It didn't mean anything to him. I don't think Bob had been sick a day in his life. Finally they made him an offer he couldn't refuse."

"What?"

"There was an old log cabin in the refuge the department had built back in the seventies," Summer said. "They had planned on letting people and organizations rent it out. The problem was, it took a lot of effort getting back there. They originally cleared a winding path down one of the creeks so you could canoe to the cabin, but it was almost impossible keeping the path clear. A few people got lost looking for it, and the mosquitoes were so bad in the summer, the ones who found it never stayed there more than once. Some boy scout troops used it in late fall and winter, but when two kids were lost for two days and almost froze to death, that ended that."

"And what did this have to do with Bob?"

"They offered to let him fix the cabin and live there," Summer said. "The department even gave him a title: Civilian Superintendent of Sandhill Slough Wildlife Refuge. It's an unpaid position of course."

"And he took it?"

"Jumped at it," Summer said. "Now he lives in the cabin, and he's pretty much self-sufficient. He has a huge garden and a wood-burning stove. In college he had a minor in botany. He knows every plant growing in the refuge and every use for it."

"How does he deal with the mosquitoes in the summer?"

"He has some Indian dope he mixes up," Summer said. "The only modern thing he has is a cellphone. The only way he can get reception is if he climbs to the top of a hill, so he keeps it turned off most of the time. But he does let us know if anything is going on in the refuge, and I leave him voicemails if I need to get information to him. But I'm not sure how often he checks them."

"So if he's self-sufficient, why do you go out there?" Aaron asked.

"I only go out there in the winter to exchange the old batteries in the cellphone for charged ones," she said. "I also bring him a few things like salt, coffee and stuff he can't get out there. He makes an Indian tea out of bark when he runs out of coffee." She made a face. "My god it's nasty."

"And he lives out there by himself?"

"Almost five years now," she said. "I fully expect one day I'll go out there and find him dead. Every time I go and he's not at the cabin, I'm afraid he went off in the refuge somewhere and died. I doubt if we'd ever find his body."

She pulled off at the edge of town into a driveway and through a gate with a white sign above it reading: IA Dot Highway Maintenance. She drove the truck around a brick building to a small white metal shed.

"The snowmobiles are in the shed," she said as she backed the pickup up to one of the two overhead garage doors.

Summer got out and unlocked a walk-in door. In a moment the overhead door rose, and Summer stood in the doorway pushing the door to the top.

Aaron figured the building was a storage shed for the DNR. It smelled of gas and dead fish. Numerous ropes, straps, chainsaws and other equipment hung from pegs on the walls. A tan camouflage Jon boat on a trailer sat in front of the other garage door with canoes hanging from steel cables suspended from the ceiling above it. In the center of the open doorway stood a green double snowmobile trailer with a red and black Polaris snowmobile and a yellow fiberglass cargo sled sitting on it.

Summer pulled a dust-covered gray tarp off a decades-old Arctic Cat El Tigre sitting against the back wall.

"I'll back the truck up here," Summer said. "You hook up the trailer, and we'll load this sled on with the other one."

She got in the pickup and backed it with a practiced ease. Aaron lined up the hitch and, when it was in position, cranked the trailer tongue jack down until the hitch rested on the hitch's ball. He secured it.

Summer came back and checked his work. Satisfied, she grabbed a rag out of a steel barrel in the corner and wiped the Arctic Cat off.

"It's been a while since this has been used," she said. "But it worked fine the last time I had it out."

Aaron didn't care. With his lack of experience on a snowmobile, he would prefer something old and slow.

Summer grabbed a gas can sitting beside the Arctic Cat and filled the machine. She pulled the starter cord a couple times. The snowmobile sputtered, popped and blew out black smoke as it made a feeble attempt at running. After a few seconds it died. She pulled the cord a few more times and each time the machine ran briefly and died. Eventually it wouldn't run at all.

"I'm not sure what's wrong," Summer said. "Maybe the plugs are fouled?"

Aaron pulled the starter cord a couple times. He didn't know if he could pull a starter cord any better than her, but he felt useless standing there doing nothing.

"Leave it. There's a storm coming in tonight," she said. "We need to get going if we want to be back before dark. We're unloading at Lester Holmgren's place. He has a couple sleds. I'm sure he'll let us use one of them."

She pulled the trailer out of the shed and shut the door.

"So who's Lester Holmgren?" Aaron asked when they were on their way again.

"He's one of the only people who would call Bob a friend," Summer said. "They did things together when they were younger. You know, hunting and fishing … that kind of stuff. Now Bob keeps his truck at Lester's when he's in the refuge."

They traveled east out of town on the state highway passed the farm service with the refuge standing out behind it.

On the third gravel road after the farm service, Summer turned south off the state highway toward the refuge.

"Lester lives a couple miles down the road," she said. "We'll stop at the house. I'm sure he'll have some stuff for Bob."

On the edge of the refuge in the shadows of the hills, Summer pulled into a farmyard with a white two-story house, a red barn and two blue silos. She stopped the truck by a red outbuilding and shut off the engine.

"Let's go talk to Lester," she said as they climbed out of the truck.

Aaron followed her to the house as Black Angus cattle watched with blank stares from a trampled-mud feedlot. The air was ripe with the stench of cow manure and the dry dusty smell of ground feed.

Before she could knock, the door opened. Standing in the doorway was a white-haired man in a gray work shirt and blue jeans.

"Hi, Summer," he said.

He was thin with a long face marked with deep vertical creases running from the corners of his eyes to the corners of his mouth. His face was dark in complexion as if he had a deep tan even in the middle of the winter, but he looked pallid, and his eyes had a dull glaze to them. Aaron guessed him to be in his seventies.

"Come on inside," he said, opening the door wider for them.

They stepped through the door into an enclosed porch. Aaron would guess they called it a mud room. A row of boots and shoes lined the far wall under a variety of coats hanging on hooks.

"Are you okay?" Summer asked. "You look a little peaked."

"I think I'm coming down with a chest cold," Lester said. He took a deep breath and coughed it out. "It's been tough breathing the last couple days."

"And breathing in this cold air I'm sure doesn't help," Summer said.

"He needs to see a doctor," A woman with short gray hair wearing black sweatpants and a red sweater with a snowman on the front said as she came into the mudroom and stood beside Lester. Aaron figured it was Lester's wife.

"Hi, Carla," Summer said.

"I ain't running to the doctor every time I get the sniffles," Lester said. "I ain't got time for that."

"All I'm saying is, it wouldn't hurt if you get it checked out before it gets out of hand," Carla said.

"If you don't feel better, it wouldn't hurt if you could get a doctor to give you something for it," Summer said. She was walking a tightrope between the two sides.

"If you don't feel better by tomorrow, I'm making an appointment," Carla said. "Summer, you might have to come and help me drag him there."

Summer smiled. "Let me know."

"Who's your friend?" Carla asked, looking at Aaron.

"This is Aaron Barnum. He's with the DCI," Summer said. "We're going out to Bob's."

They shook hands.

"DCI?" Lester asked, suddenly looking concerned. "Bob's not in trouble, is he?"

Aaron saw by the look on the old man's face that he and Wildman Bob were indeed friends.

He smiled to put him at ease. "I'm investigating the death over at the farm service," Aaron said. "I'm hoping Bob can give me some information about the refuge."

Lester nodded. He seemed satisfied. "I got some stuff for him out in the garage. Let me get my coat." He took a pair of tan insulated overalls off a line of coat hooks on the wall.

"It's such an awful thing about the poor man at the farm service," Carla said addressing Aaron. "I don't care what he was, nobody should lie out there and have the animals get at them the way they did." She shuddered.

They stood in silence for a moment while Lester struggled into the overalls.

"Summer, did my grandson Dan ever call you?" Carla asked.

"He did," Summer said, smiling. "We couldn't find a time that worked for both of us. Maybe later on."

"He's a nice boy," Carla said. "You two would make a lovely couple."

"Would you stop playing matchmaker?" Lester said, zipping the overalls. He took a green seed corn cap off a hook and put it on. "Sorry Summer. Carla thinks if you ain't married and got kids by the time you're thirty, you're committing a sin."

"It's okay," Summer said, smiling. "I'm used to it. Everyone tries to set me up with someone."

Lester slipped on a pair of camouflage rubber boots, and they went out the door into a screened-in breezeway that attached the house to the garage. The two-car garage smelled faintly of gas. A white Cadillac El Dorado stood on one side and a blue Silverado pickup on the other.

At the rear of the garage, Lester hefted a green plastic tote out of an ancient chest freezer yellowed with age. Aaron helped him lug it out the front door of the garage.

"There's meat in there for Bob," Lester said as they set the tote on the ground. "He'll holler like hell cause it's beef instead of deer, but you make him take it anyway. You got to have calories in the winter to keep you warm. Can't get calories from vegetables and fish."

"He doesn't like beef?" Aaron asked.

"Bob likes things natural," Summer said.

"Usually I give him a deer or two, but we didn't fill our tags this year," Lester said. "I let the sheriff's office know I wanted a roadkill, but there hasn't been many of them this year, either. The deer population is down."

"Too many hunters?" Aaron asked.

"Too many coyotes," Summer said. "The fur prices are down so nobody traps or hunts them. With nothing controlling their numbers, they thin the deer and rabbits quickly. We've had complaints of coyotes picking off small dogs and cats on farm places and even on the edge of Calvin."

"Eventually they'll be nothing for them to eat," Lester said. "They'll starve.

Their population thin out, and the deer and rabbits will come back. Nature has a way of working things out, but she can be a cruel bitch doing it. Excuse my language, Summer."

Summer waved it off.

"Doesn't Bob hunt deer?" Aaron asked. If he was as good of a shot and outdoorsman as Summer had said, Aaron figured he could get his own.

"You can't hunt in the refuge," Summer said.

"Bob doesn't hunt anymore," Lester said. "If he did, he would have got a deer. I never seen a better hunter or fisherman than Bob. Couple times I seen him sneak right up on deer still sleeping in their beds. He got close enough that he could have jumped on them if he had wanted to."

"Why did he stop hunting?" Aaron asked.

"Job got in the way," Lester said. "We'd be sitting in a duck blind, and a couple minutes before shooting hours began, we'd hear a shot. Bob would be done hunting. He'd go off looking for whoever had shot early. I'd tell him, 'Forget about it. You ain't working today,' but he couldn't do it. Pretty soon he stopped hunting."

"So he doesn't hunt at all?" Aaron asked.

"Hasn't hunted for years," Lester said. "Then he got the refuge in his head, and it's all he could think about. Spent all his time out there. Now that he's retired … I worry about him."

Lester paused for a moment and looked at Summer. "Usually in the spring, summer and fall when he gets his own supplies, he'll stop and chat for a spell. This last year he never stopped once. I wouldn't even known he was in town if I didn't see his pickup was out of the shed."

"Sometimes he would look me up when he was in town, too," Summer said. "But he didn't do it this year either. And he hasn't been answering my messages or texts lately."

"When you get back, stop and let me know how he's doing," Lester said. "And tell him to get in touch with me when he comes to town."

"I will," Summer said. "By the way, I couldn't get our old sled running. Could we use one of yours?"

"I'd be glad to let you, if I had one here," he said. "The boys are in northern Wisconsin snowmobiling, and they took all the sleds with them."

"All of them?"

"They didn't want to go that far and have one break down. They took mine for spares." He stopped for a minute, thinking. "You could run to Jack Simpson's. I'm sure he'd let you use one of his. In fact, I'll give him a call to see if he's home." He dug a flip phone out of his inner pants pocket.

Summer looked at her watch. "It's okay. A storm is coming in tonight. If we don't get going, we'll never be back before dark. We can double up on the one sled."

"You sure?"

Summer glanced at Aaron and looked back at Lester. "We'll be fine," she said. "Do you at least have an extra helmet we could use?"

"That I can do," Lester said. He put the phone back in his pocket and paused for a moment. "You two be careful in there." He said it seriously, as a warning, not as the polite thing to say.

Summer smiled. "I always am."

"I mean watch out for yourself," Lester said. He looked at the house and back at them. When he spoke again it was in a whisper. "I ain't even told Carla, because she'd worry, but there's something in the refuge."

"There are a lot of things in the refuge," Summer said.

Lester shook his head. "I don't mean that," he said, talking louder. "There's something strange in there."

"Strange, like what?" Aaron asked. The way he said it suggested he wasn't talking about a mountain lion.

"I don't know," Lester said. "But I seen it twice now. Once two years ago from my tree stand when I was hunting deer. It was right at sunset so I couldn't see it too good. It was hidden in the shadows, but I could see it on the side of a hill in the refuge."

"What was it?" Aaron asked.

"I'm still not sure," Lester said, whispering again. "I saw a patch of dark move at first. It looked out of place. You know what I mean? And it moved like it was walking upright. And it was big."

"How big are you talking?" Aaron asked.

Lester thought about it. "It was hard telling from up in the tree and as far away as it was, but it was big. Way taller than a deer, and it was hunting."

"How do you know it was hunting?" Aaron asked. He shot a quick glance at Summer. She stood quietly listening and trying to keep an amused look off her face.

"I've watched animals all my life," Lester said. His old eyes were excited and animated. "I know when they're hunting. It was quiet when it moved, and it picked its steps like it was sneaking up on something. It didn't make any noise, and something that big doesn't go through thick brush without making noise unless it's hunting."

Lester shot a glance at the house. "I waited for an hour after I couldn't see it before I got out of my tree stand," Lester said. "I wanted to make sure it wasn't around no more."

"Did you tell Bob about this?" Summer asked. She still fought the amused look. "Maybe he could explain it."

"I told Bob, and he laughed at me," Lester said indignantly, his voice gaining volume. "He said it was someone's cow that got into the refuge. I know cattle. They ain't quiet. They don't sneak up on nothing, and this thing was on two legs. It wasn't a cow." He glanced at the house, and his voice dropped into a whisper again. "I know Bob, too, and his eyes weren't laughing. I think he knows there's something in there."

Aaron wasn't sure about any of this, but it made Deputy Gordon's story more believable.

"And you say this thing was dark-colored?" Aaron asked. Deputy Gordon had said what he saw was white.

"That time it was," Lester said nodding. "I saw it again about a month ago, right after we had our first big snow, and it was white then. I don't know, maybe it changes color in the winter like jackrabbits and weasels."

"Where did you see it the second time?" Aaron asked.

"I had a butcher hog get out," Lester said. "It was dark, but I saw the hog's tracks in the snow headed out into the back field. I followed it and finally found it on the edge of the refuge. I tried to get behind it to run it back home. When I got close, I saw what looked like a seven or eight foot tall bush covered with snow." Lester looked at the house again. When he looked back his eyes were wide, frightened. "Only the bush was ten yards out in the field. I disked the field last fall and no bush grew that much after I turned the dirt."

"Maybe it was a pile of brush that blew out of the refuge?" Summer said.

"It wasn't no brush," Lester said, "because it took a step toward the hog. It was stalking it."

"What happened?" Aaron asked.

"Me and the hog took off for the house in a hurry," Lester said. "All I had was a stick with me, and I wasn't fighting anything off with a stick."

"Were there any tracks?" Aaron asked.

"By the time I got done shaking, I wasn't in no shape to go back out there and look in the dark," Lester said, his old eyes still wide. "I went back out in the morning when it got light, but the wind came up in the night and wiped any tracks clean."

Lester looked at the house again. He looked back and studied them for a moment.

"I think whatever it is comes out of the refuge to hunt," he said. "With game being low, it has to range further to find prey."

"Or it could have been nothing," Summer said.

"It wasn't nothing," Lester said adamantly. "There's something in there." He looked at them for a moment. When he spoke again, he was talking slowly in a loud excited whisper. "So you two be careful. It only seems to hunt after dark, so be back here before nighttime."

Summer smiled. "We should be back way before dark."

"Make sure you are," Lester said. "Now let me go get you a helmet."
~*~

They unloaded the snowmobile and hooked the cargo sled to it.

"What did Lester see?" Aaron asked. He had wanted to ask since Lester left.

Summer loaded the tote of meat into the cargo sled. "I don't know, but it wasn't Bigfoot," she said. "I've spent some time in tree stands, too. The shadows at sunset can play tricks on you."

"But he saw it move," Aaron said. "Shadows don't move."

"I believe he saw something, but he also said it was halfway up the side of a hill, which meant it was a long ways off," she said. "And it was walking on two legs. My guess is it was a hunter."

"I thought you couldn't hunt in the refuge?"

She smiled. "That's right city boy, and if nobody ever broke the law, we wouldn't have jobs, would we?"

She had a point. "Okay, but what about the second time he saw it?"

"You mean when it had magically turned white?" She chuckled. "It wasn't the same thing if it was a different color. It was night. White on white makes you lose depth perception in the dark. It was probably a bush in the refuge, and in the dark it seemed to be in the field." She loaded two canvas bags into the sled, a brown one and a green one.

"He said it moved," Aaron said.

"Right," she said and picked a folded silver tarp out of the box of the pickup along with some bungee straps. "His imagination is already going because of what he saw the other time. He sees the bush, the wind blows and abracadabra, you have a monster."

Summer unfolded the tarp and covered the sled. She handed one end of a bungee strap to Aaron. "Hook it in the hole in the corner of the sled."

When he was done she handed him the end of another strap.

"I get this all the time," she said, securing her end of the strap. "I'm always getting reports of people seeing something strange. Mountain lions, bears and even Bigfoot. When I first got here, I'd check them all out, and I never found anything that couldn't be explained. Even in snow, I wouldn't find tracks, or sometimes I'd find tracks of deer, cows or people. It doesn't take much for a person's imagination to run wild."

She secured another strap. "When I was in high school in southern Iowa, there was a legend of a grass monster at a public hunting area in our county. I knew three or four classmates who swore they'd seen it. One night a friend of mine came to me shaking like she'd seen a ghost. She said she saw the grass monster out in an open field, and it had come after her." She smiled at Aaron. "I don't believe in ghosts or anything supernatural, so I dragged her back out there. Where she said the monster had been, there was a round hay bale standing on end instead of laying on its side like the others in the field. I made her touch it, so she could see it wasn't alive."

It impressed Aaron that a high school girl would have done that. Melonie was right; she was tough as nails.

"When Wildman Bob tells me there's something in the refuge, I'll believe it." She finished securing the tarp.

"Lester said Bob knows something's living in there," Aaron said.

She laughed at him. "And Bob's protecting Bigfoot? Is that what you're thinking, city boy?"

"I guess it doesn't make much sense."

Aaron didn't believe in ghosts or goblins or Bigfoot either, but something had dragged Hemper across a field.

"I need your weapon," Summer said.

"Why?"

"Firearms aren't allowed in the refuge."

"I didn't think it applied to law enforcement," Aaron said.

"It doesn't usually," Summer said smiling. Aaron noticed she smiled more out in the country than she did in town. "But the department doesn't want Bob having a gun. If we bring one into the refuge, he might think he can do the same."

Aaron took the pistol and its holster off his belt and handed it to her. She locked it in the pickup along with hers.

The Glock .40 had been with him since his first day on the job. He kept it with him at all times, on and off duty. It was strange not having its weight hanging on his side.

They put on their helmets, and Summer started the sled. When she had it running, she sat behind the handlebars and motioned Aaron on behind her.

"There are hand holds on the side," Summer said when Aaron wrapped his arms around her waist.

Aaron grabbed the handholds and they were off. They went out into the field behind the cattle lot. There was a gate in the fence on the far side of the field. Once they went through it, they were in the refuge.

Aaron couldn't see a trail. They were riding on ice with cattails coming through it everywhere. A jumble of snow-covered reeds stretched over their heads. It was like driving in a hedge maze with tan bulrushes and brown cattails brushing against Aaron's shoulders as they went weaving between the hills. Sometimes they went partway around one hill before turning off abruptly and going in a different direction. Summer guided the sled as if she knew where she was going, winding the sled back and forth without hesitation.

"How do you know where to go?" Aaron asked, shouting over the roar of the snowmobile.

She half-turned to look at him. "What?"

"How do you know where you're going?"

She slowed the sled and finally stopped.

"This is one of three snowmobile trails running through Sandhill Slough," Summer said. "They're the only places you can legally snowmobile in the refuge. This one was the canoe trail to the cabin." She pointed at a three-foot stone and mortar pyramid covered with bull rushes. A two-foot piece of rusting angle iron stuck out of the top of the pyramid, and on top of it, an Indian-style arrow cut out of quarter inch aluminum pointed to the right. The arrowhead was faded and weathered, but specks of reflective orange paint still clung to it. "The trail is marked with these arrows," Summer said. "It's also the only trail they don't groom anymore, because it's so rough. Hardly anyone uses it."

"I see," he yelled in her ear when she didn't move on for a moment.

The sled moved forward again as Summer followed the back and forth winding path marked by the arrows.

Summer had said the cabin was ten miles inside the refuge as the crow flies, but the way the trail snaked back and forth, it had to have been twice that far.

Finally, she pulled the sled off the trail into a thick stand of cattails and shut off the snowmobile.

Summer climbed off the snowmobile. "Bob's cabin is a quarter-mile that way," she said, motioning toward a creek with high banks running east through the cattails. "We'll walk from here and pull the cargo sled." She unhooked the sled from the snowmobile.

"Why can't we take the snowmobile the rest of the way?"

Summer pulled a piece of rope out of the sled. "Because snowmobiles are only allowed on designated trails, and this isn't a designated trail."

"You're that much of a stickler for details? It's only a quarter of a mile."

"It wouldn't bother me," Summer said, tying the middle of the rope to the tongue of the cargo sled. "But believe me, Bob would have a fit. Besides, there is so much brush across the trail we'd never get the snowmobile through."

Aaron didn't relish walking a quarter-mile through knee-deep snow, but if he wanted to talk to this Wildman Bob guy, he didn't have a choice. He grabbed one of the ends of the rope while Summer grabbed the other, and they went down the creek.

Chapter Twelve

Summer hadn't been joking about the trail being blocked. Every twenty yards or so a pile of brush ran across the creek, forcing a detour up on the bank and around it. With the banks rising sharply into thick cattails, maneuvering a snowmobile around it would have been impossible. They had all they could do working the cargo sled over the obstructions.

About 100 yards into the trip to the cabin, Aaron became aware there weren't any stumps or other trees and brush along the creek. The obstructions hadn't occurred naturally. They had been dragged there for the sole purpose of blocking the trail. Wildman Bob had built a moat around his fortress to prevent easy access to the cabin and isolate himself even further from civilization.

After they had been walking for a while, the breeze brought the smell of wood smoke. Aaron knew the cabin must be close. They came to a complicated obstruction that looked like a beaver dam: a pile of rocks, branches and frozen mud, but it was clearly manmade—the branches had saw marks on them. Aaron guessed Bob had dammed the creek to make his water source deeper.

When they had passed the damn by worming their way through the cattails on one side, he could see the cabin. It stood fifty yards up the side of a hill with a southern exposure. The trees had been cleared for a hundred yards in every other direction. The ground beside the cabin had been terraced into flat steps eight feet wide and 30 yards long running to the top of the clearing. They were edged with rocks, and Aaron guessed they were raised beds for a garden.

The cabin reminded Aaron of something from a Boy Scout camp. It was made from peeled logs coated with a shiny substance—maybe varnish or polyurethane. He guessed the logs had been hauled in and not cut in the area. They were too uniform in thickness. Maybe they were made from a kit? The roof was covered in red rolled roofing that looked as if it had been replaced within the last few years. When they were closer,

Aaron could see the logs had shrunk as they aged and dried. The spaces between them had been sloppily re-packed with no thought of their appearance. Smears of gray cement ran onto the logs with clearly visible finger streaks where hands had rubbed the cement into the cracks.

There was a tiny building twenty yards from the cabin Aaron took as an outhouse. It was the only building in the clearing besides the cabin, but on the right of it stood a woodpile fully half as tall as the cabin itself. In front of it sat a chopping block. The brush blocking the trail was the refuse of what was left when Wildman Bob had chopped wood, Aaron guessed. He had used it as the material for the walls across the trail and made it as difficult as he could for people to reach the cabin.

"Bob's not here," Summer said when they reached the cabin's door.

"How do you know?"

"His snowshoes are gone," she said, motioning at two long snowshoes with pointed tails hanging by the door.

"The snowshoes are there," Aaron said.

"Those are his beaver-tails," she said. She pointed at two empty nails beside the beaver-tails. "His bear paws are gone." She looked out at the hills. "He should be headed this way. I'm sure he heard the sled when we came. Bob wouldn't let it go without checking it out."

"Doesn't he know we were coming?"

"I've been sending him texts for the last few days, but he never answered them," she said. She had a worried look on her face. "Let's wait inside."

Summer went inside the cabin and Aaron followed.

The inside of the cabin was filled with a strong burnt wood smell, like a woods after a forest fire. Everything was covered with fine dark soot. The sunlight coming through the small windows displayed a thin cloud of ash floating in the air like gray snow. Candles were anchored in holders at various spots on the wall, and a kerosene lantern sat on a wood table against the right wall. None of them were lit, and it took Aaron's eyes a moment to adjust to the dim light from the small windows.

The inside of the cabin, like the outside, had a Boy Scout look. A rusting cast iron cook stove with a black pipe running through the vaulted ceiling was the centerpiece of the room. Ugly black scars where bunk beds had once been screwed into the shellacked pine walls stood out on both side walls. Now a king-sized bed filled one corner of the room with a faded green footlocker sitting at the end of the bed. Above the table were shelves filled with Mason jars of various vegetables and small canvas bags filled with what Aaron assumed were herbs or dried beans.

"The stove's still hot, so Bob's been here recently," Summer said holding her hand over the stove. She seemed relieved. It was proof he was still alive, or at least had been recently. "Shut the door. I'll light some of these candles."

Aaron shut the cabin door and noticed heavy steel U-brackets mounted on either side of the door frame with a six-foot two by four leaning against the wall that fit into the brackets.

How paranoid must Wildman Bob be to leave the cabin unlocked when he left and secure it from the inside like Fort Knox when he was there? Another barricade against civilization.

After she'd lit the candles, Summer stripped off her snowmobile suit and draped it across the back of one of the two chairs at the table. "We might as well get comfortable," she said. "Bob might not be back for a while."

Aaron took off his suit and laid it over the other chair.

"Let me give you the tour," Summer said.

She undid a huge surface bolt in the floor by the stove and lifted a trap door.

"This is the root cellar," she said, holding the door open with one hand. "Bob dug it himself to store the stuff from the garden."

Aaron looked through the four by six-foot opening. A cool earthy smell drifted from under the floorboards. It was hard seeing into the cellar. A nearly vertical wood ladder made of two-by-sixes with two-by-four rungs led into the eight foot deep hole. It was dark everywhere the faint light from the cabin didn't touch. The floor was made of flat stones grouted with sand. It led back beyond where Aaron could see. Shelves filled with glass Mason jars lined both sides of the stone walls. There were bins on the floor with potatoes and long strings of plaited onions and garlic hanging on the sides of the shelves.

"He has a lot of storage space for food," Aaron said.

"Did you see the terraces when we came in?" she asked.

Aaron nodded.

"Those are his garden spots," she said. "He dug them by hand. He grows enough to get him through the year."

"What about meat?"

"He gets some fish in the summer, crawdads and some freshwater clams. But in the summer he's pretty much a vegetarian."

"And in the winter?"

"Lester brings him meat," she said.

Summer closed the trap door and went over to a three-foot square door in the wall of the cabin. She undid four latches, two on each side, and slid the door out of the opening. The door was six inches thick, two pieces of inch plywood separated by two by fours around the sides. The cubicle stuck out from the cabin about three feet.

"This is his freezer," Summer said. "The door has insulation inside it to keep out the cold, and the inside is lined with tin to keep out mice."

Aaron looked inside. There were three plywood shelves. They were empty.

"In the summer he uses it for storage," Summer said.

She slid the door back into place and secured it.

"I hope he gets here soon," she said looking at her watch. "I'd like to get back before dark."

Aaron didn't believe in ghosts or Bigfoot, but after what Lester had told them, and even with Summer's logical explanation for it all, he wanted to be in the truck headed for Calvin before darkness came, too. "Can we unload the sled?"

"Good idea."

They went outside and took the tarp off the sled. Aaron put the brown canvas bag on top of the plastic tote of meat and picked them up.

"Leave the brown bag," Summer said. "It's the emergency kit."

Aaron put the bag back in the sled and followed Summer into the cabin. They unloaded the tote into the freezer and took everything out of the green canvas bag and set it on the table.

Summer looked at her watch again. "I know you want to talk with Bob, but if he doesn't get here in another hour or so, we're heading back. A storm's coming, and I don't want to get caught in it if we can help it."

"Won't he come back to the cabin with the storm coming?"

"I'm sure he's spent more than one night out in the refuge," she said.

"In this kind of cold?"

She smiled showing her gapped teeth. "I've spent more than a few nights out *in this kind of cold*, too."

He liked her attitude better out there in the woods. "I'd freeze to death," Aaron said.

"It's a matter of not panicking, city boy," she said. "A little common sense and knowing what you're doing will get you a long ways."

Aaron suspected the reason she didn't want to get caught in the storm had more to do with him being with her than anything else.

The cabin door suddenly banged open.

A huge man stood in the doorway, close to seven feet tall with wide shoulders that blocked out the light coming through the four-foot wide door. He was everything Aaron expected from someone called Wildman Bob. He wore a black and tan Mackinaw coat and blue jeans. His gray beard with streaks of pure white was coated with frost. It touched his chest and fanned out in all directions, unkempt and uncombed. Gray hair flopped out in matted curls from under a tan stocking cap and hung to his shoulders.

He looked them over for a second, paying special attention to Aaron before he shut the door.

"Hi, Bob," Summer said. She went over and gave him a hug. It stunned Aaron. He never thought she would hug anyone, let alone a Wildman.

"Hi, Summer," he said, in a voice deep enough to fit that big a man. His thick arms swallowed the little woman as he returned the hug. "I didn't know you were coming."

"I sent you some texts."

"The batteries have been dead in the phone for a week or so." He took off a backpack and set it beside the door, all the while still studying Aaron.

"This is Aaron Barnum from the DCI," Summer said, motioning toward Aaron.

Aaron stepped forward and shook his hand. It engulfed Aaron's, but it was a limp, confused grip.

"What does the DCI want out here?" Wildman Bob asked.

He had calm blue eyes that didn't belong to a Wildman. They were clear, intelligent eyes without a hint of the craziness Aaron had expected.

"I'm investigating the death at the Raleigh Farm Service," Aaron said. "I was hoping you could help me with some things."

"There was a death at the farm service?" Bob asked.

"I sent you a text," Summer said. "But obviously you didn't get it since your phone wasn't working."

"Who died?"

"It was one of the local meth cooks," Aaron said. "Walter Hemper." The big man showed no signs that he recognized the name, but Hemper wouldn't have come to Cossack County until after Bob had moved onto the refuge.

"How did he die?" Bob asked.

"It's what I'm trying to find out," Aaron said. "The deputy who found him said his throat was cut. He also said there were tracks by the body."

"What kind of tracks?"

"I don't know. I was hoping you could help me figure it out," Aaron said. "The deputy said they were oval. Maybe two feet long and 18 inches wide." Aaron held his hands out showing the distance. "Any idea what kind of animal would make those kind of tracks?"

"A dinosaur," Bob said.

Aaron smiled.

"I'm serious," Bob said. "Feet that large would be on something the size of a dinosaur. The feet of an animal are proportional to its size and the surface it commonly walks on. There aren't any dinosaurs in the refuge, so your deputy is mistaken. Wind and the sun can play tricks on tracks in the snow and make them bigger than they were when they were first made."

The wind theory was beginning to make sense, or at least becoming the only logical explanation for the tracks.

"Okay, maybe you can help me with something else," Aaron said. "The body was dragged after death."

"How far?"

"A quarter mile or so. I can't be sure," Aaron said. "But it was dragged from one field, across a gravel road and out into a different field."

"Are there mountain lions in the refuge?" Summer asked. "Because I know they'll move a kill."

Bob nodded. "I've seen mountain lions now and again. What kind of field did the body end up in?"

"It was a plowing," Aaron said.

"Then it wasn't a mountain lion," Bob said. "A mountain lion will drag its kill into cover so it can eat without being seen. Usually when it's finished, it covers it with grass and sticks to hide it so it can come back and feed again. It wouldn't drag it from one open field to another."

"What about bears?" Aaron asked.

"I've never seen a bear in the refuge or any signs of one," Bob said. "Were there any teeth marks?"

"There were all kinds of teeth marks," Aaron said. "It laid in the field for two days. All kinds of animals were feeding on it."

"Game is scarce right now," Bob said. "I bet the scavengers had a field day with that big a carcass."

Aaron cringed at the word *carcass*. It was like talking to Chantel. "So what is your best guess about what kind of animal would drag a body a quarter-mile?" Aaron asked. This was turning into a wasted trip.

Bob ran a hand through his beard and blew out a sigh. The smell of his breath was overpowering. It was like a wind blowing through an outhouse.

"If I had to guess, I would say wild hogs," Bob said. "There are some in the refuge."

"They would drag a kill?" Summer asked.

"Not intentionally," Bob said. "But they don't have teeth made for ripping off meat. They'd grab hold of the body, pull and shake their heads until a chunk of flesh came off. It would move the body a little at a time. Did this happen in the daytime or at night?"

"At night," Aaron answered.

"It fits," Bob said. "Wild hogs are more active at night."

"Could a wild hog kill someone?" Aaron asked.

"Definitely," Bob said. "Especially if the person fell or was knocked down. The boars have razor-sharp tusks and could easily rip someone's throat open. You said that's how the guy died, right?"

Aaron nodded.

"But would hogs be out in a blizzard?" Summer asked. "Wouldn't they stay in the shelter of the refuge?"

"You didn't say it happened during a blizzard," Bob said. He thought about it for a moment. "Hogs would normally stay in the shelter of the refuge instead of out in the wind and cold, but wild hogs can do some unpredictable things. It wouldn't surprise me if they were out in the wind. It would be unusual, but it wouldn't be surprising."

It was the first logical explanation for Hemper's death Aaron had heard. If the DNA tests Chantel was doing on the bite marks came back to a hog, this case could be over.

"Okay," Aaron said. "Thanks. You helped a lot."

They sat at the table, and Summer and Bob chit-chatted for a while, mostly about the DNR and what had been happening in the department and the personnel changes. They talked wildlife and wildlife surveys. After a little bit, Aaron became glad he hadn't brought his pistol, because he would have shot himself to get away from the boredom. He spent the time studying the cabin.

After what seemed like forever, Summer looked at her watch. "I hate rushing off, but we had a late start coming out here, and a storm is coming."

"A few flakes were falling when I came in," Bob said.

"We better get going," she said, standing. "We put some meat from Lester in the freezer—he says you need to stop and see him when you come to town. The batteries and the other stuff are sitting on the table." She picked her snowmobile suit off the back of the chair. "When you put the new batteries in your phone, go ahead and delete all the texts from me. We've discussed everything in them."

Summer slipped into her snowmobile suit.

"I do have one more thing," Aaron said and picked his suit off the chair. "The night all this happened, the deputy said he saw something as he was leaving the farm service."

"Have you ever seen Bigfoot in the refuge, Bob?" Summer asked and chuckled.

Bob smiled, revealing black teeth with a couple missing. "There isn't Bigfoot, the Abominable Snowman or werewolves in the refuge. I can guarantee that."

"I'm not looking for Bigfoot," Aaron said. "The deputy who found the body said he saw something big with long shaggy white hair. Would you have any idea what it might have been?"

Bob's eyes popped with surprise for an instant before narrowing in concentration, his forehead wrinkled in thought. But it seemed forced, the way someone does when they are *pretending* to think about something.

"If I had to guess, I would say it was a Highland cow," Bob said.

"They're in the refuge?" Summer asked.

"What are Highland cows?" Aaron asked.

"They're cattle with big horns like longhorns, but they have long shaggy coats," Summer said. "Stan MacGregor has some he breeds as a novelty."

"About ten years ago a dozen of Stan's got out of their pen and into the refuge," Bob said. "He got them all back except three, two cows and a bull. Over the years I've seen cattle tracks and always thought it might be them. I suppose they could have bred, and there could be a small feral herd living in the refuge." He shrugged. "My guess would be they could have been what the deputy saw. I can't think of anything else."

It would explain what Hemper and Pug had seen go across the road. It didn't explain Jesse seeing something ten feet tall, though stress could account for that, but it was the look of fake concentration on Bob's face that bothered Aaron.

"Anyway," Summer said zipping the front of her suit. "We better go. The storm's coming." She gave Bob another hug. "You stop and see Lester next time you're in town. He worries about you. And stop by and see me, too. We can have coffee or something."

"I'll try," Bob said. "Last summer was busy. I made quick trips to town and didn't talk with anyone."

"It was nice to meet you," Aaron said. He stepped forward and they shook hands again. This time his grip was firm.

Once outside, they grabbed the cargo sled and went back the way they had come. Snow was falling in big feathery flakes. It had already covered the bottom of the cargo sled with a half-inch blanket of fluffy white.

"We should have left sooner," Summer said. She looked at her watch. "We should still make it out of the refuge before dark, so we'll be okay."

As they followed the packed trail they'd made on the way to the cabin and with the sled empty and lighter, it was easier going.

"I notice you and Bob get along well," Aaron said. Seeing her hug Bob twice had amazed him more than anything he had seen on this case.

"He's a sweet old man," Summer said, smiling. "He reminds me of my dad. Except my dad brushed his teeth and took a bath occasionally." She laughed. "But he loves the outdoors, and he likes being by himself. I can relate."

They made it to the snowmobile and hooked up the cargo sled. The snow was falling hard enough that visibility was blurred into a white haze.

Aaron crawled on the sled behind Summer. He would do some checking on Wildman Bob when he got back to his office and depending on what he found and how the DNA tests Chantel was running came out, he planned on talking to him again.

Chapter Thirteen

Aaron guessed they were about halfway out of the refuge when the snowmobile's engine roared like a straight stick car with the clutch pushed in and the accelerator still floored. The sled quickly stopped, and Summer shut it off.

"I bet the drive belt broke," she said.

"Now what?" Aaron asked. The snow had picked up so much that he didn't know how Summer had stayed on the trail in the growing darkness. He didn't relish walking the rest of the way through increasingly deeper snow.

"Don't worry, city boy," she said. "I keep an extra belt for emergencies like this." She undid two snaps on the sled's hood and opened it.

"Just as I thought," she said and handed Aaron a broken drive belt.

She rummaged around under the hood for a moment.

"The spare belt is gone," she said. "I keep it under the hood wrapped in aluminum foil, but it's gone." She thought a moment. "I let Chad Tholkes from the district to the west use this sled for a safety class last month. I wonder if he used the spare belt on another sled and never told me."

"So how far do we walk to get out of here?" Aaron asked with the broken belt still in his hand.

"We don't walk," Summer said, looking at her watch. "It'll be full dark in less than a half hour, and the snow is piling up quickly. Our tracks from coming in are already gone, and I don't have a flashlight. If we walk, we'll miss the signposts and get lost in the dark. Then we will be in trouble."

Aaron took out his cell phone.

"It won't do any good," Summer said. "The hills block the signal."

Aaron looked at the phone: zero bars. "How about if I climb to the top of a hill and see if I can get reception?"

She shook her head. "Listen."

She paused for a moment and Aaron heard the wind screaming through the hill tops.

"It's not bad here in between the hills," Summer said. "The snow swirls around a little and drifts in, but you get out in the open or on top of a hill, and there's a full-scale blizzard going. The first thing they'll ask when you call is, are you hurt? When you say *no*, they won't risk their lives coming out here when we're safe."

"But we're not safe. Won't they send a search party when we don't show up at Lester's?"

"Lester will figure we stayed the night with Bob." She smiled. "Don't worry, city boy. I've been sleeping out in weather worse than this since middle school. I won't let you die."

But Aaron thought he could die. He had never slept out in weather like this. He had never even been a boy scout.

Summer picked the brown canvas bag out of the cargo sled. "Let's get a shelter made before it gets dark, and we can't see."

She led Aaron around to the south side of a hill where it was calm with the hill blocking the northwest wind. She stamped the snow until it was flat and sent Aaron looking for firewood. By the time he had a good pile, Summer had made a rough lean-to with the tarp from the cargo sled for the floor and another tarp for the back and sides. Shiny silver space blankets from the canvas bag lined the back and the two sides. The front side she had covered with a sheet of heavy plastic.

"We get a fire going, and this will be perfect," she said.

She built the fire six feet away from the plastic and built a short wall of logs behind it to reflect the heat into the shelter. She filled two pots with snow and melted it on the fire. After the pots had boiled, Summer produced a hunting knife from the survival bag and opened two packets. She poured a packet of dehydrated stew in one pot and a packet of hot chocolate mix in the other.

After a few minutes, Summer picked up both pots with sticks through their handles.

"We'll eat inside. The shelter should be warm by now," she said. "Take off your snowmobile suit or you'll get overheated."

The shelter was cramped, but warm. They sat on a sleeping bag spread out over a foam pad. Summer divided half the stew onto a plate and handed it to Aaron while she ate out of the pot. The stew stood slightly above a Smitty burger on the taste scale, but Aaron forced himself to eat it all. He figured the calories would help him stay warm. The hot chocolate was sickly sweet, but Aaron drank it, too.

When they were finished, Summer took the pots outside and wiped them with snow.

"Okay, here's the deal," she said as she sat again. "We only have the one sleeping bag, but I'm small, so we should both fit in it. If we share it, can I trust you'll be on your best behavior? This is about survival not romance." She had a very serious look on her face.

He was about to spend a night in weather close to zero degrees out in a woods near where Hemper had his throat ripped out by something … maybe a wild hog. He was fighting terror. Romance was never the last thing on his mind, but right now it was pretty close.

"I'll be good," he said.

"Good," she said. "Now take off your clothes."

"What?"

"Just your outer clothes. There are wet spots, like the cuffs on your pants," she said. "When you're trying to stay warm, moisture is the enemy." She sounded as if she was teaching a survival class, and Aaron figured she had. "If you get the inside of the sleeping bag wet, it'll lose its insulating properties. Once the fire dies, it'll get cold in here. You can leave your long underwear on."

Aaron undressed to his new black long underwear.

"Leave your socks on if they're not wet," Summer said. She undressed. Her underwear was baby blue. She grabbed the back of his collar, pulled it out and read the tag.

"Take off your t-shirt," she said releasing his collar. "Your long underwear is polypropylene. It wicks away moisture. The cotton t-shirt will hold it next to your skin. If you sweat you'll freeze when it cools down. If you want to wear the t-shirt, put it on top of the long underwear."

Aaron took off the t-shirt and put the long underwear back on.

"I suppose you're wearing undershorts, too?"

"I always do," Aaron said.

"That's not great," she said. "But I'm not dealing with it right now. If you're cold in the morning, I'll go outside and you can take them off."

It didn't look like she was wearing anything under her shirt, not even a bra, but her small breasts pushed the front of her shirt straight out and didn't look as if they needed one. He looked away to get his mind back on survival.

"You get in first," Summer said zipping the sleeping bag open. "I want to be by the zipper and the door."

"Maybe I should be there," Aaron said.

She gave him an amused look. "Why? Are you going to protect the little lady?"

Aaron grinned. "No. Because I might have to pee in the middle of the night."

"Get in and hold it until morning, city boy." She opened the sleeping bag wider.

Aaron crawled inside and Summer followed, zipping the sleeping bag closed. It was close quarters as they lay beside each other with their sides touching.

"Well, isn't this cozy," Aaron said.

"No it isn't," Summer snapped. "It isn't cozy, intimate, cuddly or snuggly. It's survival." She rolled to a sitting position and looked at him. "And if anything presses against me in the middle of the night that isn't an elbow or a knee, I'll rip it off. Do we understand each other?"

She didn't sound as if she was joking. "Message received," he said.

She rolled over and he rolled the other way so their backs were against each other.

Lying in the sleeping bag staring at the back slanted wall of the lean-to inches from his face, Aaron looked at his watch: 8:15. It was almost four hours earlier than his normal bedtime. With the wind howling through the hill tops and the space blankets snapping like towels in a high school locker room, he was positive he wouldn't sleep at all.

"Some animal won't get us in the middle of the night, will it?" he asked.

"There are no animals around that would attack something our size," Summer said.

"You said the coyotes have thinned out the deer," Aaron said. "If they can kill a deer, can't they kill us, too?"

"They don't go after adult deer. They get the sick ones and the fawns when they're a few days old," Summer said. "If there are no little deer. Eventually there are no big deer. It's the way it works."

He looked at his watch again: 8:17.

"Are you sure we won't freeze to death in our sleep?" Aaron asked. It worried him more than anything.

"Don't worry, I'll keep you safe, city boy," she said. "My dad had me camping out in the cold when I was six without a tent," she said. "We'd roll out a sleeping bag under a spruce tree and spend the night."

"I'm guessing your dad wanted a boy," Aaron said.

"My dad didn't want me at all … boy or girl," she said flatly.

Aaron wished he hadn't brought it up. "Sorry."

"He was my best friend growing up," she said. "We did everything together."

"I don't understand?"

"My mother and dad tried to have a baby for five years before I came along," she said. "My mother found out she was pregnant and had cancer at the same doctor's appointment."

"I'm sorry," Aaron said.

"If she'd had chemotherapy, it would have been the end of me," Summer said. "She wouldn't do it. Dad said he got on his knees and begged her to have an abortion and start chemo. She was pro-choice, but she said one of those choices was having the baby. She said there was no guarantee she'd make it even with the treatments. The best chance for life was mine."

"And here you are," Aaron said.

"And here I am," she said. "They started her chemo right after I was born, but it was too late. She died before my first birthday."

"Sorry." He knew he should have said something else but he couldn't think of anything.

She shrugged against his back. "I have tons of pictures of her, but I don't remember her at all. It's funny, she died so I could live, and I have no independent memories of her."

"So your dad raised you?"

Her back moved against his as she nodded. "He didn't plan on it at first. When it became obvious my mother wouldn't survive, he made arrangements with my aunt for me to live with her after my mother died. My mother found out and wouldn't have it. She said she didn't go through everything so her sister could have another child to raise. She made my dad swear he'd keep me with him, and he did. He had a master's degree in forestry, so he took a job teaching. I was little so I don't remember much of it, but I'd bet he hated it. He loved the outdoors. When I turned six, he took a field job in Montana, and we moved into a cabin in the mountains. He homeschooled me, and most of the time the lessons were outside."

"It had to beat sitting in a classroom."

"It did," she said. Aaron would bet she was smiling.

"Where is he now?"

"When I was 15 he was killed in a logging accident," Summer said. "I moved in with my mother's sister in southern Iowa."

"I'm surprised you didn't go back out west after high school," Aaron said.

"I did after college," she said. "I was out there a couple of years, but there was too much of Dad out there. I came back here and took this job with the DNR."

Aaron didn't say anything. He expected she would ask about his life story, but silence came from behind him. He checked his watch: 8:22.

"So, when we get out of here will some guy be after me because I slept with his girl?" Aaron asked and smiled.

"We *slept* together. We didn't *sleep together*," she said. "And no, I don't have a boyfriend … or a girlfriend either, if that's what you really wanted to know." Her voice had a bitter edge in it. "The rumors aren't true."

Aaron lay in the following hard silence and wished he'd never brought it up. He'd been joking with her and had forgotten about Melonie saying everyone thought she was gay.

"I wouldn't worry about what cops say," Aaron said. "They gossip worse than a bunch of old ladies. A young woman doesn't have a boyfriend, and they make up stories. It doesn't mean anything."

"I had a boyfriend once," she said.

"It didn't work out?"

"He killed himself," she said.

When she didn't say anything else, Aaron decided he would stop talking. He looked at his watch again: 8:25. It was going to be a long night.

Chapter Fourteen

Aaron figured he had dozed off, because the next thing he remembered was shivering. The inside of the shelter was so cold he could see his breath. He rolled over. The thick frost pattern on the plastic covering the front of the lean-to made it look like a wedding veil. The fire outside had become a dull glow. It lit the inside of the shelter with a weak orange light that silhouetted Summer sitting up on one elbow. Her body held the top of the sleeping bag open, letting in cold air. A chill went through him and made him shiver again. He guessed it was what had awakened him.

"What's—"

She cut him off by clamping a hand roughly on his arm. A twinge of uneasiness went through him as he watched her. Her body was tense, eyes wide and lips slightly parted so he could see the dark gap between the white of her front teeth. She had her head cocked sideways as if listening for something.

Aaron listened, but didn't hear anything. An absolute silence filled the darkness. The wind had died. Not even the thin space blankets ruffled. The storm must have blown itself out, he decided. It had left a surreal stillness in its wake. He could hear Summer breathing as if her smoke-like breath had a voice … then he heard it.

The noise was so faint, he didn't know what it was or even if he had heard anything at all. If he hadn't been listening for something, he wouldn't have noticed it. Even listening for it as he was, he couldn't identify it. It sounded like the wind rustling the snow against the far end of the shelter by his feet. But there wasn't any wind.

He heard it again, a sound as soft as tissue paper crumpling. Suddenly he knew what it was. Snow was being compressed. Something was walking on the new snow outside the shelter.

His arms raised in gooseflesh as any thought of it being a deer, raccoon or something harmless packed its bags and left when Summer unsheathed the hunting knife. The muscles in Aaron's neck knotted.

Summer knew wild animals. She knew what they sounded like walking in snow. If she was uneasy, so was he. He wished he had brought his .40. Screw Wildman Bob. He could have hidden it in the emergency bag.

Summer unsheathed the knife as the space blanket by their feet bowed inward with the pressure of something outside leaning against it. Aaron's nervousness jumped to fear, barely staying out of the terror range.

Another sound came from directly over their heads. He recognized it as a sniffing sound like someone with a cold snuffling to clear their nose. Some animal was checking the lean-to. A deep inhale pulled in the smells … their smells.

Aaron tensed, his heart pounding. It was so close he could have pushed against the space blanket and touched it. Its breath rubbed against the roof as it exhaled, sounding like a paint brush on canvas. Plumes of its white frosty breath came through the seam of the tarp and the plastic when it exhaled. Its breath filled the lean-to with a putrid smell. It was the smell of dead things, the smell of rotting meat.

Whatever it was had to be huge. The fact that it was standing at the end of the shelter with its nose at the center of the roof would make it at least eight feet tall.

Summer held the knife with both hands resting between her pointy breasts. She aimed it at the ceiling, ready to shove the knife upward if whatever was out there decided to come inside. Her hands shook, but determination was welded on her face.

It was the first time Aaron had seen her anywhere near fear. Her knowing the outdoors and being afraid doubled his own fear.

The brushing sounds of breath and sniffing overhead suddenly stopped. The bow in the side of the shelter disappeared.

Relief flooded Aaron. He was panting and lightheaded from not breathing. As he sucked in air, he prayed it was leaving. He couldn't hear anything outside the lean-to anymore. His heart came down from the breakneck rhythm it had been pounding.

He started to ask Summer what kind of animal it had been, when he saw her staring at the corner of the shelter with the knife pointed at the plastic, now.

A strip of black shadow touched the edge of the plastic. At first Aaron passed it off as something hanging over the corner of the lean-to. Through the plastic it appeared as a blurry shape in the top corner, but it moved. The shadow grew bigger, slowly creeping across the front of the shelter. It moved with a measured deliberateness, like a predator stalking its prey.

Aaron's heartbeat leaped back to racing mode.

With less than two feet of shadow visible, it lunged across the front of the plastic in a black flash.

Aaron gasped and tensed, waiting for the worse, but its footsteps faded in the distance. The soft crunching of long strides in the new snow vanished into the night.

For a long moment neither of them said anything.

"What was that?" Aaron whispered finally. His muscles were still so tensed they hurt.

Before Summer could answer the night was split by the gurgling squeal of a hog in agony. The sound ended abruptly, like a car radio being turned off. Aaron huddled in the lean-to beside Summer. Neither of them spoke as they listened for the footsteps coming back.

A full five minutes passed before Aaron asked again, "What was it?"

"I'm not sure," Summer whispered. "Maybe a mountain lion. Bob said they're in the refuge."

Aaron figured she was looking for a logical explanation for something that wasn't logical.

"I think it's gone," Summer said. "Let's get some sleep." She lay back in the sleeping bag, but the knife stayed in her hand.

Aaron lay beside her, but he had no intention of sleeping or even closing his eyes. He doubted he'd blink. Maybe the thing had been a hog or a mountain lion. Or maybe it was what Deputy Gordon had seen a flash of, Lester had seen twice and Summer had laughed about, because when it went in front of the shelter, Aaron was sure it had been on two legs.

Chapter Fifteen

With his chest pressed against Summer's back, Aaron watched the rising sun lighten the day. After last night's visitor, there wasn't any chance of pushing something against her, and he had been looking out through the plastic since that thing had gone. He wasn't about to turn his back on the outside.

She wasn't sleeping. Occasionally she would stir, adjusting her position in the sleeping bag. He hadn't slept either. Snow fell again shortly after they heard the hog's death scream. The flakes hit the roof of the shelter, sliding softly toward the ground. It reminded Aaron of that thing's breath against the tarp. He shuddered.

"Are you awake?" Summer asked.

"Yeah."

She crawled out of the sleeping bag. "I'll start the fire," she said pulling on her boots. "We'll let the shelter warm up before we get dressed."

She went outside in her underwear. Aaron watched her baby blue form through the blurry plastic as she worked the fire into a small orange flame. He worried at any moment the black shape from last night would streak across and grab her. But it didn't. Soon she had a fire blazing.

By the time she crawled back into the sleeping bag, she was shivering.

"You're freezing," he said, wrapping an arm around her waist and pulling her icy back against him trying to give her warmth. He hoped she wouldn't be offended. She shivered in the sleeping bag, but she didn't pull away nor snuggle into him. It was as if he was nothing but an electric blanket keeping her warm.

"The sky is clear in the west," she said. "It's going to stop snowing and get colder."

He didn't know how to ask what he wanted to know. Part of him still hoped what had happened last night had all been a dream (nightmare), and until he talked about it and Summer confirmed it, he could fool himself into believing it hadn't been real.

"Are there any tracks outside?" he asked. There was no sense putting off confirming what he already knew. It was still way too real to have been a dream.

"No," she said. "Any tracks have been covered by the snow."

They should have gone outside last night after it left and found its tracks. But they had been thinking of other things at the time, such as staying alive.

"Any new ideas on what it was?" Aaron asked.

"I've been thinking about it," she said.

No kidding? Aaron hadn't thought of anything else since it happened.

"It might have been some wild hogs," she said.

She turned and faced him. Her face inches from his upped the intimacy and made him think of himself as more than an electric blanket. Aaron took his arm off her waist and gave her room by wiggling back a couple inches.

"You did hear the hog squeal after it left?" she asked.

Aaron had heard it, but he had heard pigs squeal on farms when they were fighting each other and biting each other's ears and tails. It hadn't been that kind of squeal. It had been a liquid death sound as if its throat had been ripped out and it was sucking in its own blood. The way Hemper would have sounded as he died.

"Could a pig stand on the end of the lean-to and sniff right above us?" Aaron asked, motioning toward the foot end of the shelter. "Do they get that big?" He'd never heard of an eight-foot tall pig.

"There are cases of wild boars over a thousand pounds," Summer said. "But I think we're talking more than one pig. Maybe one leaning against the side of the lean-to and another sniffing the top. If it was standing behind the lean-to, it wouldn't have had to be that big. They run in groups, and they're curious about things. They would have checked out the shelter."

She was making what had happened fit what she wanted, the way Sheriff Thompson had made Hemper's death fit what he wanted.

Aaron suspected a careful scrutiny of everything would blow her explanation out of the water—he would still swear what had run across the front of the lean-to had been on two legs—but he told himself she knew more about the outdoors and wildlife than him. If she believed it was nothing more than *The Three Little Pigs* visiting them last night, then so would he. Until they got out of there, and they were safe with his Glock back on his belt, he'd believe whatever brought some semblance of sanity to the situation.

They didn't say anything further about it. The shelter warmed quickly.

When the shelter was heated, they crawled out of the sleeping bag and got dressed. While Summer was busy heating another packet of stew and chocolate, Aaron took down the shelter and packed it into the canvas bag. They stowed it all back on the cargo sled when they were finished eating and covered it with the tarp.

The world was coated with six inches of powder. When the wind had stopped blowing, the snow had floated straight down in big flakes. It was an undisturbed world of fallen clouds without a mark defiling the solid surface of constant white.

On the left, where the shelter had stood, was a long depression headed in the direction whatever *it* was had gone last night. It could have been nothing more than a well-worn deer trail covered with the new snow leaving a long indentation, or even the covered tracks of pigs running, but to Aaron it looked as if it was made by footprints about eighteen inches wide and two feet long and rounded on both ends. He forced himself not to think about it and looked away. It had been nothing but wild pigs, he told himself.

"Okay, we'll leave everything here," Summer said when they had everything packed and loaded on the sled. Aaron noticed she kept the hunting knife in her pocket. "It could be tough walking. Don't get sweaty. If your clothes get wet from sweat, you'll freeze when we stop and rest, and you might not get warm again." She looked at him sternly. "This is serious stuff. We're not out of here yet. Do you understand what I'm saying, city boy?"

"I thought my long underwear would keep me from getting wet?" Aaron asked. He wanted to get going. Standing there, he glanced everywhere at once to keep from being snuck up on.

"Polypropylene can only do so much," Summer said. "If you get warm, unzip your snowmobile suit and shirt or take stuff off. Do whatever you need not to sweat.

We'll stop and rest a few times, and we'll cool down."

"Let's get going," Aaron said. He wanted to get back to civilization. "I won't get sweaty. I promise. I'll get naked if I have to."

"I'd appreciate it if you stayed clothed," she said. Not even a hint of a smile crossed her face.

The walking was easier than Aaron had thought it would be. The trail the snowmobile had packed down the day before had frozen solid. It made a good base that held their weight. Occasionally his heel would go through a weak spot, but it was mainly the six inches of fluffy snow from last night that they were walking through. Stepping off the trail was another story. He sank to his thighs.

They'd gone about 50 yards from the campsite with Summer leading the way when she stopped suddenly. She was looking off to the right of the trail when Aaron came up beside her. He couldn't see anything but trees and snow.

"What's the problem?" Aaron asked. It made him nervous having her standing there staring at nothing.

"Something's wrong," she said and stepped off the snowmobile trail and sunk to her hips.

She worked her way toward a couple trees at the base of a hill, taking giant steps, raising her leg clear of the snow, knee first, before putting it down and repeating with the other leg.

Aaron watched her from the trail. He wanted to keep going and get out of there, but he couldn't let her check it out herself. He stepped off the trail into the deep snow and followed her with the same exaggerated strides.

About ten yards off the trail, two trees with light colored bark stood five feet apart. Aaron guessed birch or poplar. When he joined her, Summer was examining a quarter-sized spot of red on the side of a tree. It amazed Aaron that she had seen it from the trail, but he guessed it was something out of place she had seen and not the actual spot.

"Is it blood?" Aaron asked.

She nodded and stepped around the tree. Her eyes widened and Aaron knew before he looked what was there. The tree was covered with blood at waist level with frozen streaks running to the ground. It was as if a garden hose of blood had been sprayed on it. The tree five feet from the first also had splatters of blood. In the footprints where they had walked, the ground had chunks of red ice as if they had walked through a field of crushed cherry popsicles, but he knew it wasn't popsicles. It was a pool of blood under the covering of snow.

Something had been killed—slaughtered—there. Aaron looked back at where the snowmobile sat and where they had spent the night in the shelter. They were still within sight.

"This is where the hog we heard last night was," Aaron said.

Summer didn't answer.

She knew more about wildlife than him, but he knew pigs didn't slaughter each other. They might bite a tail or an ear, but they didn't tear each other apart. What had Wildman Bob said? They didn't have teeth made for ripping off flesh. A mountain lion would be capable of killing a hog, but most cats killed by strangulation. Whatever had done this had done it quickly and violently, ripping out its throat the way it had done to Walter Hemper.

"We better get going," Summer said, not saying anything about a new theory about what had killed the hog.

They went back to the trail, leaving a string of bloody footprints.

~*~

Three times they stopped and rested on their way out of the refuge, and they didn't talk. Summer wasn't much on small talk, and Aaron figured she was working on a logical explanation for what had happened. Aaron just wanted out of the refuge. He'd find out the results of the DNA tests and see what had made the bite marks on Hemper and go from there. If they could be identified. Aaron believed whatever had made the marks was what had killed the hog in the woods. He also needed to talk with Lester about Wildman Bob. It still bothered him how Bob had reacted when he heard what Deputy Gordon had seen. Lester had thought Bob knew something about what was in the refuge, and now Aaron did, too.

By mid-afternoon they'd walked out of the refuge and into the glare of Lester's field. The sun had come out, and with the shadows of the trees gone, Aaron squinted against a solid field of white. Summer slipped her sunglasses out of her pocket and put them on. Aaron dug out his phone, but the battery had gone dead.

When they walked into Lester's yard, a short fat man came out of the barn carrying white plastic buckets in both hands.

"Hi Jack," Summer said.

"Hi Summer," the guy said. "What are you doing?"

"We went into the refuge to see Bob yesterday, and the snowmobile broke down."

"I wondered why your truck was here." He nodded at Aaron. "Who's this?"

"This is Aaron Barnum," Summer said. "Aaron, this is Jack Simpson."

Jack set the buckets on the ground and shook hands with Aaron.

"So what are you doing here?" Summer asked.

"Carla called and asked me to do the chores," Jack said.

"What's the matter with Lester?"

"You didn't hear?" Jack asked. "Lester had a heart attack last night."

"You're kidding," Summer said, obviously shocked.

"No. The ambulance crew did the CPR on him and shocked him to get his heart going again," Jack said.

Aaron remembered how peaked the old man had looked when they left yesterday.

"Is he alright?" Summer asked.

"Don't know," Jack said. "They wanted to ship him to Sioux Falls last night, but they couldn't because of the storm. Carla said they re-started his heart twice at the hospital. When the storm cleared this morning, they life-flighted him to Sioux Falls by helicopter. He's out there now."

"Where's Carla?"

"Cindy, Randy's wife, drove her out," Jack said. "The boys are all on their way back from Wisconsin."

"Is there anything I can do?" Summer asked.

"I got the chores until Lester's boys can take over," Jack said. "I guess a prayer wouldn't hurt."

"You wouldn't have a sled I can borrow for a little bit?" she asked. "I need to get a belt and run back into the refuge to get my sled out."

"Sure," Jack said. "Let me finish the chores, and you can follow me back to my place."

~*~

"Do you want some help getting the sled out of the refuge?" Aaron asked when they were in Summer's truck headed for Jack Simpson's house.

"You sure you don't have something you need to do?" Summer asked.

Of course he had things he needed to do, but she looked as tired as he felt. He didn't want to leave her looking for someone to help her. She had saved him from freezing to death. It was the least he could do. "Nothing I can't put off for a day," Aaron said.

"I appreciate it," she said. "I should make Chad Tholkes go with me. I need to rip him a new one for not telling me he used the spare belt. But I don't know if he's in the middle of something and can't get away."

She gave him a smile and they rode in silence following Jack's truck.

"It's too bad about Lester," Aaron said finally.

"I hope he'll be okay," she said.

It seemed as if she got along far better with the old guys than the young ones. "I was hoping to talk to Lester about Bob," Aaron said.

"What do you need to know about Bob?" She sounded defensive.

Aaron wasn't sure how he should answer.

"He's an interesting guy," Aaron said, trying to sound casual. "I'd like to know some background on him." *And what he knows that he's not telling about what's going on in the refuge.*

"He grew up in Washington State," Summer said. "Other than that, I don't know much. Bob was already living at the refuge when I got here. He doesn't talk much about his past."

It didn't help him. Aaron needed someone who knew him before he had gone off the deep end and became a hermit on the refuge.

"You could ask Melonie," Summer said. "She knows him as well as anyone, I guess."

"Melonie?"

"Melonie Riggs, the dispatcher," Summer said. "She was once married to Bob."

Chapter Sixteen

They got a sled from Jack, ran into Calvin and picked up something to eat at a fast food place and bought a new belt for the snowmobile. By the time they went back into the refuge, replaced the belt, returned the snowmobile to the storage shed and the other one to Jack, it was late afternoon. Aaron offered to take Summer out to dinner, but she turned him down. He stopped at a local restaurant and ate by himself.

After not having slept all night, spending most of the day walking out of the refuge and running around retrieving the sled, Aaron was tired. But he knew after everything that had happened, and all the questions he still had about Bob, he couldn't sleep until he had some answers. He plugged his dead cell phone into its charger in his motel room, took a shower and changed into fresh clothes.

Some skinny redheaded guy named Jamie was behind the bulletproof security glass at the law center. He told Aaron it was Melonie's day off, and she wouldn't be working until tomorrow night, but Aaron couldn't wait until tomorrow. A little prodding and Jamie coughed up her home address.

At 6:30 Aaron knocked on the door of Melonie's light gray three-bedroom ranch house.

"What are you doing here?" Melonie asked when she came to the door. She wore a red Iowa State t-shirt with Cy the cardinal on the front and black sweatpants. Her hair was pulled back with a red scrunchie, and she wasn't wearing makeup.

"I hope I'm not disturbing you," Aaron said. He wished he had called first. "There are a couple things I was hoping you could help me with. May I come in for a few minutes?"

"Sure." She stepped back and let him in. "Excuse the way I look. It's my day off, and Jim is out of town." She smoothed her hair with her hand. "I didn't go anywhere today, so I haven't gotten cleaned up."

"It's okay," Aaron said, smiling as he stepped inside the house. "I do the same thing on my days off." But he didn't. Natalie had insisted he showered and shaved as soon as he got out of bed.

"You need to take off your shoes," Melonie said. "The carpet's new."

Aaron slipped them off and put them on a black and red rag rug beside the door. It already had four other pairs of shoes in neat rows.

"You've got a nice place," Aaron said looking around. It was a simple place but everything looked neat and freshly-painted. A rock fireplace came out of the far wall with various pictures sitting on the thick wood mantle.

"Jim did most of it. He's good with his hands," she said.

He followed her into a kitchen with solid oak cupboards and a matching oak table.

"Can I get you some coffee?"

"A little late for me," Aaron said. "I'll be up all night." As tired as he was, he doubted even coffee would keep him awake, but he wasn't going to chance it.

She picked an ISU cup off the granite counter. "I go back on the 2200 to 0600 shift tomorrow night. I condition myself by staying up until two or so tonight." She pulled out a chair for him. "Have a seat. Can I get you a pop? I'd offer you a beer or something, but there's none in the house. Jim is a recovering alcoholic."

"It's okay. A beer would put me to sleep."

She sat at the table, took a sip from her cup and studied him for a moment. "You look like death warmed over."

"I didn't sleep well last night," Aaron said. "Summer Conrad and I spent the night in the refuge. We went out and saw Bob Milton, and our snowmobile broke down."

She smiled. "I figured when you said you were going out to the refuge, you were going to see Bob."

"Why didn't you tell me you were married to Wildman Bob?"

"He was hubby number two," she said and took another sip from her cup. Aaron remembered hubby number two was the reason Melonie was not a deputy. "And he wasn't Wildman then," she said. "They called him that after he grew the beard and hair. When we were married, he was Big Bob."

"It certainly fits," Aaron said. "He is a big guy."

"Six-ten and over 300 pounds when we were married," she said. "He's lost a few pounds since then, but still not the kind of guy you'd want falling asleep on top of you, if you know what I mean?"

Aaron laughed.

"I met his parents at our wedding," Melonie said. "His father is under six feet tall and his mother is barely five-foot. The family joke is she had an affair with Paul Bunyan."

He laughed again.

"One of his mother's brothers is big like Bob, so it's in the family genetics," Melonie said. "A recessive gene, I imagine."

"What is Bob like?" Aaron asked. He wasn't sure how much he wanted her to know. "We only talked for a short time."

"Before or after we were married?"

"There's a difference?"

"Big difference," she said. "When we were married he was the sweetest, most caring man I'd ever met, a typical gentle giant. He changed after we divorced."

"How?"

She cradled her cup in both hands. "He got strange. He hated the law enforcement part of the job, but it was even more than that."

"Like what?"

"He spent all his time out in the refuge," she said. "When we were married it was part of the job, but after we divorced, it consumed him."

"So you two still talked?"

"We were still friends," she said.

"Can I ask why you split?"

She gave a sad smile. "Babies."

"Babies?"

"Before we got married, Bob told me he'd had a vasectomy a few years after he graduated from college, so there wouldn't be any kids," Melonie said. "I told him it was okay. If I wanted something to take care of, I'd get a dog." She smiled sadly again. "But there's a difference between being in your early thirties and being in your late-thirties— the old biological clock thing. It was getting into now-or-never time for babies. I did some research and found they could reverse a vasectomy."

"I take it he wasn't for it?"

"He said his genes were screwed up, and it wouldn't go well if he had kids," Melonie said. She took another sip of coffee. "I always thought it was an excuse not to have babies. He'd had the vasectomy way back before they'd done any mapping of the human genome. There was no way he could have known what his genes were like."

"So how did this break up your marriage?"

"I kept after him, and after him, and after him about it," she said and huffed out a laugh. "You might find this hard to believe, but I can be a persistent bitch if I try."

Aaron smiled. "And he still wouldn't go for it?"

"No," she said, shaking her head. "But I kept after him anyway. One day Josh Franklin, our civil deputy, came to my door with divorce papers."

"Really?"

"It came out of the blue," she said. "We never had a big fight or anything." She set the cup on the table and toyed with the handle for a moment but didn't take a drink. "I still think he did it for me. He was letting me go so I could find someone and have a baby."

"Did you see him much after the divorce?" Aaron asked.

"He still stopped by, here and at work. He even helped me out when hubby number three got sick," she said. "Like I said, we remained friends. It's the kind of guy Bob is. He was still friends with his first wife, too. When she died a few years back, Bob drove out to Washington State for her funeral."

"He drove?"

"Bob's big time claustrophobic," she said. "I'd lie on top of him and pin his arms down. He would freak out." She laughed. "Of course he'd throw me off in two seconds, but I can't imagine him cramped into an airplane seat for two or three hours."

She stopped for a moment and looked off sadly at nothing.

"His first wife's death hit him hard," she said, still looking away. "I guess she was his one true love." She said it sadly. "It was when he came back from Washington that he started spending all his time out in the refuge."

"I thought he always loved the refuge?"

"He thought of it as a nuisance when we were married," she said, looking back at

Aaron. "The state always wanted wildlife surveys done, and of course there were always people hunting the edges, which was illegal. Only part of it was in his district, but I always thought he wished none of it was."

"Did Bob ever say anything about seeing anything unusual in the refuge?" Aaron asked.

She laughed. "Did he tell you about the Skookum?"

"What?"

"It was a joke we had," she said. "He did a raccoon survey for the state one year. He'd drive along the edge of the refuge with a spotlight and count how many raccoon eyes he'd see shining. One night he saw something big and black moving inside the refuge. To scare me, he said it was a Skookum."

"What's a Skookum?"

"It's a Chinook term," she said. "I guess it's an evil spirit, something like a Bigfoot of the Pacific Northwest. After that, every time I couldn't find something or someone would eat the last of anything and put the empty box back in the cupboard, Bob would say, 'The Skookum did it.'"

She drained the last from her cup and stood. "I need a refill. Are you sure there isn't something I can get you?"

"I'm fine, thanks."

She went and refilled her cup.

Bob had seen something. It had been black like the first thing Lester had seen, not white like Jesse's thing, but he had still seen something. Aaron knew he'd been right about the look on Bob's face.

"So what did Bob see?" Aaron asked when she had sat at the table again.

"I don't know." She blew on her coffee and cautiously sipped from her newly-heated cup. When she raised her head she had a curious smile on her face. "Surely you're not giving Jesse's Bigfoot tracks credibility, are you?"

"You said Bob saw something."

She laughed. "If you spend enough time in the woods you'll see things you can't explain," she said. "Bob was always taking reports from people who had seen strange things. Most of them had logical explanations. In the dark and at sunset and sunrise, shadows play tricks on you."

"But you said yourself … Bob … saw … something."

"He was joking," she said. "You're the hot shot investigator and you think Bigfoot killed Hemper?" She laughed again.

Any other time Aaron would have been laughing along with her, but last night had changed that.

"Get some sleep," Melonie said. "When you get up in the morning, you'll see how ridiculous what you're saying sounds."

"Maybe you're right," Aaron said standing. *And maybe you're not, because something big that kills things had been outside the lean-to last night.*

~*~

Aaron went back to his motel room, more curious about Wildman Bob than before he had talked with Melonie.

His phone was charged, and he checked the texts. Many of them were insignificant. A lot of office stuff and mass texts to the entire department from his supervisor. He could view them later. The ones he thought might need immediate attention, he opened.

Dr. Chantel Moore:

The DNA results on the bite marks are in. They are up on the lab's website. Call me so I can explain them to you.

He looked at his watch. 8:30. He wanted to know the results, but Chantel wouldn't be at the office, and he hated bothering her at home if the bite marks were from a hog. He'd call her first thing in the morning. He went through the rest of the messages.

Paul Taylor:

I have set up a meeting with your wife and her attorney at 3PM next Friday at their office. Let me know if it works for you?

Aaron sent a text back saying it would be fine unless something came up. Aaron hoped this would be the last of it until the judge signed the decree, and they would be free of each other. He still didn't have any animosity toward Nat. He just wanted to get on with his life. He looked back at the messages.

Natalie Barnum:

We have another appointment at my attorney's office next Friday at three. It should be the last time before the judge signs the order. Maybe we can get together and have a few drinks to celebrate afterward.

Now that the divorce was close, she seemed in a hurry to get it over with, too. He wasn't sure what she meant by getting together for drinks. Maybe she wanted to hook up one more time for old time's sake before they were officially split? He had heard of other divorcing couples doing it. Jerry Masters had said the best sex he and his ex-wife ever had was after they had separated. Aaron wasn't going there. He looked back at the phone.

Dr. Chantel Moore:

Aaron, we need to talk about the DNA results on Hemper. I've tried calling you numerous times but it goes straight to voicemail. Please call me as soon as possible.

Aaron checked his missed calls. There were twelve from Chantel. A sense of dread came over him. It had to be important.

She wouldn't have tried to reach him so many times if the bites were from a hog. He had her private cell phone number and could have called her. If it had been a normal night and he was only normally tired, he would have. But he had slipped into exhaustion, and he couldn't deal with knowing they had found Skookum's DNA when he was this tired. It would be hard enough trying to sleep not knowing. It would be impossible if he knew.

Aaron put the phone on the nightstand and crawled into bed.

Chapter Seventeen

The next morning Aaron took his laptop out of its case and plugged it into the wall socket in his makeshift office. As soon as it booted, he went online and brought up the lab's reports. He opened the one marked HEMPER DEATH INVESTIGATION, but he didn't open the file marked DNA RESULTS.

He knew a little more about DNA than the average person, but he had a suspicion the results would come back as *unknown animal*, because he doubted Bigfoot's or Skookum's DNA were on file anywhere. After the incident in the lean-to, he didn't know if Deputy Gordon and Lester had seen Bigfoot, but he suspected it was what had visited the lean-to the night he and Summer spent in the refuge. He needed someone with knowledge of DNA walking him through the report. There was too much that didn't make rational sense, and too much had happened for him to make mistakes now.

He checked his watch. It was 9:10. Chantel should be in her office. Aaron picked up his phone and punched in her office number.

"Dr. Moore," she answered.

"Hi Chantel, it's Aaron."

"Aaron, I've been trying to get in touch with you since yesterday," she said. The excitement in her voice told him he was right. "Have you seen the DNA results?"

"No, I have it on the screen right now," he said and opened the file. "But I thought it would be better if you explained them to me."

"The bite marks on Hemper are human," she said.

"What?" It shocked him more than if she had said they were from Bigfoot or the Abominable Snowman. "There must be a mistake."

"There is no doubt the bite marks were made by a person," she said. "You have a murder and cannibalism." She paused a moment. "This is front page stuff, Aaron."

"Are you sure?" he asked. "You're certain it's not Hemper's DNA?"

"It is not possible," she said. "This DNA is unique in its genomic duplication of the XQ26.3 chromosome. It is not in the victim's DNA. They are far too dissimilar to be the same."

He didn't have a clue what she had said. "What does that mean in plain English?"

"It means the murderer suffers from Launois' Syndrome," she said.

Aaron jotted down *Lonwah*, spelling it phonetically. He'd Google it later, but he needed to know what it meant now. "And that means … what?"

"He has gigantism," she said. "He is abnormally large."

A chill went through Aaron. Wildman Bob was abnormally large. Big Bob was huge. "You mean someone who would be six-ten or so and 300 pounds?"

"There have been documented cases of specimens over eight feet tall," she said.

She was doing the coroner talk again, specimen instead of person or patient. Aaron was so stunned he barely noticed.

"You gave an exact height," she said. "Do you have a suspect?"

"Maybe." *It had to be.*

"What does the guy's head look like?" she asked.

Of his list of top 50 questions she might ask, that one wasn't on it. "What do you mean?"

"There is also a mutation of the NSD1 gene," she said. "It is an indication of acromegaly or Sotos Syndrome."

He wrote *Sotos Syndrome*. "What is that?"

"His eyelids would have an antimongoloid slant, hypertelorism and he could have macrocephaly and ADHD."

Other than the ADHD, Aaron didn't understand any of it. "Say it again in English, please."

"Sotos is sometimes called cerebral gigantism," she said. "It usually occurs in adulthood while Launois occurs in younger people. If he has acromegaly, his head would be abnormally large or deformed. Do his eyelids droop or are his eyes wide-set? They could be far enough apart that you could put your hand between his eyes without touching either of them."

"Is this pretty common?" Aaron asked. "Because you know a lot about it?"

She gave a little laugh. Aaron could picture her smiling. "It is an extremely rare condition. I've been researching it since the test results came back."

Aaron was relieved she didn't know it all off the top of her head. He already considered her at least twice as smart as him.

"Well, the guy I'm thinking of has a normal head for his body size." Aaron said. "He's big all over."

"It's possible the Sotos is recessive," she said.

Something suddenly occurred to Aaron. "Could he pass it on to his children?"

"He could," she said. "It would depend on the mother."

"And those children would be deformed?

"If they had Sotos Syndrome, their heads could be grossly deformed," she said.

It was why Bob didn't want children. Somehow he had found out he had those genetic defects, and he didn't want them passed on. "If I get a sample of DNA, can you positively connect it with the DNA from the bite marks?" Aaron asked.

"Absolutely," she said. "With those unique markers, we can get it as close to one hundred per cent as you can statistically get."

"Would a simple cheek swab be enough for the test?"

"That should be fine," she said. "When are you going to get the sample?"

"I don't know," Aaron said. "The guy lives in the woods out in the middle of nowhere. The only ways of getting there are by snowmobile or walking."

She didn't answer for a moment, and Aaron knew she was thinking about something.

"Aaron," she said finally. Her voice had an underlying concern in it. "Take someone with you when you go, especially if you're out in the middle of nowhere."

"I'll definitely have backup with me," Aaron said.

"Good," she said, but she still sounded worried. "From what you say, it doesn't look as if there are any physical indications of Sotos Syndrome, but maybe it is because the Launois hid the physical signs. Someone with Sotos often has intellectual impairments. They are prone to violence and tantrums. Remember, if this is the guy who killed your victim, he kills and eats people. He's mentally unstable, large and dangerous. So be careful."

"Thanks for the warning," Aaron said.

"Also, they often have physical disabilities and frequent headaches which would put them in a poor mood," she said. "So again, be careful."

"I always am," Aaron said.

"Good, she said. "Do you have any other questions?"

"Not right now," he said. "I'll send you a text if I need something later."

"I'll be waiting for your call," she said. "Watch yourself, Aaron. Goodbye."

Aaron hung up. He needed a DNA sample from Bob. He didn't know if he had enough probable cause for a search warrant. In a perfect world he would go out and have Bob come back, give the sample and be questioned. But Bob had law enforcement experience. Dirty cops and ex-cons usually lawyered up as soon as they were read their rights. Aaron had dealt with enough of both of them to know that. And what was going through the head of someone who not only killed people but ate them? Aaron couldn't even guess. This went beyond insanity. It was like Ted Bundy or Dennis Rader who appeared as good guys to everyone they met, while a creature lived inside them that went nutso and committed cold-blooded murders.

Chantel had said it was possible Bob had some kind of intellectual disability. Could it mean a psychological disability that came and went? Could he be normal one minute and out hunting people the next? Maybe it was why he spent his time in the refuge and stopped seeing people? It hadn't occurred to him when he talked to Chantel so he hadn't asked her, but could it be the change Melonie had talked about when he came back from Washington State after his ex-wife's funeral? There were too many questions he couldn't answer. He hadn't had enough time to think it through.

He had to get a sample of Bob's DNA and have it tested—this time when he went, he would have his pistol with him. Summer knew Bob well and was as close to a friend as a hermit could have. She could keep him calm … maybe. It might go smoothly without any trouble, and it might not. You never knew when you were dealing with crazy.

~*~

Aaron had gone to the county attorney's office for help with the application for the search warrant. He wasn't sure if he had enough probable cause. The county attorney had listened wide-eyed as he explained the DNA results and the cannibalism. She assured him they had plenty of probable cause. They'd filled out the application, and sure enough, the magistrate, a retired attorney with thick glasses, a bald head and a full beard, looked through it briefly and issued the warrant. Aaron had forgotten how much of a rubber stamp some of the small-county magistrates could be.

It still bothered him. Even though the magistrate had issued the warrant, it didn't mean some trial or appellate court judge couldn't declare the warrant invalid later and throw out the DNA tests. He had mentioned it to the county attorney, and her response was not to worry about it. Although before he left her office with the warrant in his hand, she had suggested he ask Bob for a voluntary sample before reading him the warrant.

After Aaron had locked the warrant in his temporary office, he went into the control room. Jana was working.

"Can you have Summer Conrad meet me here?" Aaron asked.

"You're spending a lot of time with her," Jana said.

Aaron struggled keeping the smile off his face. She sounded like a jealous wife. "I need her expertise for all the wildlife stuff," Aaron said, sounding like a guilty husband. "Could you have her meet me here sometime today?"

Jana had a hurt, angry look on her face. "You know she's a lesbian," she said.

"Just have her meet me here," Aaron said curtly. He wasn't fighting the smile anymore. His taste for lasagna had suddenly left.

He walked out of the control room.

"She's out back," Jana yelled after him.

He poked his head back in the room. Jana looked at the radios in front of her and not at him.

"What's she doing back there?" Aaron asked.

"The sheriff got some snowshoes from the military," Jana said. "Summer is in the back teaching the deputies how to use them."

Aaron went out the door and around the back of the law center. In the new snow from yesterday, seven deputies were standing in a loose line wearing light-colored snowshoes with aircraft cable bindings. They were rounded on top and pointed like a tail in the back. Summer stood in front of the group wearing a pair of rounder wood snowshoes with leather webbing.

"The snowshoes are wider than your feet," she said to the group. "When you walk, take a wide stance. Keep your feet apart or you'll step on the frame of the other snowshoe and trip yourself. Also lift your snowshoe clear of the snow, but don't lift them any higher than necessary."

She demonstrated a few steps away from them and turned around again.

"If you do it long enough, you'll feel it tomorrow in your hips and groin. These things can get heavy after a while" She saw Aaron and gave him a smile. "Work on it for a little bit. Practice walking and making turns."

She left them practicing and went over by Aaron. Before she was there, two of the deputies had run into each other and had fallen into a giggling pile.

"Be careful," she said over her shoulder. "We don't want anyone getting hurt."

She looked at Aaron and rolled her eyes. "They'll never use them," she whispered. "They'll stick them in the trunks of their squad cars and forget they have them."

Aaron laughed, but he knew it was true. He had things in the trunk of his car the state had issued him he had never used.

"So you survived our little camping trip?" she said and gave him an actual smile. Aaron guessed spending the night in the woods had put him into some sort of club.

He returned her smile. "It was an experience," he said. "Did you get ahold of the guy who used the spare belt and didn't tell you?"

"I talked with him this morning. He swore he didn't use it," she said. "Maybe I didn't have it secured well enough under the hood, and it fell off."

"Could be," Aaron said.

He wished he had examined the broken belt closer. It could have been cut partway through. It had been poor police work. He hadn't been in a familiar environment, and people bowed to the experts in unfamiliar situations. At the time he had been worried about getting out of the refuge and surviving. The belt being cut had never occurred to him. Now he was suspicious of everything. The belt breaking and the spare one falling off on the same trip suddenly seemed a very big coincidence.

"Are you ready to take me back out there and do it again?" Aaron asked.

"You want to spend another night in the woods?" She looked amazed.

"No. A quick trip out and back," Aaron said. "I have a few more questions for Bob."

She looked suspicious. It was what Aaron had worried about since he'd gotten the warrant. "Why?"

He didn't know how much he should tell her. She had said Bob reminded her of her father. Bob was the only person he had ever seen her hug, and she was the only one who called him regularly on the phone. How she'd react if she found out Bob had suddenly become the number one suspect in Hemper's murder was anyone's guess.

He smiled to put her at ease. "I have a few more questions," Aaron said. He'd never had a good poker face, but he made it sound as innocent as he could. If she suspected something was up, she might let Bob know they were coming, and it would be easier getting the sample if he didn't know about it beforehand.

"What questions?" She sounded suspicious.

"I was wondering if he had any ideas about our midnight visitor," Aaron said. "It's possible whatever killed the hog might have killed Hemper."

He said it with a straight face. He could have passed a polygraph, because the more he thought about it, the more he was convinced it had been Bob outside their lean-to. But why had he run off and killed the hog instead of finishing them off? He could only guess it was because he had smelled Summer in the tent with him. Maybe whatever human still remained in him prevented him from killing her?

"I can give him a call and ask him," Summer said. "I'll leave him a message. It might be a few days before he answers back."

"I'd rather do it in person," Aaron said. "You know how it goes. Each answer brings another question."

She studied him for a moment, and he knew she suspected there was more.

"I like seeing people's faces when I interview them," Aaron said. "Sometimes their inflections can mean more than their words." The angry look that wrinkled her face told him he had said the wrong thing.

"Do you think Bob is hiding something?" she asked in an accusatory tone, like a mother defending a child.

"Not intentionally," Aaron lied. "But Melonie said he once saw something black in the refuge. I want to ask him about it. I'm sure it'll be embarrassing admitting he might have seen Bigfoot. I'd like to be able to prod him when I ask him about it."

She seemed satisfied. After what they had gone through in the lean-to, the existence of Bigfoot wasn't so far-fetched anymore.

"So when do you want to go?" she asked.

"The sooner the better."

"Can you wait until tomorrow morning?"

"That'd be fine." He debated for a moment whether to tell her not to call Bob and tell him they were coming, but he knew she would suspect something if he did. This way even if she called Bob, she couldn't tell him anything more than they were coming out with a few more questions. It wasn't perfect, but it would have to do.

"Okay. We'll meet here tomorrow morning at eight," she said. "We'll get an early start so we can get back at a decent time. I have things I need to do."

"That'll work fine," Aaron said. "I have things I need to get done, too."

"By the way, I changed the plugs in the other sled, and it runs fine," she said. "So we won't be doubling up on the one sled this time." She gave him a smile and walked away toward the group of deputies.

Aaron watched her go and a shiver went through him. The hair on his arms raised in gooseflesh.

"I have another question," he called, making an effort to keep his voice smooth.

She turned around and faced him. "What?"

"What kind of snowshoes are those?" he asked.

"Why do you want to know?"

"You've got me curious about all this outdoorsy stuff."

"The guys have modified beavertail snowshoes with magnesium frames," she said. She lifted one of her wooden snowshoes out of the snow, balancing on one leg. "These are bear paws."

"Aren't bear paws what you said Bob had?"

"He has bear paws and beavertails. The bear paws work better than beavertails in the woods, because they're smaller and easier maneuvering around things. The beavertails are good in deep snow."

Aaron smiled. "Thanks for the lesson."

She gave him a wide, gap-toothed smile. "Maybe we'll get the city boy out of you yet." She went back to her students.

As soon as she turned her back, the smile slipped from Aaron's face. The tracks Summer left in the snow with her bear paw snowshoes were a foot to a foot and a half wide, two feet long and rounded on both ends. Aaron knew exactly what tracks Deputy Gordon had seen the night he found Hemper's body, and he had a pretty good idea who had made them.

Chapter Eighteen

As they closed in on the creek where they would leave the snowmobiles and walk the rest of the way to Bob's cabin, Aaron hoped he hadn't made a huge mistake. He had slipped his backup 9mm Smith and Wesson into the brown emergency bag in the cargo sled when Summer had backed the truck up to the snowmobile trailer at the state shed. If she knew he was taking a weapon along, she would know the trip wasn't for *a few more questions*. So he had put the 9mm in the bag without her knowing and handed her his .40 Glock for the glove compartment. He didn't believe she was involved in Hemper's murder, but she knew Bob better than she knew him, and he couldn't take the chance she'd do something stupid.

When they unloaded the sleds at Lester's place, Aaron had slid the cargo sled off the trailer when Summer stopped him.

"We're not going to need that bulky thing," she had said. "We're not taking anything to Bob."

Suddenly Aaron saw his plan disappear. "But what if we break down again?"

"We have two sleds. I doubt if both of them will break down," she said with a smile. Aaron had a sinking feeling. "And if they do, we're leaving early enough that we can walk out before it gets dark."

He never had a chance to retrieve the 9mm. Thinking back, he should have come clean with her right then and told her about the warrant. But it had all happened so fast. She had jumped on her sled, he had gotten on the other Arctic Cat, and they were off. The pistol was still in the brown canvas bag on the cargo sled sitting in Lester's yard. He hoped wanting to bring it had been an overreaction. But Chantel's warning about Bob possibly being mentally unstable kept haunting him.

He wasn't unarmed. The Taser from the trunk of his car was in the pocket of his snowmobile suit. It was one of those pieces of equipment the state had given him that he had never used. It might come in handy if Bob wouldn't give a sample willingly. The Wildman might be old, but he was huge. If Bob refused to cooperate, Summer and he could not restrain him and forcibly take a cheek swab—Aaron figured subduing someone's Bob's size would take five to ten men. When Aaron had certified with the Taser, he had been shot with it. It had knocked him down and stunned him for a few moments. If the worst happened and Bob resisted, the Taser would stun him long enough for them to get the sample, but he was hoping against hope everything would go smoothly.

Now the Taser was in his pocket with two copies of the search warrant—one for Bob and one for the court's return. He needed the DNA sample if he was going to prove what he already knew: Wildman Bob was a crazy person who killed and ate people. So he stuck the Taser in his pocket in case he needed it. He should have put the 9mm in there too, but the pistol was heavy and Summer would have noticed it when he put on his snowmobile suit. He hoped he hadn't made a mistake.

Summer pulled her snowmobile off on the side of the trail and stopped. Aaron pulled the old Arctic Cat behind it and shut it off.

"Are you ready?" she asked getting off the sled.

"We need to talk for a minute," Aaron said. He would need her help convincing Bob to voluntarily give a sample. It was time she knew what they were really doing there, and she needed to know how dangerous Bob might be. He didn't know how Bob would react when he was read the warrant and asked for a cheek swab. She couldn't be caught off guard if Bob became violent. He pulled the search warrant out of his pocket and handed it to her.

Summer open the warrant and read it carefully.

"What's this all about?" she asked, shaking the paper at him as she looked over the top of it at him with confused eyes. "A cheek swab from Robert Allen Milton for DNA testing," she said, reading from the warrant. "Why do you need a cheek swab?"

Aaron decided that not telling her about the warrant before had been the right decision.

"I believe Bob was there when Hemper was killed," Aaron said. He didn't tell her how flimsy the probable cause was, and he didn't mention the cannibalism. She wouldn't take it well, and he didn't want to deal with it right now.

She looked shocked and didn't say anything for a moment, looking at him, back at the warrant and back at him. "What evidence do you have?"

"They found human DNA on Hemper's body," Aaron said.

"So what?" She sounded defensive. "Why do you think it's Bob's?"

"The DNA shows the person has gigantism," Aaron said. "It makes a person large like a giant. It's a rare condition, and Bob's a huge guy."

"So what?" she asked again, anger creeping into her voice. "You don't know Bob has gigantism." She pronounced it *giantism*."

"Both of Bob's parents are under six feet tall, and he's six-ten," Aaron said. "How did that happen?"

"It doesn't mean anything." Her voice grew louder. "Kids are always bigger than their parents."

"Not that much bigger," Aaron said.

"Maybe you don't know who his real father is?" Summer said.

She was rationalizing, trying to make it fit the way she wanted it to fit.

"All I know for sure is Bob wouldn't kill someone," she said. "He doesn't even hunt anymore, for god's sake."

"This isn't personal. I have nothing against Bob," Aaron said. "I didn't even know him until a couple days ago." He studied her for a moment, but her attitude didn't look as if it was improving. "I'm doing my job," he continued. "I check out all the possibilities, get rid of the ones that don't work and what's left is the solution. Bob is a suspect. I have to check him out until he's eliminated."

She didn't say anything. He could tell she was fuming by the death stare she gave him.

"I'm not saying he killed Hemper," Aaron said, lying to try and calm her. "But if his DNA was there, it means he was there. Which means he knows something about it."

For a moment he thought she would crumple the warrant and throw it at him. Instead she shoved it towards him.

"This is the only reason we're out here, isn't it?"

Aaron took the warrant and nodded. "It's the main reason."

"Why didn't you tell me about the warrant before we left?" she asked.

"I work on a need to know basis," he said. "I didn't feel you needed to know until now."

"You were afraid I'd tip him off, weren't you?"

"I know you and Bob are friends," he said. "I wanted him caught off guard. I didn't want him knowing we were coming."

"Well, he knows we're coming," Summer said. "I left him a voicemail and a text."

"I wish you hadn't," Aaron said. If Bob had murdered Hemper, unless all guilt and conscience had left him, he would be suspicious about them coming back so soon.

"Did you want him to be at the cabin or not?" Summer asked. "I told you before, Bob doesn't spend all his nights in the cabin. If I hadn't left him the messages, he might not have been there, and it would have been a wasted trip."

She had a point, but now he didn't know what was waiting for them at Bob's cabin. "Did he say anything?"

"He never responded," she said. "But that's not unusual."

Aaron didn't know if not getting a response from him was good or bad … it felt bad. "So can we get the sample and have it tested?"

"It won't be Bob's DNA," she said. "I guarantee it."

"If it's not, both you and he will get my sincerest apology," Aaron said and gave her a big smile that she didn't return.

~*~

They made the walk to the cabin in a silence colder than the outside temperature that hovered around zero. Without having the cargo sled and muscling it around and over the brush blocking the trail, the walking was easier and faster than the first time they'd come out.

When they made it to the cabin, the first thing Aaron noticed was both sets of snowshoes, the beavertails and the bear paws—which looked like they would make the exact marks Deputy Gordon had seen the night Hemper was killed—were hanging on their pegs.

"Bob," Summer yelled, pounding on the door.

Nobody answered. Nothing but silence greeted them from inside the cabin.

"He has to be here," Summer said. She pushed the door open and went inside.

Aaron cautiously followed her inside the dark cabin. The one-room cabin didn't have much in it, which was good. Someone Summer's size could have found something to hide behind and ambush them, but not a six-ten, 300-pound man.

"Bob?" she called out again.

The cabin looked exactly as it had the last time they had been there, as if nobody had been there since. The room had the same wood smoke smell, but it was chilly enough in the cabin for Aaron to see his breath. Before Summer walked over to the stove and put her hand on it, Aaron knew it was cold.

"He hasn't been here for a while," she said, gingerly tapping the cold metal with her fingers before she laid them on it.

She opened the door on the front of the stove.

"There are a few coals left," she said. "But it's been a long time since he's been here."

"Where would he go?" Aaron hoped he hadn't gone off somewhere on one of his jaunts in the woods. They couldn't wait for days until he got back, and the warrant had an expiration date.

"He couldn't have gone too far," she said. "He didn't take his snowshoes, and his pack is still here." She gestured toward a khaki pack and frame leaning against the wall by the door. "Maybe he climbed to the top of the hill and checked his messages."

"So what do we do?" Aaron asked.

"Wait," she said. "And I'll get this fire going again."

In a few minutes she had coaxed the warmth back into the stove. The cabin warmed quickly. Within minutes they had taken off their snowmobile suits. The fire crackled in the stove, but it was the only sound in the cabin. He sat at the table while she sat on Bob's bunk. She wouldn't look at him. Aaron figured she was still ticked.

"I'm sorry about not telling you about the warrant," Aaron said. "It isn't that I don't trust you—"

"You might think I'm just a deer cop, but I'm still a cop," she snapped, cutting him off, bitterness coming out in her voice. "I went through the same law enforcement academy as every police officer and deputy in the state. How could you think I would have tipped Bob off about the warrant?"

"I know you wouldn't have," he said. Fences needed mending. He would need her help convincing Bob to give a voluntary sample. If it meant prostrating himself in front of her, he'd do it. "I work alone most of the time," he said, sounding as apologetic as he could. "Sometimes I don't think anyone but me needs to know everything. I'm sorry. It was nothing personal against you."

"Well, it feels like a slap in the face," she said. "Getting a sample from Bob doesn't bother me. I'll guarantee you he had nothing to do with Hemper's death. The sample will only prove it."

"You might be right," he said, although he doubted it.

Her gray eyes narrowed. "What else aren't you telling me?"

"Nothing," he said.

"I don't believe you," she said. "I haven't applied for many search warrants, but

I know you couldn't get one just because Bob is big. What else do you have?"

Aaron figured he might as well lay it all out. "The DNA showed another abnormality which could disfigure the person's children," Aaron said. "Melonie said Bob had a vasectomy years ago because he had something wrong with his DNA that would affect his children." He looked at her again and decided to give her everything. "Also, I don't know how much you read of Deputy Gordon's report, but he saw some big tracks the night he found Hemper's body."

"The Bigfoot tracks," she said.

"They weren't from Bigfoot," Aaron said. "They were bear paw snowshoe tracks … like the ones hanging outside the cabin door."

It caught her off guard. She didn't say anything for a moment, and Aaron figured part of it was her not having connected the tracks and snowshoes before.

"A bunch of people around here have snowshoes like those, even me," she said. "It doesn't mean they were Bob's."

"And we'll find out with the DNA test," Aaron said.

She didn't look angry anymore. A better word would be hurt, Aaron decided.

"Again, I'm sorry about not trusting you," he said. "Usually I trust the women I've slept with."

It bought him a gap-toothed smile. "We never slept together," she said. "We *slept ... together*."

"Enjoyable either way you say it," Aaron said.

She gave a small laugh, and he knew it was good between them again.

"What was that?" she asked suddenly, the smile dropping from her face.

Aaron heard things all the time when they were in the woods. At first he had jumped at every sound. Now he ignored them unless they sounded loud or violent.

"Maybe Bob is back," Aaron said. He stood and stepped toward the door.

"It didn't sound like it came from outside," she said.

Aaron looked around the cabin. Whatever she heard couldn't have come from the cabin. There was the stove, bed, table, piles of clothes and other things on the floor and various stuff hanging on the walls, but the rest was open.

"Maybe it was a mouse," Aaron said, as he heard it too. A slow muffled swish, with no hard sounds, like a big sack of flour being dragged across a floor.

"It came from over there," Summer said, pointing toward the root cellar door.

"Maybe Bob is in the root cellar?" Aaron asked and dismissed it as quickly as he had said it. Why would Bob go in the root cellar and close the trap door over him? It didn't make sense, but who else could it be? It wasn't as if a mouse would be dragging a 50-pound bag across the cellar floor.

Before they'd made it to the trap door, the sound came again. It *was* coming from the root cellar.

"Bob," Summer called out.

No answer from below and the sound stopped.

Aaron grabbed the trap door, swinging it open and laying it on the floor. The square shaft of light from above lit the area directly below the opening with a dim light, but it was enough for Aaron to see Bob laying on his belly on the floor of the cellar.

Chapter Nineteen

Aaron beat Summer to the ladder by a step. She tried following him into the cellar, but he stopped her.

"There's not enough room for both of us," he said as he climbed into the cellar. Bob filled most of the floor space.

Aaron hit the stone floor a couple steps from Bob. He lay with his head by Aaron's feet and his legs fading off into darkness at the rear of the cellar. Even in the dimly-lit cellar, Aaron could see a pool of dark dried blood running out from under his head. It covered the stones under it and ran into the sand grouted cracks between.

His best guess was Bob had tripped and done a header into the cellar. He didn't know how the trap door got closed—maybe Bob had been holding it open when it happened and it slammed shut when he fell in? The sounds they'd heard must have been him pulling himself across the floor. Aaron knelt on one knee and as soon as he touched an arm, his theory about Bob making the dragging sounds vanished. The body was rigor mortis hard. Dried blood had gathered in his ears and nose in dried black crusts. His head was turned away from Aaron. When he shifted to Bob's other side, he could see a deep indentation in his head above the right temple. Aaron didn't need Chantel's expertise to confirm Bob had died instantly. Bob hadn't dragged himself anywhere.

"Is he okay?" Summer asked.

"No," Aaron said, looking at her standing framed in the hole. He didn't know how to put it delicately, so he just put it. "He's dead."

A small gasp came from above. When you didn't have many friends, losing one hit you hard, Aaron imagined.

Aaron the investigator looked back at Bob's body. He could still get the DNA sample, but he'd wait until they took the body in for examination. He'd let Chantel take the sample. She had more experience.

It would be tough getting Bob's big body out of there. Lifting 300 pounds straight up without equipment would take at least five men.

He suddenly felt morbid. Summer was still sobbing in the cabin above and already he had moved on. Sympathy became a casualty of the job; it desensitized him, and he guessed even more so with Chantel, because she always dealt with dead people.

Aaron's eyes had adjusted to the darkness in the cellar. Before he could see to Bob's waist, now he could see his feet. Ten feet beyond Bob's body was the back wall of the cellar. It was covered with some type of hairy fungus, long stringy and light-colored. After a few moments, Aaron saw it was a fur robe hanging on the far wall, or maybe a curtain separating this room from a deeper room. As he studied it longer, features materialized. He could see arms, legs, and a head … It moved!

Aaron stopped breathing. His hands shook. His skin jumped into gooseflesh.

A low growl came from the back wall that wasn't a wall.

Aaron slowly stood, moving deliberately and not making any quick movements. His eyes were glued to the thing at the back of the cellar. He backed away as you'd back away from a wild dog or a grizzly. His eyes never left the creature. When his calves bumped into the bottom rung of the ladder, it took every ounce of self-control he had in him to keep from fleeing up the ladder into the cabin.

"What's the matter?" Summer asked, her voice thick with tears.

"There's something down here," Aaron said. He said it softly so whatever it was wouldn't read the terror in him and take it as a weakness, but his voice broke.

"Get up here," Summer said. He knew the break in his voice had tipped her off that it was more than an opossum, because she suddenly sounded panicked.

"No," Aaron said. Some instinct told him as soon as he turned his back and climbed the ladder, the thing would see it as an opening. It was like a buffalo holding off a pack of wolves. As long as it faces them it's alright, but as soon as it turns and runs, it loses the advantage and guarantees its doom.

He wished to god he had found a way to bring his 9mm.

"Summer," Aaron said, still talking calmly. "There's a Taser in the pocket of my snowmobile suit. Go get it."

"What?"

"Get me the Taser, now!" he screamed. Any attempt at staying calm vanished as the thing worked its foot over the top of Bob's body and took a step toward him. "It's in my snowmobile suit pocket! Hurry!"

She was so small and light he couldn't hear her footsteps crossing the floor. He couldn't tell if she had gone after the Taser or had frozen and was still watching him through the cellar door. His eyes never left the creature as it slowly worked its way toward him. He still couldn't make out any distinct features. The same shaggy white hair covering the rest of its body, hung over its face. It crouched to keep from hitting its head on the eight-foot ceiling while its broad shoulders brushed the strings of plaited onions and garlic hanging from the shelves on both walls. The cellar filled with a pungent garlic smell.

"Here's the Taser," Summer said from above, her voice shaking. "What do you want me to do with it?"

She couldn't see the thing from where she stood. Aaron held out his cupped hands as if waiting to catch manna from Heaven. He didn't take his eyes off the creature for even a second. "Drop it in my hands."

The Taser fell from above and hit his hands. Aaron looked at his hands and secured it. When he looked back the creature was in full charge. Aaron pointed, found the trigger and pulled it in one motion. Its momentum carried the creature within touching distance of Aaron. He could smell its rancid breath, but the Taser gave out a vicious electrical crackling. Sparks jumped from the two probes as the Taser clicked its way through its five-second cycle.

The thing shook for a moment before stumbling backward and tripping over Bob's body. It hit the floor with a thump. The impact vibrated the stone floor under Aaron's feet.

Aaron jerked the Taser and broke the micro-thin copper wires attached to the probes and fled up the ladder. When his feet hit the floorboards above, he flung the Taser to the side. With both hands, he jerked the ladder out of the hole and slammed the trap door shut. He sat on top of it.

Summer's gray eyes were wide with terror. Aaron was sure if they had gotten any wider her eyeballs would have fallen out and rolled across the floor. "What was tha—"

The trap door lurched a foot, throwing Aaron into the air. He landed with a thump, driving the door closed again.

"Jump on the door. Jump on it," Aaron screamed as the door came up again.

Summer jumped and the trap door went flat. Aaron threw the surface bolt into the staple. They sat on the door as the creature pounded on it from below, bouncing them as if the door was being hit by a sledgehammer. Even with both of them sitting on it, Aaron could see the screws in the surface bolt coming loose a little bit each time the monster's weight slammed against it. It wouldn't hold for long. He looked around the room for something heavy to help keep it from coming through the floor.

"Can you reach the nail apron and hammer?" Aaron shouted, pointing at a gray canvas one hanging on the wall.

Summer stretched out without getting off the door and grabbed the apron and hammer.

Aaron snatched it from her and looked inside. One pocket overflowed with two-inch roofing nails, too short. The other pocket had a couple handfuls of 16-penny nails. Aaron grabbed the ladder, tipped it on one two by six rail and laid it across the center of the trap door. He nailed it on both ends and in the middle. He added two more nails at the ends and another in the center. The pounding continued from below, but the door didn't budge. After a little bit the banging stopped.

"We've got it trapped," Aaron said, looking at Summer's stunned face.

"The root cellar has an outside entrance on the north side," she said in a scared whisper.

The words weren't out of her mouth when Aaron saw a blurry figure go across the frosted window.

"It's headed for the door," Aaron shouted.

Summer beat him to the door and threw the deadbolt right before the creature slammed into the door, making it sound like thunder in the cabin. The frame cracked and the lock bent. Aaron hefted the two-by-four leaning against the wall and jammed it into the U-brackets on either side of the door. He got it in place as the creature hit the door again. The two-by-four held, but the brackets pulled slightly away from the frame.

Aaron wasn't sure how much pounding the brackets could take. He grabbed the hammer from the floor and pounded off the top riser on the nailed-down ladder. He ripped out two of the two by four rungs and lugged them to the door. One rung he pounded into the middle of the door while the creature banged away at it—he bent two nails before he got two to hold. He wedged one end of the ladder rail under it, slammed it tight and nailed the other rung to the floor to hold it in place. The thing continued to bang, but nothing moved. After a little bit the banging stopped.

"I hope it left," Summer said when they hadn't heard anything for a few minutes.

"I don't know," Aaron said. He prayed it had, but why would it leave after trying so hard to get to them?

The sound of wood being torn came to them. Aaron couldn't figure it out.

"It's trying to come in through the freezer!" Summer yelled.

They ran to the wall. The freezer door was held on by wimpy latches. One good punch and the thing would be inside.

Aaron tore off another ladder rung and nailed it to the floor, blocking the bottom of the freezer door. He grabbed another rung, but before he could nail it across a top corner, the door bulged inward. One of its latches popped off with a metallic ping and flew across the room, clattering across the floor to the opposite wall. The top right corner of the door pushed in three inches. Aaron could see stringy white hair through the crack. He slammed his shoulder against the corner of the freezer door.

"Nail a rung across the corner!" he yelled.

Summer nailed a rung across both top corners and used the rest of the rungs to further secure the door.

The banging on the freezer door stopped. There was nothing but silence outside the cabin.

Its blurry form went by the windows, first on one side then on the other as it circled the cabin.

"What's it doing?" Summer asked.

"It's looking for a way in," Aaron said, and since it knew about the freezer, it knew the cabin. Eventually it would find an opening.

A Death in a Snowstorm

Chapter Twenty

It circled the cabin for an hour. They watched its blur as it repeatedly passed by the frosted windows. Aaron was glad the windows in the cabin were small. Summer would have had a hard time squeezing through them. The creature couldn't have gotten more than an arm through.

Another hour went by and they didn't see or hear anything.

"Is it gone?" Summer asked, her voice a nervous whisper.

"I don't know." Aaron hoped it had left, but he knew it could be right outside the cabin door waiting.

"We should try to make it to the sleds before it comes back," Summer said.

Aaron didn't know. He wished they knew where it was. Not knowing gave *it* the advantage. They didn't have much for defense. There were a few knives in the cabin, hunting knives as well as some butcher knives in a wood block on the table but using a knife against something that big was a last resort option at best. His Taser had a second cartridge stored in the handle, but its effective range was ten feet or less, way too close. And when the second cartridge was gone, he could use the Taser as a stun gun, but if it came to that, the knife would be a better option.

Aaron decided they could open the door and see if it was there. If it was outside waiting for them and charged, he could shoot it with the Taser. It should stun it long enough for them to get the door closed and barred before it recovered, but hand-to-hand combat with a knife would be their only option remaining. He didn't like it, but he didn't see what other choice they had.

He started telling Summer his plan when she held a finger to her lips, shushing him.

It took a moment before he heard it, too. The same soft sound as a bag of flour being dragged across a floor.

Summer tiptoed over to the trap door. She squatted, listening. After a moment she pointed at the floor and mouthed the words: *It's down there.*

Aaron shuddered at the possibility it was feeding on Bob's body.

She came back to him and stood on her toes to whisper in his ear. "Let's get to the sleds while it's in the cellar."

Aaron nodded. The only other choice was to stay there, and that wasn't a choice.

Quietly they slipped into their snowmobile suits. Aaron picked his Taser off the floor and reloaded it with the second cartridge from the handle. Summer grabbed a butcher knife out of the block, and Aaron picked a hunting knife in a sheath off Bob's bed and stowed it in the pocket of his suit.

"Go make sure it's still there while I open the door," Aaron whispered.

Summer went and kneeled by the trap door. After a moment she looked at Aaron and nodded.

As silently as he could, he eased a nail out of the ladder rung on the floor. It gave out a sharp screech and filled the cabin with its scream before the nail let go.

Summer looked at him with panic all over her face, but she listened for a few seconds and nodded again. It was still down there.

Aaron rotated the rung on the remaining nail, removed the rail blocking the door and laid it gently on the floor. Lifting the cross bar out of the U-brackets, he leaned it against the wall. Nothing protected them from the outside but a bent deadbolt lock. He looked at Summer again.

She cocked her head to the side listening for a moment. Her head moved closer to the floor trying to hear. Aaron's heart jumped into his throat. Had it heard the nail and left the cellar? He grabbed the cross bar, ready to slam it back into place.

Finally Summer nodded at him, gestured at the floor, stood and came over to him.

"It's still there," she whispered. "Let's go."

Aaron stuck his head out the door and looked both ways. Nothing. They slipped out of the cabin and walked quietly away from the cabin, glancing back frequently. When the cabin was out of sight, they took off at a run, or as close as they could do in the deep snow. Aaron's longer legs would have allowed him to outdistance Summer, but they had a better chance of defending themselves if they stayed together. He held back and let her lead the way so she could set the pace while he watched their rear.

They covered the quarter-mile to the sleds in less than half the time it took coming out. A sense of relief came over Aaron as he rounded the last brush pile blocking the creek. The feeling left quickly. Summer's Polaris was tipped over and the track had been sliced through. It lay in a pile like a black carpet runner at the back of the sled. His Arctic Cat's hood was smashed. The motor's aluminum cylinders were broken off. Parts were strewn everywhere. It looked as if someone had taken a sledgehammer to it. Snowshoe tracks covered the ground. Aaron knew what it had been doing for the hour when they couldn't find it.

Summer barely looked at the sleds. Instead she nervously watched the woods around them. "Now what do we do?" she asked, whispering.

"We walk out," Aaron said.

She looked at her wristwatch. "It'll be way after dark before we get out of here, and he has longer legs than we do. He'll run us down out in the open."

"What do you mean, *he*?" Aaron asked.

"We're dealing with a person," she said, still looking into the woods. "He uses snowshoes, and he used some kind of tool, a hammer or something, to do this much damage to the sleds. It's not an animal. It's a person."

Aaron had been thinking something unexplained like Bigfoot or a Skookum. It walked upright like a person, but it was huge, at least eight feet tall. And it didn't have the characteristics of a man. However, it did explain the DNA results. It would be a person with gigantism and mental disabilities. And even a person with mental disabilities was smarter than most animals. That wasn't good for them.

"We can't stay here. It … he will track us," Aaron said. He was whispering. "Let's go back to the cabin."

"Okay, but let's go back a different way in case he's tracking us," she said. "I don't want to run into him out here in the open."

Aaron agreed. They had the Taser with one cartridge left and the two knives. They wouldn't be much defense against whatever He had that did this much damage to the sleds.

~*~

They stayed on the creek bank on the way back to the cabin. Summer led the way with Aaron following. It was slow going because a trail hadn't been broken through the deep snow and brush. They fought their way through the bulrushes and the stacks of branches piled on the side of the creek.

About halfway back, Summer stopped abruptly and held up her hand, listening. Aaron couldn't hear anything but the normal noises of the woods, but he didn't have as much experience in the outdoors as her.

Suddenly her eyes popped wide. She pointed frantically at the ground and dropped on her belly in the snow. Aaron didn't know what was going on. She grabbed his pants' leg and pulled him in the snow beside her. They lay side by side on their stomachs with an ember of apprehension laying in Aaron.

"Something's coming," she whispered in his ear.

The feeling of apprehension doubled in size. He couldn't see anything, and he had no idea what had tipped Summer off, but he trusted her. If she said something was coming, something was coming. A hard knot filled his stomach. He wiggled deeper into the snow to cover as much of himself as possible.

Aaron never heard Him coming. He traveled with the silence of smoke drifting across the top of the snow. It was amazing something so big could travel so quietly. At first Aaron saw His head towering over the top of the branches and bulrushes as it came down the center of the frozen creek. He was all of eight feet tall with wide shoulders that would have had to turn sideways to make it through an average door. Aaron still doubted it was a man until He was directly across from them. In the bright daylight, Aaron could see He wore a white fur coat with a hood of the same stringy white fur that partially covered his face. His forehead was deformed, bulging and knobby like a hunk of cauliflower. It sat atop a long face with bumps and wrinkles covering everything not hidden by His long brown beard. His eyes were wide apart and as Chantel had said, "You could put the palm of your hand between his eyes without touching either of them." In his left hand He carried a corn sorghum knife on the end of a heavy axe handle. It could easily slice a wild hog in two or Hemper's throat wide open. It looked heavy, but He carried it in one hand with no more effort than a kid would carry a baseball bat.

When He was directly across from them, he stopped and sniffed the breeze with the sound of a person with a cold snuffling. Aaron knew little about hunting, but with the breeze blowing in his face he knew He couldn't scent them. It seemed a little preposterous that a human could smell them, but he remembered the night in the lean-to and the snuffling sounds he had heard.

Aaron lay still, putting his head on the snow. He couldn't see the middle of the creek or the trail where He was, but he didn't want to give them away. He watched Summer and by her eyes he could tell He was moving towards the sleds. In a moment she raised to her knees.

"Let's go," she whispered as she stood. "As soon as he gets to the sleds, he'll know we went back to the cabin."

Summer took the lead again while Aaron followed, glancing frequently over his shoulder. After a few minutes, Summer stopped.

"Let's go on the creek," she said, still whispering. "It'll be faster walking."

On the creek ice, Aaron could see the snowshoe tracks He had made. They were big oval shaped marks that sank only a few inches into the snow. He was moving faster than they were, because he didn't sink in the snow as much, and His longer legs with a longer stride let him cover ground faster than them. There were two sets of snowshoes hanging by Bob's door. They should have put them on. As it was, they sank two feet in the snow and fought getting through the deep drifts. Even though they had busted trail on the way in and back to the sleds, any progress was a struggle.

He was gaining on them. Aaron couldn't see him yet, but he knew He was coming. He would have found the spot where they went on the creek bank trail and followed their footprints back. Aaron looked over his shoulder again. He hoped they could get to the cabin before He caught them.

When they broke through into the clearing where the cabin stood, relief flooded through Aaron. Safety was fifty yards away. He didn't know what they'd do once they were barricaded in the cabin again, but at least they could think it through behind the safety of a barricaded door. He glanced over his shoulder one more time and relief abandoned all hope. A shaggy white head bobbed over the top of the bulrushes and slough grass.

"He's coming," Aaron said. "Hurry."

The trail was more defined and easier walking in the clearing. They tried running, but the snow was still deep. Summer fell face first.

Aaron glanced back again. Now a whole head and part of shoulders towered over the top of the rushes. He could see them and had quickened his pace, running now. Aaron could hear the flip flopping of the snowshoes, sounding like sandals on a beach as He came on, not trying to be quiet anymore.

Aaron grabbed Summer's arm and jerked her to her feet. "We have to get going," he yelled.

Aaron looked over his shoulder again as He broke through the brush into the cabin's clearing. They were twenty-five yards from the cabin. He was twenty-five yards from them.

"We're not going to make it," Aaron yelled.

Aaron turned toward it, like the buffalo facing the wolves again, and dug the Taser out of his pocket.

It stopped ten yards from them, panting from the running. His breath came out in white bursts in the cold air like a steam engine huffing and puffing as it climbed a hill.

"We don't want to hurt you," Summer said, speaking calmly as if talking to a wild animal, but her normally deep raspy voice squeaked.

His face was unmoved as if He couldn't hear. It reminded Aaron of the face of Frankenstein's monster, no bolts or scars, but the absolute lack of emotion in it. Its wide-set eyes weren't angry or filled with rage. They were blank, as if it had nothing against them like the wolves have nothing against the buffalo. They were prey, another meal.

"Get to the cabin," Aaron said. "I'll hold it off."

"I'm not going without you," Summer said. She grabbed the elbow of his free arm and pulled on it.

He shook it loose. "Get going. I'll be along. Get the two by four ready to block the door as soon as I get inside. It'll crash through before we get a chance to secure it if you don't have it ready." But more than anything, he wanted at least one of them to survive, and she had the best chance.

Summer left him and headed for the cabin by herself.

He might have had a mental disability as Chantel had guessed, but He wasn't stupid. As soon as Summer went toward the cabin, He tried flanking Aaron by going to his right and staying five yards away, right outside the range of the Taser.

His legs were longer than Aaron's. Aaron took three steps for every two of his. Summer took four. In ten yards Aaron had caught Summer.

"He's trying to cut us off," Aaron yelled as he went past her, and it looked as if He would win the race.

Aaron thought about running toward him and shooting him with the Taser, but He had on the thick shaggy robe. The Taser's probes had penetrated it in the root cellar, but it had been more luck than anything else. Now the robe bounced and swelled as He ran.

Aaron doubted the probes would penetrate and deliver a jolt. They had one cartridge left. Once it was gone, they'd be left with hand-to-hand combat with their knives against the corn sorghum knife. It didn't take much guessing to know how that would turn out.

Suddenly Aaron had an idea. He pulled the cartridge off the front of the Taser, pointed it towards Him and pulled the trigger in stun gun mode. Angry blue sparks crackled harmlessly between the electrodes as the Taser clicked rapidly through its five-second cycle.

He cringed and stopped for a moment. Aaron was aware of Summer passing by. He kept moving after her without taking his eyes off him, standing stunned for a few moments as if waiting for the shock. Aaron heard the creak of the wood steps at the front of the cabin as Summer ran onto the porch and the door creaked open. Within moments He realized the Taser wasn't hurting him and came after Aaron on a dead run. Aaron popped the Taser off again. It crackled, but He never slowed. He had already figured out it couldn't hurt him.

Aaron fled through the open door. Summer stood holding the cross bar. Aaron slammed the door shut and Summer put the cross bar in place. A great thump hit the door. The screws on the U-brackets moved some more. Aaron grabbed the rail and wedged it against the door as Summer drove the nail in the rung on the floor solid. He hit the door one more time and stopped. He had already learned he couldn't get through the door.

Summer looked at Aaron with wide, terror-filled eyes. She was panting. "Now what?"

"I don't know," he said as his heart pounded against his sternum.

Chapter Twenty One

Summer crouched by the root cellar door listening with her head cocked sideways like the RCA Victor dog. Her fright showed in her eyes. He was there again. The light through the windows was fading. Daylight was dissolving as darkness approached. Aaron figured there might be an hour or two of light left, then they would spend the night with him outside the cabin or in the root cellar trying to get inside. And He *would* get inside. The wood pile had been cut and split with something, an axe … maybe a chainsaw. Aaron couldn't see it in the cabin which meant it was outside. It was only a matter of time before He figured out a chainsaw or axe would make short work of the wood door. They couldn't wait until daylight.

Aaron checked his cell phone for the twentieth time, still zero bars. He only had one feasible option. He picked his snowmobile suit off the back of the chair and put it on.

"I'm going to the top of the hill and calling the sheriff's office," Aaron whispered so He couldn't hear. "We can't stay here. Eventually he'll figure out a way in."

Summer picked her snowmobile suit off the chair.

"You're staying here," Aaron said.

She looked confused. "Why?"

"Because, if he follows me, you'll put on Bob's snowshoes and walk out of here," Aaron said.

"He'll still catch me even if I have the snowshoes," she said.

"Not if I can keep him busy long enough to give you a big head start," Aaron said.

"How are you going to do that?"

"If he follows me, I'll lead him away from you," Aaron said. "Maybe I can keep him busy for an hour or so. It should give you enough of a head start that he won't catch you."

"But he'll catch *you*," she said.

"Maybe," Aaron said. He hadn't thought it out fully, but as he saw it, it was their only option. "I have the Taser. It should keep him at bay." *I hope.*

"Why don't you let me make the call, and you walk out of here?"

Aaron shook his head. "Won't work."

"Because I'm a woman?"

"No, because you have short legs," Aaron said. "If you were a basketball player, we'd flip a coin to see who goes which way." *If I had a two-headed coin.* "You had trouble getting back to the cabin because of the deep snow. I don't know much about snowshoes, but I figure they can't do well climbing hills, right?"

"Not without crampons."

"We have no idea how deep the snow is on the hill or if there's a path through it," Aaron said. "But however deep it is, you'll have more trouble getting through it than I will. He can catch you quicker than me."

She nodded.

"And besides, I've never been on snowshoes in my life," Aaron said. "If I tried walking out of here with them, I'd spend more time falling than walking. You'll have a better chance of getting out of here than me."

She nodded again.

Aaron looked out a window but couldn't see anything through the frosted glass. He forced it open a crack. It creaked and bits of frost fell off the pane like snowflakes.

"You can watch me go from here," he said. "If he follows me, as soon as he's out of sight you get out of here. Keep going and don't look back."

She moved a chair over by the root cellar door. "I can listen to him in the cellar. If I hear the outside cellar door open, I'll check the window." She walked back over and studied Aaron seriously for a moment. "You are coming back, right? You're not planning on doing something stupid?"

He gave her a wide smile. "If you're worried about me being a hero, it's not going to happen," he said, but he knew his only defense was the last Taser cartridge. After he had used it, there was little chance he could outrun Him. And with the snow, losing or hiding from Him would be impossible. Their only hope was if Aaron could make him waste time and give Summer a big enough lead that He couldn't catch her. Aaron didn't relish being a meal for that thing, but he couldn't see another option that got at least one of them out of there. "If I get the call made—"

"If?" She cut him off. Her face filled with worry.

"*When* I make the call," Aaron said. "Help will be headed this way, so you'll meet them somewhere on the trail." *And if you don't, you'll know he caught me before I made the call.* "Have the rescue party keep coming. I'll come back to the cabin when I lose him. If I'm not here, you can follow my tracks and pick me up." *Or pick up whatever's left of my carcass.*

"You be careful," she whispered, her eyes suddenly watery. She knew exactly what was at stake. "I plan on seeing you again."

For a moment Aaron thought he might be the second person he had ever seen her hug. Instead she went over and crouched by the root cellar door again.

After a moment she mouthed the words: *He's still there.*

Aaron zipped the front of his snowmobile suit and put on his stocking cap and gloves. He patted his pocket and the hard plastic of the Taser greeted him.

Aaron eased the nail out of the ladder rung on the floor. It came out quieter this time without the screech. He rotated it sideways and removed the rail wedged against the door.

"Don't pound the nail back in," Aaron whispered. "Slide it in the hole in the rung so he doesn't hear. It should hold it. If he tries to get in, you can pound it solid."

"Be careful," she whispered.

Aaron tried smiling to put her at ease. But by the way she looked, he guessed it had made it to his face as a grimace or something worse. He opened the door and looked outside. Nothing in any direction. With his heart pounding, he stepped out onto the wooden stoop, took the bear paw snowshoes off their pegs and leaned them against the inside of the cabin wall.

"Is he still there?" Aaron asked.

Summer leaned her head toward the floor again. She pointed and nodded. Aaron quietly closed the door and stepped off the stoop.

Aaron had the Taser in his hand pointed out in front of him as he picked his way slowly to the rear of the cabin and peeked around the corner. The outside cellar door sat at the end of a dirt mound. It was a heavy door made of two-by-sixes and leaning at a 45-degree angle. Snowshoe tracks covered the stomped snow in front of the door and a pair of snowshoes leaned against the door's rock and mortar framing.

Aaron looked around for something heavy he could use to barricade the cellar door. If they could trap him inside, they would both have a chance of walking out of there, but he couldn't see anything.

Aaron edged by the door, never taking his eyes off it, backing up the hill until he had passed the garden terraces and was standing in the trees at the top of the clearing. He stopped by a brush pile and studied the outside entrance from a distance. For a second he considered yelling and clapping his hands. If he got his attention and made him come up the hill and away from the cabin, Summer might have a chance of getting back. But Aaron truly was not a hero, and if He didn't hear him leave, maybe He wouldn't know he was gone, and he could make the call for help and get back to the cabin before He knew he was gone. It would be the best chance for both of them to get out alive. Once help was on its way, they could barricade the cabin door. There was a table and chairs and a bed with a mattress they could put against the door. It wouldn't stop him from chopping his way through, but it might slow him long enough for help to arrive.

Aaron backed into the woods and kept backing until the cabin was buried by the trees. He put the Taser in his pocket and ran up the hill as fast as he could.

Chapter Twenty Two

"Cossack County Sheriff's Office. How may I help you?"

Aaron recognized Melonie's voice. "Melonie, this is Aaron Barnum. I need to talk with Sheriff Thompson right away," Aaron said, crouching behind a broken off tree trunk at the top of the hill, staying hidden and all the time watching downhill for signs he was being followed.

"I'll buzz him, but he might have gone home." The tone of his voice tipped her off to the seriousness of the situation, because she was all business. "I'm going to put you on hold, Aaron. Don't hang up."

The phone went dead, not even elevator music. For a moment Aaron worried he'd lost the call. Ten yards before he'd reached the top of the hill, he'd had zero bars on his phone. He checked the display, where a full five bars greeted him. Everything was still good.

"Hi Aaron, what's going on?" Sheriff Thompson's voice came abruptly out of the silence, making Aaron jump. "I was getting ready to leave. You're lucky—"

"I need you to listen," Aaron said, raising his voice. There was no time for politeness. "I'm at the refuge at Wildman Bob's place with Summer Conrad. Get some officers with snowmobiles and guns and get out here right away."

"What's the problem?" He sounded confused.

"The guy who killed Hemper is out here," Aaron said.

There was silence. Aaron checked his phone again, still five bars.

He was about to say something when the sheriff came back on.

"Is it Wildman Bob?"

"No. Bob's dead," Aaron said. "This guy might have killed him, too."

"Who is he?" the sheriff asked nervously.

"I don't know," Aaron said. "He's a big guy. Eight feet tall and he must weigh around four hundred pounds."

There was silence on the phone again.

"Okay, you got me," the sheriff said and laughed. "I guess I deserve it after all the ribbing I gave Jesse about Big—"

"THIS IS NOT A FRIGGIN' JOKE!" Aaron screamed. He wanted to reach through the phone and slap him. "This is a real man and he has us trapped in Bob's cabin. He destroyed our snowmobiles so we can't get back, and we're unarmed, and he's trying to kill us, and you need to get some men with guns and snowmobiles and get out here NOW!" Aaron sucked in a breath.

"You're serious about this?" the sheriff asked. "An eight-foot tall man?"

"Yes. I'm serious." Aaron knew how ridiculous it sounded, but he went ahead anyway. The sheriff didn't have to believe him. He just needed to come and bring help. "I know it sounds incredible, but it's true," Aaron said, softer now that the sheriff was coming around. "Do you know where Bob's cabin is?"

"No. I'm afraid I don't," the sheriff said. "But I can find someone who does." He sounded nervous now. That was good. Aaron wanted him nervous. It meant he was taking it seriously.

"Get your people together and get coming this way as soon as possible," Aaron said.

"It's going to be dark soon," the sheriff said.

"I know," Aaron said. "But it'll be a clear night. If you have someone who knows how to get to the cabin, they should be able to find the arrows."

"Arrows?"

"I don't have time to explain," Aaron said and stopped suddenly. He was sure one of the snow-covered bushes twenty-five yards downhill had moved. His eyes stayed focused on it and nothing else.

"Aaron?"

Aaron never took his eyes off the bush.

"Aaron?"

Aaron decided the bush was too small for Him to hide behind. "Get your people together and get out here," he said.

"We'll be on our way within the hour," the sheriff said.

"I appreciate it," Aaron said. He thought about telling them to watch for Summer, but he didn't know if she was walking out of the refuge or not. It would slow them down if they spent the trip looking for her. And if she was walking out, it meant He was somewhere coming up the hill. "You need to hurry."

"I'm on it," the sheriff said. "We'll be there as soon as we can."

Aaron put the phone back in his pocket. He studied the hill again, carefully this time, looking at every white blob of snow-covered brush to see if it looked different from the others ... to see if it moved. He considered staying crouched there hidden until help arrived. From where he was at the top of the hill, he could hear the snowmobiles when they came. But Aaron didn't know if He was coming up the hill. The sun was already behind the far west hills. Twilight had crept into the lowlands covering everything in shadows. Soon night would be there. The thought of being out in the woods in the dark made Aaron cautiously stand and walk downhill toward the cabin.

~*~

The trip back was slow. Aaron took a step and looked and listened before taking another one. Halfway there, he decided if He had come out of the root cellar and followed him, He would have already caught him. By the time Aaron reached the top of the terraces above the cabin, he was convinced He had never left the cellar.

Aaron stopped for a moment in the shelter of the trees, checking everything out before stepping into the clearing. The one thing he didn't want was to step into view as He came out the cellar door.

Daylight had all but vanished, but the white snow accentuated dark objects. The cellar door was still closed with the snowshoes leaning against its rock arch frame as they had been when Aaron left. The cabin door was shut. He guessed Summer was still in there. She would have left the door open if she had left the cabin so he'd know she was gone. Maybe He had never left the root cellar. It meant there were fifty yards between Aaron and the safety of the cabin. Once he was inside, they could barricade the door with everything they could find and wait for help to arrive.

Aaron stepped out into the open, concentrating on nothing but the closed cellar door. Suddenly the cabin door banged opened and Summer stepped outside and waved at him. Aaron half raised his hand in a return wave when he realized she wasn't waving *at him*. She was waving him away as if she wanted him to go back up the hill.

He saw it first from the corner of his eye, a white blur in his peripheral vision 15 yards on the left rushing toward him from a brush pile in the fading light. Before even looking, Aaron knew it was Him. He fumbled in his pocket for the Taser. By the time he had it out and pointed at Him, less than ten feet separated them. Aaron pulled the trigger.

The probes flew out and stuck in the white robe. Sparks flew as the Taser clicked furiously through its five-second cycle.

He stepped back, his white robe shaking as he tensed and dropped the corn knife—it vanished in the snow—but Aaron knew the probes hadn't found their way through the thick fur coat. The monster didn't jerk or stiffen. When He knew he hadn't been hurt, He lunged toward Aaron.

Aaron took off toward the cabin, running in big terrified strides. It caught him by the back of his snowmobile suit before he'd taken a dozen steps and dragged him backwards, lifting him off the ground by his collar. Aaron hung suspended in the air by one huge hand. The other hand grabbed for Aaron's throat. Aaron tucked his chin to his chest. A hand smothered Aaron's mouth and another found the back of his neck and squeezed.

Aaron dangled in the air, yelling muffled screams into the gloved hand over his mouth. The pain was excruciating; fire bolts shot into his ears and eyes. He was afraid his jaw would shatter.

He shook Aaron the way a terrier shakes a rat. Both of Aaron's hands grasped the hand over his mouth so his neck wouldn't break from the shaking.

Out of the corner of his eye Aaron could see a mutated face. Light blue, dull eyes glared out from under the protruding forehead like the eyes of a demon looking out from under the bill of a cap. The disgusting smell of rancid meat came from a mouth full of dark teeth. The smell engulfed Aaron. His stomach lurched. Bile filled his mouth. His consciousness blurred, came back and went as he slipped into blackness.

A wire from the Taser hung from Aaron's arm. The Taser dangled in the air flopping back and forth against Aaron's chest as he was shaken. It brought him around for a moment. The spent cartridge had two electrodes on its front he could use to drive stun. Aaron let go with one hand and grabbed the Taser. He shoved the electrodes against the hand over his mouth and pulled the trigger.

With a roar of pain He let go, and Aaron flopped on the frozen ground hard, gasping for air. It stunned him for a moment. The blackness threatened to overwhelm him again. When it cleared, he found that he still had the Taser in his hand. Aaron shoved the Taser under His fur robe and pressed it against the inner thigh. He pulled the trigger. The Taser clicked through its cycle. Sparks crackled under the robe. With a sharp shriek, He slapped the Taser from Aaron's grasp.

Something popped in Aaron's wrist from the blow. His fingers went numb followed by dragsters of pain racing up to his elbow.

The giant's leg stopped working from the stun. He fell on one knee.

Aaron was on his feet in a second and running for the cabin. At the bottom of the hill, Summer was away from the cabin coming up the hill with a butcher knife in her hand.

"Get back inside," Aaron screamed.

She stopped. Her terror-filled eyes told him He was back on his feet and coming. Aaron didn't turn around. It would slow him down. Instead he poured on the coals, holding his throbbing right hand against his body to keep it from hitting anything.

Aaron leaped on the cabin's steps not knowing how much of a lead he had. He went through the door, slammed it shut with his good hand, and rammed his shoulder against the door as Summer threw the two by four cross piece in place. When He hit the door, the concussion sent Aaron sprawling.

He fell on his injured wrist and cried out as pain screeched through his arm. Sobbing from the pain and holding his hurt hand against his stomach, he got off the floor and threw his back against the door, holding it while Summer wedged the ladder rail in place and nailed the rung on the floor solid. For the next ten minutes He banged on the door with his fists, but mainly roaring his anger from being hurt by the Taser. The door held.

When He was gone—or when they thought He was gone, because they never knew for sure unless He was in the root cellar, and He wasn't there—they sat with their backs against the door shaking.

"He didn't leave the root cellar until right before you came back," Summer said. Tears glistened on her cheeks. She was shaking. "It followed your tracks, and he must have heard you coming. It's when he hid behind the brush pile. I'm sorry. I tried warning you. I'm so sorry."

"It's okay," Aaron said.

He put his good arm around her shoulder and gave it a squeeze. She might not need a hug, but right now, *he* needed one.

She slid closer, put her arms around his waist and hugged him back. "Did you get the call made?" she asked, looking at him.

Aaron nodded. "They should be on their way soon." He flexed his sore wrist. It was throbbing. He could close it in a loose fist, but he couldn't squeeze it tight.

"What happened to your hand?" she asked.

"I broke something."

Summer took his hand and, starting at his fingers, squeezed it gently, working her way down the hand. "Does that hurt?"

"No."

When she got to below his thumb, Aaron winced.

"There it is," he said. It was swelling already.

She let go of his hand and stood. "While I was waiting, I went through Bob's things," she said. "He has some bandages over there. Let me see if I can fix you up a little."

She went over and opened the green footlocker sitting on the floor by the bed. In a moment she was back with a clear plastic container, a garden seed catalog and a *Field and Stream* magazine.

"We'll use these as a splint," she said holding up the catalog and magazine. She folded the catalog in half and held it out to Aaron.

Aaron put his hurt wrist in the catalog and held it in place with the other hand. She placed the folded magazine on top of the catalog, opened the container, took out a roll of white tape and taped the two of them together.

"This should at least stabilize it," she said as she wrapped everything tightly with a beige elastic bandage from the container. She stopped suddenly and looked at him with her eyes wide again. "I forgot to tell you," she said. "I know who *he* is."

Chapter Twenty Three

"He's Bob's son, Bridger," Summer said as she continued wrapping the elastic bandage around Aaron's wrist.

Her concentration was on getting the wrist wrapped right, but Aaron couldn't see any sign she was joking, and this wasn't a joking situation. "How do you know?"

"I found some spiral notebooks Bob had been using as journals," Summer said. "He detailed everything from the time he picked his son up in Washington State until yesterday. It was the last entry in the journal." She stopped wrapping and looked at him. "I think he was leaving a record so people would know what was going on if he died and they found his son out here. Anyway, the last entry in the journal was made right before he died."

"How do you know?"

"Because it says he was going in the cellar to kill his son," Summer said.

"Then he was going to kill himself."

It didn't clarify anything. "Start at the beginning," Aaron said. "Because I didn't know Bob had any kids."

"I didn't either," she said, "but according to the notebooks, he married his high school sweetheart after he graduated from college. The kid was born normal, but as he grew, his body deformed. It must have been that gigantism thing you were talking about." Again she pronounced it *giantism*. "By the time he was five, they could tell he would be grossly deformed by the time he was an adult. His head grew in unusual ways, and he had some mental problems as well."

Aaron nodded. It would explain how Bob knew he carried a genetic defect.

"In the notebooks, Bob says Bridger couldn't talk, and he didn't have any emotions except extreme ones," Summer said. "Bob called it alexithymia—I'm not sure I'm pronouncing it right. He had no empathy or emotional attachment to anyone, but he would fly into rages at times. Dysphoria is what Bob called it."

It was like listening to Chantel. "How can he not have emotions and still fly into a rage? A rage is an emotion isn't it?"

"I don't know. I'm telling you what I read," Summer said. "There are places in the journals where Bob locked himself in the cabin for hours because Bridger was in a rage. He would drag his bed against the wall with two legs on the trap door and the headboard against the freezer door. He'd sit on the bed so Bridger couldn't break into the cabin." She looked up from her wrapping. "Bob didn't come right out and say it, but I think he was afraid of Bridger."

It explained why the two-by-four cross bar had been put on the door. "So how did Bridger get here?"

"When he got older, they knew they couldn't care of him at home. They finally put him in a private institution, The Gettford Sanitarium." Summer said. "It was a pricey place, but the way it sounds his first wife's family had money and could afford it.

"Bob divorced his wife shortly afterward and moved here," Summer said. "It sounds as if he went back out there a few times at first and saw his son, but with Bridger not forming any attachments, Bob said it was as if he was some stranger. It sounds like Bridger treated everyone like a stranger, even his mother. He didn't make any connections on an emotional level, so Bob stopped going."

It would be part of the decreased mental capacity Chantel had talked about, Aaron decided. "Go on."

"Bob's first wife got remarried. She got brain cancer, and as soon as she lost coherency, her husband put Bridger in a state institution. My guess is he wasn't about to shell out money for Gettford. He sounded like a real ass," Summer said. "When Bob went out for the funeral, he stopped and saw Bridger. Bob wrote they were treating his son like an animal. They kept him locked in a little room and heavily sedated twenty-four-seven."

"How could they get away with it?" Aaron asked. "Every state must have rules governing the care of patients."

"I'm sure they do," Summer said. "But they were afraid of him, because Bridger is so big and powerful. I guess when he first went into the state institution, he went into a rage. It took the entire staff to subdue him. People were injured with broken bones and one guy was put in a coma for a time. After that, they didn't take any chances, and they used the safety of the institution as an excuse."

"His mother didn't leave a trust or something for the son's care?"

"The way I read it, her family had something in their will about Bridger being cared for, but she left it at the discretion of her husband. He must've fooled her into believing he cared about the kid," Summer said. "If anyone contested what he did, the husband would argue that as long as Bridger was being cared for, he met the terms of the will."

"Was Bob going to contest it?"

"He wanted to, but the guy had more money than Bob," Summer said.

She finished with the elastic bandage and wrapped a layer of tape over it.

"Bob spoke with a Dr. Newton at Gettford. He was the one who had been in charge of Bridger's case. He said Bridger needed to be kept busy all the time. He had ADHD and a lot of energy. They had kept him busy doing something all the time when he was at Gettford, sweeping or walking around the grounds. They never had a problem with him. He was fine."

She finished with the tape. "Is that going to work?"

Aaron tried flexing his wrist. The splint held it rigid. It still hurt, but much better than before. "It'll work," he said. "Thanks."

She put the tape back in the container. "Anyway, Bob wanted to bring Bridger back to Iowa and take care of him," Summer said, "but the doctor said Bridger couldn't survive out in public. He had no emotional attachments, so he couldn't adapt to being around people. He'd never adjust to their customs and mores. Also, if he went into a rage, they would throw him in jail, and he would spend the rest of his life there, or in another state institution."

"And that's where the refuge comes in," Aaron said. "It would keep him isolated from people."

"Exactly," Summer said. "The doctor said Bridger could learn basic things, and he didn't need human companionship. In fact, he spurned it. Bob figured the refuge would be the perfect place for him."

It was Bob rationalizing. He didn't have the money to put Bridger in a private place where he could do things and live a normal life. The only other choice was leaving him in the state institution in a drug-induced coma.

"So how did Bob get them to let him take Bridger?" Aaron asked. "If the state was paying for his care, I'm sure there was some court order giving the state guardianship."

"That part wasn't clear," Summer said. "Bob mentions an attorney and a judge out in Washington, but nothing specific."

Since Bob was the father, Aaron imagined it wouldn't take much to get the guardianship transferred to him. He'd give them a story about moving Bridger to a facility in Iowa. Nobody would fight it. The state institution would gladly get rid of him. The entire staff, including the doctors, were worried that one day they would walk into Bridger's room and somebody would have forgotten to give him his medication, or maybe his body would develop a resistance to the drug, and they would be the next one in a coma.

"So how did Bob get him back here?" Aaron asked.

"He rented an enclosed trailer," Summer said.

"You're kidding?"

"No," Summer said. "He threw a mattress in the back and away they went."

Aaron figured the institution would jump at the chance of getting rid of Bridger. They would have given Bridger enough medication to make a gorilla into a house pet. They wouldn't have cared as long as he was gone. Once the U-Haul was out of their state, he was someone else's problem. "And it worked?"

"Bob wasn't specific, but it sounded as if he might have had a problem or two along the way," Summer said. "But they finally made it."

"And that's why Bob spent all his time at the refuge?"

"Exactly," Summer said. "Bob was getting Bridger settled in. Bob planned from the beginning to put Bridger at this cabin. He knew no one had used it in years. He dug the cellar with the outside entrance so Bridger could hide there if anyone came around. He must have put in the door in the floor later."

"And it went well?"

"Bob wrote he was extremely pleased with the results," Summer said. "Although he was disappointed because they never had any kind of connection. The way it sounded, Bridger tolerated Bob, but Bob was hoping there would be a father and son bond. It never happened."

Because of his mental condition, he didn't have the emotions to develop a connection with anyone. Aaron made a mental note to ask Chantel about all of this when they got out of there … if they got out of there.

"He taught Bridger how to hunt," Summer said. "Bob wrote he was amazed how good of a hunter he was."

"Bob allowed hunting in the refuge?"

"It surprised me, too," Summer said. "But Bob wrote that Bridger was like an animal. He didn't use any weapon but the corn knife, and he hunted for food only. Bob still didn't hunt. By the way, the robe Bridger wears is made from Scottish Highland cattle. Bob found the ones that got away from Stan McGregor frozen in the refuge. He skinned them and made the robe. He thought it would be good winter camouflage for Bridger."

Aaron nodded. It was how Bob came up with the bogus story about Jesse seeing a Highland cow at the farm service.

"Bob wrote that Bridger was ranging farther and farther because game was scarce," Summer said. "It worried Bob. He was afraid Bridger would go off the refuge and people would see him. By the way, the reason Bob didn't want beef at the cabin was because he was afraid Bridger would get the taste for beef and hunt some farmer's cattle. Many farmers put their cattle out in the fields in the fall to clean up the corn the combines missed."

It made sense. A farmer who found a half-eaten steer out in his field would demand answers. "What about the wild hogs?" Aaron asked. "Wasn't he afraid Bridger would go after domesticated hogs if he got the taste for pork?"

Summer shrugged. "He doesn't mention anything about it. My guess would be that most farmers raise hogs in confinements, and there aren't any confinements around the refuge.

"After Bob got his retirement deal and moved out here in the cabin, there's not much in the journals," Summer said. "Their lives must have been fairly routine. There are long periods of time in the journals where Bob didn't write anything. A few times there would be a date and a short notation: *Bridger was in one of his moods. I spent the day locked in the cabin.* Other than things like that, there is nothing for a long time until after we left here two days ago."

"He knew Bridger killed Hemper," Aaron said. He had known Bob knew something when he saw the look on his face.

"I don't know if he knew right away," Summer said. "He might have suspected something, but when he was out getting wood for the stove, he saw Bridger twenty yards away crouched and trying to stay hidden as he slowly came toward Bob. Bob wrote he had seen predators stalking prey, and Bridger was stalking him."

"And *then* he knew Bridger had killed Hemper."

She nodded. "Bob thought Bridger couldn't have seen well in the blizzard. He saw a form and investigated. If Hemper ran or made panicky noises, it would have triggered the predator instinct in Bridger."

Pug had said Hemper was sobbing and crying when he butt-dialed him. "So Bob was going to kill Bridger."

"I don't think he knew what else to do," Summer said. "He wouldn't lock him in another mental institution or the psychiatric ward of a prison hospital."

And something happened. Either Bob was nervous, tripped and did the header into the root cellar, or Bridger did something and caused his fall. Aaron didn't know, and it didn't matter at this point. Maybe Bridger killed him outright.

"When we leave, make sure we take the journals with us," Aaron said. "I'll go through them in detail when we get back, no matter how this turns out."

"They're over by the cellar door," she said, standing. "I was reading them when I was listening for Bridger to leave."

She stepped toward the cellar door and stopped suddenly. "Do you hear that?"

Aaron expected to hear the despicable sound like a bag of flour being dragged across the floor. Instead he heard the faint but unmistakable roar of distant snowmobiles.

Chapter Twenty Four

If Aaron hadn't looked at his watch when he first heard the snowmobiles, it would have seemed hours had passed before the knock came at the door. It was 23 minutes. And even though they were waiting for them, they both jumped at the pounding.

"Aaron, are you in there?" Sheriff Thompson's voice asked nervously from the other side of the door.

"We're here," Aaron said.

They stood and Summer helped him remove the barricades on the door. When they opened it, Aaron was surprised how dark it was outside. They had lit a few candles after Bridger had gone, but the windows were so small in the cabin that after a certain point it was hard to notice the difference in the outside light.

Sheriff Thompson stood in the doorway holding an old M-16 rifle. Aaron guessed he had gotten it from the military in one of their lend programs. The guy beside the sheriff was shorter and heavyset. He wore a black snowmobile suit with gold Cossack County Sheriff Department shoulder patches on the sleeves and sergeant's stripes below them. A black stocking cap was pulled over his ears, and Aaron would have bet it covered a bald head, he had that look. A Bushmaster M4 lay nonchalantly over his shoulder. His relaxed posture told Aaron he didn't believe a word about an eight-foot tall homicidal maniac.

The sheriff stepped inside. "Are you two okay?" he asked, looking at Aaron's wrapped wrist. The heavyset guy followed with the rifle still on his shoulder.

Aaron held up his wrist. "I'll be okay."

"So, where's this monster?" the heavyset guy asked, his voice filled with skepticism.

"We don't know," Summer said.

"Monsters are like that," the guy said smirking. "They just disappear sometimes."

If Aaron's dominant hand hadn't been injured, he might have knocked the smirk off the guy's face. Summer stepped toward the guy, and Aaron thought she might have a go at it.

"It's Bob's son, Bridger," she said loudly. "He has gigantism and mental problems. Do you think we would make this stuff up?"

"I'm not saying there's not someone out here," the guy said, still smirking, "It's the eight feet, four hundred pounds I'm having trouble with. When people get scared, their imagination runs wild. They see all kinds of things that aren't there."

"And who are you?" Aaron asked.

"This is my sergeant, John Sanders," the sheriff said.

Aaron didn't offer his hand because his right hand was bandaged, but he doubted he would have shaken his hand even if it hadn't been. This was the guy who had made Jesse change his first report about the tracks and who had let a dispatcher sit in on an interrogation, so he could have some lasagna, Aaron guessed.

"We have notebooks Bob left detailing everything," Aaron said. He could have told him about the DNA tests and the footprints Jesse had seen, but he didn't care if the guy believed him or not. He decided he'd ignore Sanders as much as possible. "Is it just the two of you?" Aaron asked the sheriff.

"Jack Simpson is back with the snowmobiles. He's the one who got us out here." Sheriff Thompson said. "When we saw what happened to your snowmobiles, we left him with ours. John wanted to bring the SWAT team, but I didn't want to take the time to get them all together. You sounded urgent on the phone."

"It wouldn't have taken long," Sanders said. "We train for quick responses."

Aaron had hoped they would have brought more people and a cargo sled so they could have taken Bob's body with them, but he hadn't said anything about it when he'd called. He hadn't been thinking clearly. Watching your back to see if a monster is stalking you spoils your concentration. It didn't matter now. They could get out of here and come back with more officers. Aaron would get an arrest warrant for Bridger. He still couldn't prove he had killed Hemper or Bob, but he could get a warrant for attempted murder. There was plenty of probable cause from when Bridger had grabbed him by the throat. It didn't matter what the warrant was for. There would never be a trial. If Bridger was as mentally handicapped as Bob's writings suggested, he'd be committed to some mental institution. When they came back, they'd take Bob's body and Bridger … if they could take him alive.

"I hope Jack is armed," Summer said.

"He's got a shotgun with double ought buckshot," Sanders said.

Summer nodded.

"So Cal here says Bob's dead," Sanders said. "Where's his body?"

"It's in the root cellar," Summer said pointing at the chair by the cellar door on the other side of the room.

"Let's check it out," Sanders said. "I want to see for myself."

"Let's get out of here," the sheriff said, looking around nervously. "We can come back when it's light out, and we have more people."

Sanders ignored him and went over to the cellar door. "I see you got this thing secured pretty good." He kicked the ladder rail nailed across the trap door and looked over at the freezer door nailed shut.

"He tried to get in," Summer said. "We secured everything so he couldn't." She kneeled by the cellar door and listened.

"Usually we can hear him moving around if he's there. I don't hear anything now."

A smirk touched Sanders' face. "So you've never actually had a good look at him?"

"When he had me by the throat, I got a good up-close-and-personal look," Aaron said.

"It must have scared the hell out of you?" Sanders asked.

Aaron didn't answer. He knew what he was insinuating: he was scared and fear enhanced things; it had made the guy bigger than he was, but Aaron knew what he had seen and what Bob had written in his journals. He no longer cared what Sanders thought. The more he talked, the less Aaron liked this guy and his cocky attitude.

"You got something we can open this with?" Sanders asked, easing his bulk on one knee beside the ladder rail.

Summer got the hammer by the door and pulled the nails out of the ladder rail. Sanders jerked the hammer away from her as if she was a ten-year-old and an adult needed to finish the job. She was visibly offended and looked at Aaron for support.

He shrugged. Welcome to the club.

After Sanders removed the rail, he tried to open the door, but it caught on the surface bolt. Aaron bent over and with his good hand slid it out of the way.

Sanders produced a Maglite from inside his snowmobile suit, opened the cellar door and shined it in the cellar. The light produced a brilliant white cone like a spotlight, ending abruptly on the edge of the circle of light.

Bob's body had been moved. The top of his head was the only thing visible through the opening. A dark stain of dried blood covered two stones on the floor where his head had laid before.

"That's Bob, I assume?" Sanders said.

Summer nodded. "Yeah."

"It looks like he just fell," Sanders said. "What makes you think he was murdered?"

"I never said he was murdered," Aaron said. "How he died doesn't change anything." This guy was cocky and dumb. An interesting combination that Aaron liked less and less all the time.

"Well I'm going down to check this out," Sanders said.

"I've already checked him out," Aaron said. "I guarantee he's dead." There was no logical reason for him going in the cellar.

"I want to look things over myself," Sanders said.

"Watch out," Summer said. "There's an outside entrance. He could come in from there."

Sanders smiled. "I'm not worried." He displayed the M4 with one hand.

"Do you want me to go with you?" Sheriff Thompson asked, sounding as if he wanted the answer to be *no*.

"It's okay, Cal," Sanders said. "There's not enough room for both of us. Cover me from up here while I check it out."

He got on his knees and shined the flashlight toward the back of the cellar, putting his head through the opening in the floor and looking as far as he could to the back. "Grab my belt, Cal," he said.

The sheriff got on his knees beside Sanders and grabbed the back of Sanders' belt through his snowmobile suit.

Sanders leaned even farther into the hole. "I don't see nothing there but Bob." He pulled his head out of the hole and stood. "You got a ladder?"

"We took it apart," Summer said. She pushed the rail they'd taken off the cellar door with her toe.

"Never mind," Sanders said. He handed the sheriff his M4. "Hold this, Cal."

He put a hand on the floor and dropped through the opening into the cellar. A loud thump came from the darkness below followed by a quick stumbling sound. Something bumped into something. Sanders cursed, followed by loud machine gun-like pops, as if Sanders had knocked over a shelf of glass jars.

"You okay?" the sheriff asked.

"I twisted my ankle," Sanders called out from the dark.

Aaron wasn't surprised. He couldn't believe he would drop into a dark place without even a weapon.

The Sheriff pulled his Maglite out of his pocket and lit the cellar from above. The floor was littered with broken glass, yellow Mason jar rims, and dark wet spots spreading across the stone floor. The pungent smell of sauerkraut floated out of the hole.

"Can you walk?" Sheriff Thompson asked.

"Yeah. It's sprained, but not too bad," Sanders said. He stood against the wall with one hand holding his ankle. He limped a few steps. "I'll be okay."

"Do you need your rifle?" the sheriff asked.

"No, let me check the body, and I'll get out of here," Sanders said.

He turned on his Maglite, limped over to the body and knelt on one knee. The glow of the flashlight filled the cellar with shadows.

"He cracked his head open," Sanders said. His voice sounded hollow coming through the opening. "This isn't a murder."

Aaron didn't argue with him. He'd have to care what Sanders thought to argue with him.

"Can we get him out of there so we can take him back?" Sheriff Thompson asked.

"Did you bring a cargo sled?" Summer asked.

"No. But we could put him on one of the snowmobiles," the sheriff said.

"Are you going to strap him across the hood like a deer?" Summer asked.

"Well, no," the sheriff said sounding sheepish.

"You say there's a back door out of this?" Sanders asked. The glow of the Maglite disappeared for a moment as he shined it at the back of the cellar. "Okay. I see it. We could—"

The way he cut off the end of the sentence and the strange pause that followed sent a shiver through Aaron. Something was wrong.

"John, are you okay?" Sheriff Thompson asked. No answer. "John?"

"His legs are gone," Sanders said in a shocked whisper. "Something's been eating his legs. All that's left is the bones." He stood and backed away from the body. His light never left the back of the cellar. "Get me out of here."

Sanders glanced at them and his wide eyes showed he had become a true believer in an eight foot-tall, 400-pound man who killed and ate people.

"Get me out of here," he said again, shouting. "Find something I can stand on."

Summer grabbed a chair and handed it through the cellar opening. "Try this."

Sanders stood on the chair, but his arms didn't go through the hole even to his elbows. The sheriff and Summer tried pulling him up. It appeared the fat man had a better chance of pulling them into the cellar then they had of getting him out. With his injured hand, Aaron could only watch.

"You'll have to go through the outside entrance," Summer said.

Sanders looked nervously at the back of the cellar. "Hand me my rifle."

The sheriff handed him the M4.

"You guys go outside and make sure nothing is out there waiting for me," Sanders said. "I'll be coming out of here blind."

The sheriff released him and stood. "We'll meet you outside."

Sanders disappeared from view as he limped toward the back of the cellar.

Sheriff Thompson closed the trap door and picked his M16 off the floor. "Let's go."

"Wait a minute," Summer said, grabbing the sheriff's sleeve. "Do you have a pistol under your snowmobile suit?"

"Yeah. Why?"

"It would be nice to have a weapon."

Sheriff Thompson dug a pistol out from under his suit. He handed it to Summer.

She checked the magazine, slapped it back into place and racked the weapon so a round was in the chamber. "Thanks. Let's go," she said.

The outside had turned black. With a heavy cloud cover, everything was dark, even the white snow didn't show up. Sheriff Thompson turned on his flashlight. He whipped it around continuously, checking everywhere. The light's beam went across Aaron eyes, blinding him for a second and destroying his night vision. For a moment he couldn't see anything. He closed his eyes and waited for the white spots to leave.

"Are you guys out there?" Sanders yelled from the far side of the cabin.

"We're around the side of the cabin," Sheriff Thompson yelled back.

"You're clear this way," Summer yelled.

Aaron opened his eyes and the beam from Sanders' Maglite came around the cabin. The light was now mounted on the barrel of the M4. The deep snow made

Sanders' limp more pronounced than it had been on the level cellar floor.

"Let's go back inside and I'll wrap your ankle," Summer said.

Sanders shook his head. "It's okay. I'll be fine. Let's get to the sleds and get out of here," Sanders said. "I'll get my SWAT team together, and we'll come back out in the morning when it's light."

Aaron didn't know what this local SWAT team of Sanders' was like. He'd watched the state's SWAT team train a few times. Usually they ran a mile and a half and did calisthenics before they started. Most team members ran on their own daily and lifted weights off-duty. Sanders was at least 30 pounds overweight, didn't have enough strength to crawl out of the cellar and Aaron doubted he could run a mile and a half if Bridger was chasing him with the corn knife. When they got back, Aaron would get in touch with the highway patrol's SWAT team. If they wanted Sanders' team assisting, that was their call, but Aaron wouldn't put this in the hands of any team Sanders headed.

"Do you have a pistol?" Aaron asked.

"Yeah. Why?" Sanders asked.

"It would be nice to have a weapon."

"Can you shoot left-handed?" For a moment Aaron didn't think Sanders was going to let him have the pistol.

"The state course requires we shoot with the strong and weak hand," Aaron said. "You should know that."

Sanders dug a .40 Smith and Wesson out from inside his snowmobile suit and handed it to Aaron.

Tyler Brown, the department's firearms instructor, had once told Aaron he'd be better off throwing the gun at the bad guy than trying to shoot him with his weak hand. He would have a better chance of doing damage, because he was that bad at shooting with his weak hand. But Aaron figured if Bridger grabbed him by the throat again, he could hit him at that range with either hand.

Aaron handed Summer the pistol. "Check it and make sure it's ready to go?" He couldn't pop the magazine or operate the slide one-handed.

She checked it quickly and handed it back to him. "It's good to go," she said. "There's already one in the chamber."

"I'll take the lead," Sanders said. "Summer you follow me and watch the right side. Aaron you have the left. Cal, you cover our six."

The sheriff looked nervous, still whipping the Maglite around. Aaron kept his head down so he wouldn't be blinded again.

The trail from the cabin was well-worn now. Aaron and Summer had made three trips on it, and Sanders and the sheriff had made one, and that didn't count the ones Bridger had made. Walking was easy on the packed snow, but the absolute black of the night gave Bridger a thousand places he could hide and ambush them. It bothered Aaron that they hadn't seen him since before the snowmobiles had arrived. He hoped Bridger had heard the snowmobiles and had gone off someplace more solitary to avoid all the people who were suddenly there. Those hopes were dashed when they came over the last pile of brush where the snowmobiles were parked.

"What the hell happened?" Sanders said. The snowmobiles lay methodically smashed, not overturned in a rage the way Aaron's and Summer's had been. The hoods were ripped off and wire and spark plugs had been broken. Bridger had learned something.

"Where's Jack?" the sheriff asked in a breathless whisper.

"Jack?" Summer called.

"Jack?" Sanders repeated.

"Shine your light this way," Summer said.

Sanders joined her and shined his light on the ground as she knelt in the snow.

"I have Bridger's snowshoe tracks going south," she said. "And Jack must have gotten a shot off before he ran." She picked up a piece of snow and rubbed it between her gloved fingers and studied it. "There's a blood trail alongside the footprints."

"How much blood?" Aaron asked.

"A lot," she answered. "If this was a deer, I'd find it within fifty yards with it bleeding this much."

"Let's follow it," Sanders said.

"No. We're going back and getting help. We'll come back when we have more people," Sheriff Thompson said, saying it as an order.

Sanders ignored him and followed the blood trail with Summer beside him like a professional tracker following wounded game. Aaron dropped in behind them, and reluctantly the sheriff brought up the rear.

The trail led around the side of a hill into trees much bigger than the scrub oak that had filled the refuge in all the areas Aaron had been before. Back there it was thick and overgrown without a trail. Most of the limbs overlapped. They barely squeezed through, brush and tree limbs dragging across them and scratching their faces as they passed. Aaron was amazed Bridger could squeeze his huge bulk through it. The sheriff still whipped his flashlight around in all directions. Occasionally the Maglite's beam lit blood smears on branches.

Aaron examined them as he went by. A shotgun with double ought buck shot does a lot of damage. Jack had to have gotten a solid hit for there to be that much blood. Aaron was expecting they'd find Bridger's body ahead somewhere. He hoped they'd find Bridger's body.

After fifty yards, Summer abruptly stopped. She studied the ground with Sanders guiding the Maglite.

"The blood trail's gone," she said. "I still have footprints, but there's no blood."

"Did he stop bleeding?" Aaron asked.

"I don't know," she said. "There was a lot of blood a little bit ago. Now there's none. You wouldn't think he'd stop bleeding all at once."

"I've got a big smear of blood back here on this tree," The sheriff said from the rear of the line.

His flashlight lit the trunk of an oak tree five yards behind where Summer stood. The sheriff shined it into the tree and screamed.

Chapter Twenty Five

The sheriff's scream was long and shrill. He turned away from the tree, staggered a few steps, dropped to his knees and vomited.

Aaron ran over with the other two and looked into the tree. Wedged in a crotch ten feet off the ground was Jack Simpson. His head hung down with the back of it cleaved open. Grayish white brains, like a slimy mushroom, oozed out of the crack in his skull.

"That explains the blood trail," Summer said in a shocked voice. "He was carrying Jack."

Aaron looked at the sheriff on his knees still whimpering. He hadn't come up through the ranks. When you haven't been a road deputy there are a lot of things you never see. Most of what a sheriff did was done in the office and at meetings. When he was called out on something, everything was already over but the shouting. The ambulance crew or coroner had hauled the victim away, the danger had passed, things had been cleaned up and there were enough officers around that he was never in danger. Cal Thompson hadn't signed up for any of this when he ran for sheriff.

Sanders dropped beside the sheriff, grabbed him by the shoulders and shook him. "You got to pull yourself together, Cal." It looked as if he might slap the sheriff.

"We have to get out of here," Sheriff Thompson said. He sounded on the verge of hysteria. "We have to get back to Calvin."

"We'll go back to the cabin," Aaron said.

"No. We're getting out of here," the sheriff said shouting. He was crying. "We're not going back to the damn cabin."

"We'll go back to the cabin," Aaron said again. "We'll wait until daylight and walk out of here."

"No," the sheriff shouted. "I'm not spending the night out here. We're getting out of here now. I'm the sheriff. I order it."

"Cal look at your Maglite," Sanders said, taking the sheriff's hand and holding it and the flashlight in front of his face. "It's already pissing a yellow stream. In another hour the battery will be dead. Mine is the same way. Do you want to be out here stumbling around in the dark without any lights? Let's go back to the cabin and wait until daylight."

The sheriff's eyes were wild. "*He* could be at the cabin."

"I hope so," Sanders said. The terror in the sheriff's face was matched by the anger in Sanders' voice. "I'll run a Mozambique Drill on his ass. Double tap the chest and one to the head. Then we won't have to worry about the son of a bitch."

"What do we do about Jack?" the sheriff asked in a softer voice as Sanders helped him to his feet.

"We'll leave him here until we come back tomorrow," Aaron said. "He's in the tree so the coyotes can't get at him."

"It's why Bridger put him there," Summer whispered so only Aaron could hear. "He was caching his food."

It made Aaron shudder, but he guessed she was right.

"Cal, why don't you give your rifle and flashlight to Aaron," Sanders said and looked at Aaron's wrapped hand. "Or give it to Summer. She can cover the rear, and we'll put you in the middle where you'll be safer."

"No," the sheriff said and clutched the M-16 tightly to his chest. It was obvious he wasn't going to trade down in firepower.

"At least give her the flashlight," Aaron suggested.

"No," he said again and blew out an anguished sob. "I'm sorry I lost it for a minute. I've known Jack all my life." His voice broke on the last word, and he paused a moment regaining his composure. "But I'll be all right. I'm okay now."

Aaron nodded as did the other two, but he didn't believe the sheriff could have hit *okay* with a sniper's rifle. There wasn't much they could do short of forcibly taking the rifle and flashlight away from him. That wasn't something they needed right then.

"Okay, everybody huddle up here," Sanders said. Everybody gathered together. "Here's what we're going to do. His tracks run toward the cabin. We'll follow them."

"No," the sheriff said. "Let's go back the way we came."

Sanders shook his head. "I want to know where he is, Cal. We keep him in front of us, and we know the threat will come from the front. If we go off another way, he can come at us from any side."

Aaron suspected Sanders didn't want Bridger attacking from the rear where the sheriff was. Sanders was overweight, out-of-shape, and he told rookies to change their reports, but he knew his stuff. Aaron had gained some respect for him.

"If he changes direction, we'll break off and go straight for the cabin," Sanders said. "Everybody understand?"

Aaron nodded.

"Okay, we'll go with the same order in the stack as before," Sanders said. "Me first, then Summer, followed by Aaron, and Cal watching our rear. Everybody pay attention to your area. You two in the center without lights, if you see something move or something suspicious, sing out and we'll check it before we move on."

They got in their line, huddled together so close they touched, and moved slowly forward with Sanders limping and lighting the front with the Maglite mounted on his M4. After a couple hundred yards when the trees got smaller and the brush came in clumps, Sanders stopped.

"Summer, what was he doing here?" Sanders asked.

Summer looked around his shoulder at the tracks.

"He turned around and checked his back trail," she said. "He might know we're following him."

The sheriff let out a gasp.

"It's okay. Cal," Sanders said calmly. "He's still going in the same direction, so we should be okay. He's running from us and we have him outnumbered. Cover your area. Pay attention to our rear."

But Sheriff Thompson didn't pay attention to the rear. His flashlight's beam went everywhere as they moved, flashing both sides, the rear and even lighting up Sanders in the front. After putting up with it for a while, Sanders abruptly stopped. His weapon was still pointed toward the front but his head was turned as he glared at the sheriff.

"Dammit, Cal," Sanders shouted. Aaron could tell he'd had it. "You've got to keep your light to the rear. And get your finger off that friggin' trigger. You're going to kill someo—"

His words were cut short. Aaron saw a flash of white, and Sanders' head left his shoulders, spinning in one full revolution and spraying blood like a fireworks pinwheel. Blood shot straight up from his severed neck. His body collapsed, the knees buckling first and the rest of the body folding on the ground in a heap. Sanders' loose head hit his chest and bounced off into the snow.

"John?" the sheriff gasped, his face drained of color and filled with horror.

For a moment he stared in shock at the grisly sight twitching on the ground. He gasped and pulled the trigger of the M-16 with the selector switch on full-auto.

The concussion of the muzzle blasts banged against Aaron's back and neck like a jackhammer. The bullets zipped by within inches of his ear. Aaron grabbed Summer by the waist and tackled her to the ground out of the line of fire. He landed hard on his sore wrist, his screams of pain drowned out by the popping of the M-16 as the sheriff emptied the twenty-shot magazine in one long burst. The last bullets rattled in the top tree branches as the muzzle of the M16 climbed skyward.

Sheriff Thompson stood in stunned silence with the smoking breech of the rifle locked open and empty. Anything resembling *okay* had vanished. His flight response kicked in. He fled back the way they'd come. His flashlight bounced through the trees, growing fainter and fainter as the distance grew. Twice he tripped, fell and quickly scrambled to his feet and kept running.

Summer crawled to her knees, pointing her pistol where Bridger had been when he decapitated Sanders. She stuffed the pistol in her pocket and grabbed the M4 off the ground. The attached Maglite on the barrel glowed a dull pink from Sanders' blood covering the lens. She wiped it with snow and stood, checking in all directions. Sanders' quivering body lay in front of her. His loose head face-up in the snow beside his waist, the shiny, unblinking eyes lit by the glow of the Maglite.

"I think Bridger's gone." Summer said, her voice and hands shook. She pointed the M4 and flashlight at the ground. "Here's where he waited for us."

Behind a chest-high bush were the melted knee and handprints where Bridger had crouched. Beside them in the snow was the imprint where the corn knife had lain.

"He backtracked and set up the ambush," Summer said.

Aaron studied the impressions. Bridger may have been mentally challenged, but he could plan.

"He went that way," Summer said, motioning at a right angle from the way they had been going. "His footprints are far apart. He's running."

There was a good chance Bridger had never heard a gun before. Bob didn't have any, and firearms weren't allowed on the refuge. Maybe Bridger had heard some from a distance during hunting season, but Aaron doubted he'd ever heard one as up close as he just had. Aaron hoped it had scared the hell out of him and sent him running a long ways away to hide for a while. Maybe for a couple days … or at least until they got out of the refuge.

"Is there any blood?" Aaron asked. "Did Sheriff Thompson hit him?"

Summer cautiously followed the tracks a little ways. "I don't see anything. That spray and pray stuff normally doesn't get you anything."

She stopped and looked back at Aaron. Splatters of Sanders' blood dotted her face. She was doing a good job of holding it together, but she looked terrified. And why wouldn't she be? This was not how she thought the day would go when they'd gotten on the snowmobiles to ask Bob a few more questions.

"What do we do now?" she asked.

"We keep going to the cabin and wait for daylight," Aaron said.

"What about Cal?"

"There's nothing we can do for him," Aaron said. "We don't know where he is, and we don't have enough battery life in the flashlight to look for him." Aaron knew it was a butthole thing to do, but as Mr. Spock said: "The needs of the many outweighs the needs of the few." There were only two of them, but right now they were the many.

Summer nodded in agreement. "I don't think we're far from the cabin. If I'm right, we go around this hill and we should hit the creek leading to it."

She was right. They rounded the hill and there lay the creek with the well-beaten path in the center of it.

"Do you see any of Bridger's tracks?" Aaron asked as he stepped into the path.

Summer looked around with the flashlight. "Nothing new. There are some of his snowshoe tracks, but our footprints from when we left the cabin are over the top of them. He hasn't been this way since we came through."

That was good. Aaron hoped he was still running from the gunfire and had found a place to hide on the other side of the refuge. He didn't want him back in this area until tomorrow after they had walked out.

Summer led the way to the cabin with Aaron following. She kept the M4 locked on her shoulder at the ready and checked everything carefully before moving on. The Maglite was quickly losing power and didn't light anything beyond ten yards. The cloud cover had drawn back and opened the sky. A sliver of silver moon brightened the snow enough to fool Aaron into believing he could see.

When they reached the cabin, the door stood wide open.

"Didn't we close the door when we left?" Summer asked. Her voice trembled.

Aaron couldn't remember, but they couldn't stay outside all night. "Let's check it out."

"I'll go in first," Summer said. "You watch the left side, and I'll take the right."

Aaron swallowed. His arms puckered with gooseflesh. "Remember, two to the chest and one to the head," Aaron whispered.

Summer went into the cabin and Aaron followed going left. The darkness inside the cabin made Aaron blind. Even the pistol in his hand was invisible. Bridger could have been standing in front of him within touching distance holding the corn knife cocked back and ready to swing, and Aaron wouldn't have known it. Summer swung the Maglite around the inside of the cabin, lighting it as much as the weak yellow stream could. When it lit the area in front of him, Aaron cringed, but it was empty.

The cabin didn't have any place big enough to hide someone eight feet tall. As soon as they were sure it was empty, they barred the door with the crosspiece and ladder rail.

"Now what?" Summer asked.

Aaron laid his pistol on the table. It had gotten heavy carrying it all this time. "Now we get a fire going in the stove, light some lamps and wait until daylight."

Chapter Twenty Six

Summer tried getting the stove going, but there wasn't any wood left. Neither of them suggested going outside and getting more. Instead they left their snowmobile suits on. After Summer had the lamps going, Aaron sat on the floor with his back against the door. A moment later she sat beside him and sobbed into her hands. It had finally gotten to her.

Aaron put an arm around her shoulder and pulled her closer. Within minutes she had cried herself to sleep. Exhaustion conquers everything after a while, but he knew he'd never sleep until they were out of there for good.

The next thing he knew he awoke still sitting against the door. Summer was across the room standing over the cellar door listening. She didn't have to tell him for Aaron to know Bridger was in the cellar. The scared look on Summer's face shouted it. A tidal wave of disappointment crashed over him. He had hoped Bridger was off somewhere hiding on the other side of the refuge, and they wouldn't deal with him again until they had made it out of the refuge and came back with a SWAT team. Now they would be watching every tree and bush all the way out tomorrow. Ambushing them would be harder for Bridger in the daylight, but predators ambushed prey in the daytime on a regular basis.

His disappointment suddenly flipped to anger. They didn't deserve this. They hadn't threatened Bridger, and any pain he received from the Taser was done in self-defense. If Aaron's right hand had been in good shape he would have gotten the M4 off the table and pumped rounds through the floor. Maybe he'd hit him. Maybe he'd kill him. Maybe he'd at least scare him enough to get him out of there again. But he couldn't control the rifle with one hand. He could use Sander's .40, but shooting left-handed, he doubted he could hit the floor, and wounding Bridger would only make him angrier. What did they say about nothing being more dangerous than a wounded animal?

Aaron stood and tiptoed over by Summer, cringing at each creak the floor made from his weight.

"Is he there?" Aaron asked, mouthing the words more than saying them. He already knew the answer.

She nodded. He could see she was as frustrated as him. It showed even through the fear in her eyes. "What do we do now?" she whispered.

Aaron didn't know. Summer could take the rifle, throw open the cellar door and spray bullets into the cellar. But as soon as Bridger heard the surface bolt slide he might—

Aaron stopped. The surface bolt wasn't in place. They hadn't slid it back after the sheriff closed the door when Sanders had left through the outside entrance. There was nothing stopping Bridger from coming into the cabin through the cellar door.

"We need to lock the door," Aaron whispered, motioning toward the surface bolt.

Summer saw the unlocked bolt and bent to secure it.

When she slid the bolt, it made a creaking sound. The door burst open and

Bridger's arms came through the opening and grabbed for Summer. She lunged away knocking Aaron on the floor. Aaron scrambled to his feet and his first move was toward the table and the pistol. But before he could get there, Bridger had Summer by the left ankle. He dragged her toward the dark hole in the floor with Summer screaming and beating on his hands.

Aaron grabbed her by her snowmobile suit with his good hand and held on. It barely slowed her as they slid across the floor. He wrapped his arms under her shoulders to the crook of his elbows and dug his heels into the wood floor. They were dragged toward the opening like the tongue of a giant pulling them into its mouth.

Summer gasped when she slipped into the hole. Aaron braced his feet on the opposite side of the cellar's opening. She twisted around and wrapped her arms around his neck and clung to him, hanging from his neck.

The sheer weight took his breath away. Aaron screamed as sharp talons of pain gripped his spine and neck. It was like holding up a Buick, but it stopped them for a moment. Summer hung suspended between

Aaron above and Bridger below in the black of the cellar. He jerked on her the way a terrier plays tug-of-war with a rag, sharp, hard pulls. Aaron almost lost his footing. Something popped below, sounding like the muffled snap of a stick encased in cotton. Summer screamed in his ear. Her grip slipped. Fingernails tore bloody grooves in his neck. He grabbed the back of her belt through her snowmobile suit to get a better grip. His hand bumped against something hard and metallic. When he had her belt, he realized Sheriff Thompson's pistol was still in her pocket. He let go of her belt, reached in her pocket and grabbed the pistol. She slipped further into the cellar. Her head and arms were in the cabin. Everything else was below with Bridger.

Aaron found the pistol with his good hand. He grabbed it, but it wouldn't come out of her pocket. It was caught on the pocket's lining. His frantic jerks produced the ripping sounds of fabric tearing, but it wouldn't come loose. He canted the pistol to the side, hoping it wouldn't hit her leg, but even if it did, it would be better than the fate awaiting her below. Aaron pulled the trigger.

The weight on Summer left abruptly. They shot out of the hole as if coming out of a Jack-in-the-box. With the weight off Summer, Aaron worked the pistol out of her pocket. He pointed it in the cellar and kept pulling the trigger until it was empty. The pistol flashed into the dark space like a strobe light, absolute brightness followed by absolute darkness. Bullets bounced off the stone floor, and Aaron didn't know if he'd hit anything.

Summer sat sobbing and holding her knee. She tried standing, but her leg wouldn't hold her weight. "Get the rifle," she screamed.

Aaron grabbed the M4 from the table and handed it to her. She dragged herself across the floor until she could look into the cellar and turned on the flashlight. The dim yellow light lit Bridger laying on top of Bob's body. He was moving, trying to get to his feet. A stream of blood poured out of his right shoulder. Summer popped off a quick round and Bridger twitched and went flat on his back. She methodically squeezed off rounds, taking careful aim after each bark of the rifle and making sure every bullet went where she wanted it: twice to the chest, one to the head, twice to the chest, one to the head …

Aaron believed she would have emptied the magazine if he hadn't stopped her.

"We might need some of that ammunition," he said, putting his hand across her line of sight.

She stopped firing.

Bridger lay in the cellar on top of Bob's body. A pool of dark blood spread quickly from the two bodies and ran across the stone floor, but *he* wasn't moving.

Aaron closed the cellar door, slid the surface bolt into place and collapsed beside Summer. They sat in silence for a long time, holding each other and both of them shaking. "What are we going to do?" Summer asked after a little bit with tears still running down her face. "He did something to my knee. I can't walk out of here."

"I'll build some kind of sled and pull you out," Aaron said.

"Maybe you should leave me here and go get help," she said. "I'll be okay until you get back."

It wasn't going to happen. They had come here together and even if he had to carry her on his back, they were going out together.

They both jumped at the all too familiar sound of someone trying to break down the cabin door.

Summer's face filled with horror. "When's it going to end?" she sobbed. "Can't he be killed?" She put her head into Aaron's chest and cried.

"Summer, are you in there?" a voice yelled from the other side of the door.

The confusion on her face wiped out any remaining horror. "Chad, is that you?"

"Yeah, it's me, Summer," the voice said. "We heard shots. Are you okay?"

"We're okay," Summer shouted. She looked at Aaron and wiped her eyes with her wrists. "It's Chad Tholkes. Go let him in."

Aaron took the barricades off the door and opened it. The first five people through the door were dressed in black helmets and goggles. Each of them held M4s at the ready with bright Maglites attached. Aaron figured it was the county SWAT team … minus Sanders. The last guy through the door was a young guy with dark hair under a green stocking cap with an Iowa DNR emblem.

"Chad, you're the best sight I've ever seen," Summer said. She was doing everything she could to keep from crying again. "But why are you here?"

Chad knelt beside her. "The dispatcher, Melonie Riggs, got worried when you guys and the sheriff didn't come back. She called the SWAT team. I'm the only one she was sure knew how to get out here."

Aaron smiled. Way to go Mom.

Chapter Twenty Seven

Every time Aaron saw Chantel he was sure she was more beautiful than the last time. He hadn't known her in her modeling days, but he'd seen some pictures of her on the internet—a couple in bikinis that were unbelievable. He knew they could do wonders with air brushing and digital photography, but he didn't know how you could improve on what sat across the desk from him. Even in a lab coat over simple green hospital scrubs with her hair pulled back in a loose ponytail, he couldn't see anything that needed fixing.

"So how's your wrist?" she asked and smiled, her violet eyes closing to slits.

Aaron held up the cast. "They had to pin it. The scaphoid and trap—" He stopped.

"The trapezium or trapezoid?" Chantel asked.

"The *zium* one," Aaron said smiling. "Anyway, it was fractured, and they pinned it. I have an x-ray of it at home. I'm going to have some wallet-sized ones made and hand them out."

Chantel laughed. "Put me down for one."

Aaron smiled. "You're on the list."

"Will it affect your shooting?" she asked. "It is your strong hand."

He shrugged. "The orthopedic surgeon says with physical therapy I should be as good as new."

She nodded. "That's good. How long will you be off?"

"I'm told four to six weeks, depending on how everything goes."

"Great," she said, smiling. "It sounds like a vacation." She paused and got serious for a moment. "So what is it you need from me?"

"I need to clear some stuff up before I close this case and go off on my … vacation." Aaron said. He smiled.

She returned it. "Such as?"

"Was it Bridger Milton's DNA on Hemper's body?" Aaron asked.

Definitely," she said. "As close to 100% positive as I can get. And there is not a forensic pathologist in the world who would not concur."

A wave of relief washed over Aaron. He had been positive it was Bridger's, but there was always a nagging doubt. If it had come back as not his, he didn't know what he would have done. He wasn't sure he could have taken it, but it was. Case closed on Hemper's death.

"What did Sheriff Thompson die from?" Aaron asked.

"Exposure and hypothermia," Chantel said. "From the report it sounded as if they found him about two miles from where you last saw him?"

"They took me straight back, so I wasn't there when they found him," Aaron said. "But it's what I heard, too."

"I imagine he ran until he dropped from exhaustion," Chantel said. "If he worked up a good sweat from running, and as cold as it was, it wouldn't take long for his body to dissipate its heat when he stopped."

"I heard they did CPR."

"There is an old saying in emergency medicine," Chantel said. "'You're not dead until you're warm and dead.' The cold minimizes the damage to the brain even after the heart stops beating. I'm sure they warmed him and tried to resuscitate him. It didn't work."

Aaron had mixed feelings about the sheriff. He had screwed up the Hemper case from the beginning by looking for a solution he wanted instead of finding a solution dictated by the evidence. But he had come out personally to rescue them. He could have sent one of his underlings, but he didn't. It took courage, even if at times Sheriff Thompson didn't seem to have any.

"Is there anything else?" Chantel asked.

"I don't think so," Aaron said. "If I think of something while I'm writing the final report, I'll give you a call."

"Anytime," she said, smiling. The smile fell from her face and was replaced by one of concern. "After reading your initial report, I can't imagine what it was like going through what you did."

"It was an experience," Aaron said smiling, but the memories swamped him for a moment. His hands shook. He looked away, pretending he was looking at her diplomas on the wall. If she saw his eyes, he was afraid she had enough psychiatric training to know about the nightmares.

He looked back at her, and the sympathy on her face told him she already knew.

"I know someone who can get us a couple tickets to the *Jersey Boys* this weekend if you're interested," she said, smiling. "It would be a good time. We could make a night of it. Dinner first, and afterward we could talk."

He couldn't fault her for wanting to help, but he hadn't wanted to talk with the department's psychiatrist, and they'd made him. He had no desire to go out with someone and be psychoanalyzed. It was another thing on his list of reasons why he would never date Dr. Moore.

"I appreciate the offer," Aaron said. "But I have plans this weekend. I'm going ice fishing."

She laughed. "I would have thought you would have all the cold you could take for a while."

"It's not bad if you dress right," Aaron said.

"What about your hand?"

He held it up again. "I'm told we'll be fishing shallow, and I shouldn't have any problem," he said. "Besides, my fishing partner has a bum knee."

Chantel laughed. "You two should be quite the pair."

"That's what *I* thought," Aaron said.

THE END